the
deepest
roots

the deepest roots

MIRANDA ASEBEDO

HARPER TEEN
An Imprint of HarperCollinsPublishers

HarperTeen is an imprint of HarperCollins Publishers.

Library of Congress Control Number: 2018939994

ISBN 978-0-06-274707-5

Typography by Jenna Stempel-Lobell
18 19 20 21 22 PC/LSCH 10 9 8 7 6 5 4 3 2 1
❖
First Edition

For Antonio, who believed in me always
and
for my daughters, may you grow to be
as brave as Rome,
as strong as Lux,
and as compassionate as Mercy

the
deepest
roots

ONE

THE THING ABOUT TORNADOES IS that they're a game of odds. Every die cast has to fall against you at the perfect moment. And when you live in the small, rural town of Cottonwood Hollow, Kansas, you think, *What are the odds it'll hit here out of all the places in the county?*

Well, my odds have been shit lately.

"Why aren't you at the shelter, Mom?" I yell as I slam the front door shut behind me. She's got all the windows of our old single-wide trailer open, and they seem to suck in and amplify the tornado siren. The sky outside is a greenish gold, the color of an old bruise that is faded but still tender to the touch.

Mom should have left twenty minutes ago, when we were first put under the tornado warning, the radio blaring an advisory to take immediate shelter. Red let me off my shift at the auto shop early so I could beat the storm home, but when I passed

Cottonwood Hollow's community tornado shelter and didn't see Mom's car, I knew something was wrong.

Mom's face when she sees me is one of surprise, quickly overshadowed by a tightening of her mouth, that face she makes when she's afraid. "What are you doing here?" she shouts back, her voice accusatory, as if I'm the one who's done something wrong. "You should have stayed in Evanston. I texted you to stay put. You would've been safe in the shop." She holds Steven's halter with one hand. Steven is a giant, beastly mix of generations of mutts who's begun to howl in concert with the tornado siren.

"My phone's out of minutes! I came back to meet you in the shelter," I shout back. "What the hell are you still doing here?"

"Garrett told me no pets allowed in the tornado shelter after Missy Underwood's dog bit one of the Pelter kids." Garrett Remington is the mayor of Cottonwood Hollow, and also our landlord. He may or may not have been one of Mom's previous boyfriends, too. He brags around town that he's descended from *the* Remingtons, and I think that's probably the only reason a creep like him got elected mayor.

"Tell Garrett to screw off." I bellow over the sirens and Steven's howls.

This is the most communication we've had in days. Mom has been conveniently away when I've been home, or sleeping, which is a sure sign that things are going to shit. Mom faces problems like an ostrich, head in the sand.

"I thought you would stay at the shop!" she yells again, looking frustrated, as if I've spoiled her plans. "It's too dangerous to go

2

back out now!" The wind outside picks up, careening through the open windows and knocking over a lamp near the couch.

"This isn't the safest place to be, either!" I retort.

Mom avoids answering me, instead shouting back, "We have to close the windows!"

Tornadoes make you realize your priorities, too. So as Mom and I are running around closing windows, she's dragging Steven with one hand, as if he might run off and be lost forever in the storm. With her other hand, she gathers her beloved, yellowed, dog-eared paperbacks and stows them away in drawers and cupboards like that will save them if the tornado sucks us up. I'm thinking of Lux and Mercy, and wondering if they're okay. I'm hoping neither of them does anything stupid when I don't show up in the tornado shelter, like coming to look for me and getting stuck in this deathtrap with me and Mom. And I'm still hoping that wherever this tornado touches down, it won't be here.

The screams of the siren subside, as if to make sure that we hear the first ball of hail like a bullet cracking against the shingles. A few vengeful shots follow, and then what sounds like all-out war.

I run to the window to look at my car, a 1972 Mach 1 Mustang parked in the front yard. I'd rescued it out of a barn and meticulously restored it. If we had a garage, or even a carport, it might survive this. All I can think about as I watch the chunks of ice pounding down is the force with which they collide into metal that I've spent years of my life Fixing. I feel the ache in my muscles, in my bones, of every hour spent under the hood of that car. Every dent, every chip from the crash of hail might as well be on my own body. That car and I are one and the same. Years of work, years of struggle. Damn the odds. Damn this day.

My attention is torn from the Mach because behind it, nearly a mile to the north near the old Remington homestead just outside of town, I see the dark funnel stretch toward the pasture like a hesitant finger. When it touches down, a shadowy cloud of debris builds around it. Maybe for once luck will be on our side and it'll suck up the curse along with the old Remington place.

A massive gust of wind hits the trailer like a slap, and it reels in response, rocking back against the tie-downs holding it in place. A punch of fear-soaked adrenaline bursts and spreads through my middle. Mom's breath catches, and she steadies us both with a hand on my shoulder.

"We should probably move away from the windows," I say, as the trailer rocks again.

I follow Mom into the hallway, the only part of the house without windows or furniture, a place we might survive if the tie-downs don't hold and the trailer rolls. Steven sits beside us, wagging his tail like we're all just hanging out together on a typical Sunday.

"What's going on?" I ask quietly, staring at the faded wallpaper, hands clenched around my knees. If we're going to die here, I want to know why.

Maybe it's because she thinks this might be the end, but for once Mom doesn't sidestep. "I didn't want to run into Garrett at the tornado shelter. We're late on the rent." She can't even look me in the eye when she says it. "This storm might buy us a couple more days if he's out checking damages on his other properties."

"I gave you my half!" I grind out.

"I didn't have mine." Her voice is barely a whisper over the roar of the wind and rain.

Mom shuts down again, her eyes closed, as if she's waiting for the end. She tries to hold my hand as the trailer rocks, the windows shaking.

But I pull away. "We'd better not die in this trailer."

Twenty minutes later, the storm has passed and there's a fist pounding on our front door.

"Jesus," Mom swears, opening her eyes. "If that's Garrett, don't answer it."

"Jesus isn't going to save us from Garrett." I pull myself up from where we've been hunched in silence, hoping the trailer didn't get thrown across Cottonwood Hollow.

The cheap, faux-gold doorknob turns as I approach it, and Lux pushes in, and then despite the tornado missing us, I know my odds are really going to shit today. When things are bad, I try to keep Lux and Mercy from stopping by. There's nothing worse than the way Lux's green eyes watch my mom laugh too loudly, or make too many jokes to cover up the fact that we're huddling around space heaters because we don't have the cash to fill the propane tank. And Mercy, well, she'll start to poke around in the kitchen, quietly note the empty cupboards, and then the dinner invitations will start.

"What the hell?" Lux says, brandishing her phone above the large, voluminous mass of strawberry-blond hair balled into a messy bun on the top of her head. Strands have fallen loose to frame her heart-shaped face and dimpled chin. "You don't know how to use one of these anymore?" She shoves her phone nearly into my face.

Mercy follows Lux inside, squeezing me in a fierce hug that constricts painfully around my waist as she smashes her cheek against my chest. "Rome!" When she says my name, it's half reprimand, half exultation. "Why in the world did you stay in this *trai—*" She stops, casting an uncomfortable look at Lux and continuing her tirade of concern. "*House* when you know it's not safe? And why didn't you answer your phone?"

"I need to put more minutes on my phone," I mutter, irritated that she can't say *trailer* without thinking she'll offend me. And because somehow it does, a little. I give her a quick squeeze and then step away.

"Lame," Lux remarks with a roll of her eyes. "Next time let someone know what's up."

Mom got up from the floor of the hall while Lux and Mercy were talking, and now she sits down on the couch, pulling one of her books up from between the cushions like nothing is wrong.

"Did you see how close it got?" Mercy asks. She senses something is wrong, I can tell by the way she's inching toward the kitchen, trying to get a look around. "Dad stayed out on the front porch and watched while we were in the basement. He said it touched down about a mile north, not far from the Remington place."

I nod, heading off Mercy and pretending I'm really just putting the fallen lamp back on the end table rather than herding her. "Yeah, I watched it. Then we went to the hall." I gesture nonchalantly toward where we'd just been cowering, trying to divert Mercy's attention from the kitchen and its empty cupboards. "Really makes you evaluate your life goals, though, right? Of all the places to die, I don't want it to be in a trailer." I laugh too loudly.

Lux raises one eyebrow, like my forced humor isn't fooling her. Mercy purses her lips, like it's all she can do not to start lecturing me again about how dangerous it was for us to stay here.

"I've got to go check on the Mach," I announce suddenly, pushing past them both and putting my hand on the knob of the front door. It's better if I get Mercy and Lux out of here.

I look back over my shoulder at Mom, who's reading with Steven's head in her lap like nothing happened.

"See you later," Mom says, giving me a lazy wave. As if she's carefree, as if we aren't behind on the rent, as if we didn't just wonder if we were going to die together in this tin can.

"Lock the door," I tell her. "Don't answer it." Garrett is just dick enough to throw us out for being late. Holding that kind of power over his poor female tenants is something he savors.

As I open the door, Steven's ears prick up and he leaps off the couch, squeezing between me and the door and bounding down the rickety front steps.

"Steven!" I yell. "Stay!" Steven's not really one for commands, though, and he continues to trot out to the yard, sniffing at downed branches and licking stray bits of hail.

Outside, Mercy's little sister, Neveah, is stacking larger chunks of hail near the dirt road, making an impossible army of tiny snowmen at the beginning of May. Neveah is eight, and a miniature copy of Mercy. Thick black hair, tan skin, dark-brown eyes, and arched, expressive brows. She must have begged Mercy to tag along when they came out to check on me. Steven sticks his snout against the nape of Neveah's neck where she crouches with her snowman army, and she laughs and waves him off.

I make a beeline for the Mach, relieved when I see that there are far fewer dents and dings in the heavy metal of the car than I thought there would be.

"I guess we should be getting home," Mercy says. "It's almost eight. We just wanted to make sure you were okay."

Lux is still looking back at the trailer, probably wondering why I told Mom to lock the door and not answer it.

Fluffernut, the Ruizes' cat from a couple trailers down the road, slinks out from underneath the Mach, where she must have been riding out the storm. She yowls pitifully.

"Oh, little kitty, you poor thing!" Neveah croons, coming to pet her.

At the sound of Neveah's voice, Steven halts his investigation of a stray branch and heads back in her direction. He spots Fluffernut and lets out a sound that is half snort, half gleeful bark. Fluffernut puffs up and hisses, arching her back, but Steven doesn't recognize anything but a new friend and charges toward her anyway. Fluffernut shoots out of the yard and into the dirt road with Steven in pursuit, barking joyfully.

"Steven!" I call. "No! Stay!" But once again, Steven has his own plans.

"I'll get him!" Neveah shouts, and she races after him. The sight of Neveah chasing him spurs Steven on, and he abandons his hunt for Fluffernut and charges off toward the open pastures of

Remington land in the direction of where the tornado just touched down.

"Neveah, wait!" Mercy calls. She looks helplessly at me, and I shrug.

"She'll be fine," Lux says. "There's nothing out there but dirt and grass."

"There's snakes," Mercy retorts. "And who knows what the tornado sucked up and spit out over there."

Lux's full mouth twists in amusement, and her green eyes meet mine. "We'll go get her. Come on."

There's no sidewalks out here on the edge of Cottonwood Hollow, so we walk along the edge of the dirt road, kicking chunks of hail along the way. Cottonwoods line the road, their leaves quaking and sighing as if they're relieved that they survived the storm.

Before we reach the farthest edge of town, Rick Ruiz stops me outside of his double-wide. It's the nicest one out here, with real siding and little green shutters on the windows. He's fixing some of the white plastic skirting around the bottom, standing it back up where it's been blown in by the storm. I'd given up years ago trying to keep the cheap skirting on our old trailer nice and put up plywood around the bottom instead to keep out the possums and the stray cats. It's not pretty, but it's functional.

Rick is still in his sheriff's deputy uniform, which means he must have rushed home to make sure Marisol and Letty were okay. When he and Marisol moved here seven years ago, they'd known that the girls of Cottonwood Hollow were different, but two years later when they had their daughter, Letty, it was up to Mom and me to explain to them exactly why their daughter could name all the American presidents in order after reading a book from the library at the age of three. Letty was a Wit.

"Rome?" he asks me. "Everything okay? Marisol said she didn't see you or your mom and Steven at the tornado shelter. She and Letty were worried."

"Need a hand?" I ask, changing the subject as I gesture at the electrical box that's hanging off the side of their house by one bent screw. A cottonwood branch fell on the power line during the storm, and the force nearly yanked the box clean off. Wires tangle behind it, some exposed and partially severed, wet and glistening.

"Would you mind?" Relief softens his features.

"Of course not," I reply, wiping my hands on my jeans.

Rick hurries over to the small shed near his back deck to get his toolbox.

"We'll wait," Lux says, stopping and crossing her arms. Thanks to Rick, she's thinking again about why I wasn't in the tornado shelter, and I know she's waiting to see if I give anything up. But Mercy, eyebrows bunched, looks concerned about letting Neveah get too far away. I can see the top of Neveah's head out in the pasture, and fleeting glimpses of Steven loping through the tall grass.

"Go on," I tell Mercy with a jerk of my chin. One ruddy curl falls loose from my ponytail and bounces against my cheek. "We'll catch up."

Mercy nods gratefully and chases after her sister. From a distance, she's so tiny she looks much younger than seventeen. The dark clouds have moved out, and the setting sun casts a lambent glow over the pasture where they're headed.

Rick brings me his toolbox. He's only a little taller than me and built as wide as a door, all of it muscle. My talent for Fixing has come in handy for both of us over the years since our mutual landlord isn't known for his prompt responses to things like maintenance requests.

Lux is careful not to smile at Rick, using what Mercy and I call her Stone Face. Rick knows what will happen if a Siren smiles at him, though, and doesn't take it personally. He gives her a hesitant wave.

I run my hands along the wires that go into the house behind the box, smoothing the thin metal hairs together with my fingers, twisting them back into firm, capable strands. I barely feel a rush of electricity beneath the pads of my fingertips. It licks with a swift, teasing tongue. Then I push the box back up to the house and take the power drill from Rick. He's already found the screws I need and holds them in his wide palm, waiting to hand them to me when I'm ready. Holding the box against the house with my forearm, I use the drill to reattach the box to the house.

I don't need a test to know when something is Fixed, but I tell Rick, "Give the lights inside a try."

Before he can run back around the double-wide to the front door to yell at Marisol to hit the lights, she comes out on their front stoop. "The power's back!" she shouts with a relieved wave. "Thank you, Rome!"

"How much do I owe you?" Rick asks.

I am surprised, because so few people offer money. The

currency in Cottonwood Hollow is usually food or favors between neighbors and friends.

"Nothing," I tell Rick, though we are behind on the rent. "Just being neighborly."

Marisol is undeterred, and she calls from the front door, "I've got the fixings for a casserole, so Letty and I will bring one by later."

"I'll do you one better," Rick promises. "The next time I catch you racing the Mach, I'll be sure to look the other way."

"What more could a girl ask for, Deputy Ruiz?" I ask with a grin as we leave. "See you later."

"I don't think you needed to Stone Face Rick," I tell Lux as I wipe my dirty hands on my jeans.

This immediately nettles her, and she tightens her arms across her chest. "Better safe than sorry," she huffs. "You should've heard what the man at the gas station promised me this morning."

"I hope it was free gas. The Mach needs a fill-up."

"It was pumping he offered," Lux says, "but not that kind."

"Gross," I reply, sticking out my tongue. "That dude is a meth head."

"Yeah. Well, my pretty face doesn't care. I was laughing at that text message you sent before your phone ran out. And he was just *there* in the crossfire." She frowns, her full mouth tightening. "I've gotten good at controlling it. I hate it when it happens out of the blue like that."

Lux is what we call a Siren, and flirting from her—devastating smiles, sparkling laughter, or what Mercy calls her "sexy voice"—leads men to profess their undying love. Or at least to do whatever she wants. When we were younger, we thought it was funny, letting Lux charm our math teacher into believing we'd turned in our algebra homework and that he'd just misplaced it. It was less funny when the forty-year-old teacher declared he was in love with her.

The irony is that Lux doesn't even like boys. She told Mercy and me last summer, as if we hadn't known for years already. The three of us have always been friends. Lux's and Mercy's faces are as familiar to me as my own, every expression a story written in a language that only we three can understand.

The more generous locals say the daughters of Cottonwood Hollow have unique talents. Fixers, Finders, Sirens, Enoughs, Strong Backs, Wits, Sights, Readers, and Healers. Some are talents that I've heard of but never seen. Ten years ago, when I was only seven, the townspeople thought maybe it had something to do with the water, and they had bake sales and softball tournaments and hot-dog-eating contests to raise the money to get it tested. But nothing in the water was out of the ordinary. Only the girls were.

Mercy is an Enough, and just her presence can make, well, Enough. Once when we were kids, she wanted to share her Kool-Aid with Lux and me. Of course since she was Mercy, she'd already shared the Kool-Aid with anyone close enough to look thirsty, so the pitcher was nearly empty. But when we held out our plastic cups, she just kept pouring, and the Kool-Aid kept coming out, filling our cups to the brim. There was just enough. She can't make more money appear in my wallet, or in Mom's bank account. But whatever she has seems to always be Enough for what she needs. And sometimes for what *we* need, too. I've

13

driven the Mach on an empty tank more times than I can count with Mercy in the back seat.

And my story is nearly just like everyone else's. Mom moved to Cottonwood Hollow when she was an unwed, pregnant seventeen-year-old who could afford a trailer when rented with two roommates. Years passed and the two roommates left, and then it was just me and Mom. She'd heard the stories, followed the gazes of the other mothers watching me, waiting to see what talent I would have. And so she hadn't missed a beat when I'd Fixed the microwave at the age of four, sliding my hand over the grease-slicked buttons and tugging gently at wires in the back. When I plugged it back in, the microwave *worked*, and that was all that mattered.

We ate microwave popcorn for supper that night.

TWO

AHEAD, MERCY IS A WATCHFUL statue as she stands on a small rise, the setting sun casting her in a dark silhouette. When we get to the barbed-wire fence that separates us from the Remington pasture ground, I hold the middle strand of wire down with my worn sneaker and pull the top strand up with my hand, careful not to nick myself on the rusty barbs. Lux squeezes through the opening. One of the barbs catches in her messy bun, and she mutters a couple of curse words as she tugs away, leaving a few strands of hair. Then she returns the favor for me, holding the wires apart with a dubious expression.

"I never understand why this is fenced off, anyway," Lux complains when we're both through. She dusts her hands off on her jeans, trying to remove the tawny smudges of rust and dirt from her hands. "It's not like there are cattle out here. It's just a big empty field with only the Remington house and the junky old ruins."

I shrug.

Everyone knows the story about the Remingtons. Long ago a woman named Emmeline Remington lived here. She and her husband were newly married and settled on eighty acres of prairie near Cottonwood Hollow, which back then was no more than a main street with a general store, a schoolhouse, and a saloon, not the bustling metropolis of two hundred and fifty citizens that it is now. Supposedly, the husband up and left Emmeline for another woman. Some say the other woman was a saloon girl, and others say she was the new schoolteacher. Either way, Emmeline cursed the women of Cottonwood Hollow. She cursed us to be strange and unwanted because one of us had stolen her husband. And ever since then, the girls born here have been a little peculiar.

"So why weren't you in the tornado shelter?"

Damn.

"Mom was sleeping and didn't know we were in a warning until the sirens went off. I drove straight from work to get her, but by then it was too dangerous to go back out."

"Are you sure that's all? It seems like your mom is always sleeping lately," Lux says, her green eyes fixed on my brown ones.

"Because she's tired. People who work get tired. You should try it sometime," I jab. Neither Lux nor Mercy have a job like I do, and neither one of them knows almost my entire paycheck goes to helping with the rent now. We've sworn to tell each other everything, but this is a secret that I can't share. I can't see the pity in their eyes and still feel like we're sisters, pieces of the same whole. "It's not a big deal."

We walk until we reach Mercy. "Check it out," she says,

pointing at the trail carved in the pasture where the tornado touched down. Neveah is cavorting along it, exclaiming over the way the grass has been scoured from the ground. Steven is following her now, sniffing at everything she points out. Debris lies scattered along both sides of the path, mostly cottonwood branches and dirt. But there are a few strange objects, too, and she delights in pulling things out of the mess. Part of a rake, a raincoat, a tricycle with a missing wheel, and what looks like a baking sheet that's been bent into a U shape.

"It must have hit a house," Mercy murmurs as her sister shouts about each rare treasure she recovers. A broken bottle, a crutch. A deflated soccer ball.

"No, look," Lux says, pointing to the rusted trailers stacked together on the eastern edge of the Remingtons' fenced-off land. "It wasn't a house. It hit the ruins."

We turn toward the cluster of abandoned trailers, which aren't much bigger than Lego blocks from this far out. They're wedged up against a few small hills on the edge of Remington land, and in winter they look like they're huddling together to keep warm. Mom said there used to be a lot of trailers out where ours is on the edge of town, but eventually the town voted to remove the abandoned, dilapidated ones. So they raised funds to hire a semi to come out and drag the run-down mobile homes onto the eastern corner of Remington land. Now the trailers perch alongside each other on stacks of cinder blocks, lined close enough together that you could pass through each one to get to the other, a maze of tiny, narrow halls and cramped rooms. There had been a debate about whether they should be burned, or taken apart for scrap, but no one had committed to a plan. So the trailers were just left there, abandoned a second time.

In the distance, one of the trailers looks like it's been tipped onto its side, guts spilling out. There's a twist in my own gut when I think of what Mom and I recently risked, riding out the storm in our own trailer.

"Next time, come over to my house," Mercy chides gently, squeezing my hand like she's read my mind.

Casual affection comes naturally to Mercy. Hugging is like breathing to her, or maybe like smiling at someone. I squeeze her hand back, give her a small smile to show her that everything is okay, that Mom and I are fine.

Lux puts her hand on my shoulder, connecting the three of us as we have always been. "And get a better phone."

Mercy and I laugh, and she releases my hand. Lux's hand stays on my shoulder a while longer, her touch firm, and I know that even though she doesn't say it outright, she was scared for me, too.

It's almost twilight now, and though it's early in the season, the fireflies are beginning to come out, tiny greenish-gold lights floating between sweet-smelling clumps of tall grass. A breeze pushes through the pasture as if nudging us back toward Cottonwood Hollow, pulling more curls from my messy ponytail. We all turn back to where Neveah is exploring.

"Rome," Neveah calls from a distance down the wide path. "Look at this," she says, galloping over to me with something in her hands. Steven chases after her, probably hoping they're going to play some more.

The crickets are out in force now, their songs loud in the silence after the storm.

"What is it?" I ask.

Neveah is carrying something small in both hands, but it's hard to see what it is in the dim light. "The latch is stuck. Do you think you can Fix it?"

Mercy puts one hand on her hip. "You shouldn't be picking up weird things. You know that."

"Yeah, but I *Found* it," Neveah retorts. She turns back to me, her dark eyes serious. Neveah is a Finder, locating things that are lost or hidden with the accuracy of a bloodhound. "I saw a lady, too."

"What lady?" Lux asks, scanning the pasture.

"She didn't say her name," Neveah answers.

"But where is she?" Mercy asks.

Neveah looks back over her shoulder toward the piles of branches. "She's gone." She thrusts the thing into my hands and runs off.

I look down. It's a small wooden chest, not much bigger than a jewelry box. The wood is scarred and dirty, and the hinges are rusted metal. I can barely make out what looks like a set of initials carved into the lid, but there's too much dirt caked on it to read them. There's a rusted latch on the front. I can't explain it, but the tug I feel in my gut is tremendous. I get that feeling sometimes when something really needs to be Fixed. My fingers are nearly twitching to fiddle with the latch and see if I can open it. But the wood is almost cold to the touch, and fear sends a small shiver down my spine. Sometimes the things we think we want end up hurting us.

"Wonder what's in it," Lux says, her interest kindled.

"Nothing good," Mercy says, wrinkling her nose. "It probably got sucked up and dropped here from the ruins."

"What about the lady?" Lux asks.

"Neveah is eight, Lux. She still has imaginary friends," Mercy replies.

"Could've been a ghost," Lux whispers, reaching up a hand to tug on my ponytail from behind, as if I couldn't tell it was her.

"If it's a ghost from the ruins, it's probably just a nice box of black mold," I reply. But I can't stop myself from looking around the pasture again. Who was the lady Neveah thought she saw?

"Maybe it's money," Lux hypothesizes. "If it's money, promise me we'll use it to drive away into the sunset. Far, far away from Cottonwood Hollow." There's something strange in the set of her mouth, something I haven't seen before.

"Come on," Mercy says, putting her hand at the small of Lux's back to nudge her along. "It's starting to get dark. Let's go home." She looks down at Steven and says firmly, "Heel, Steven. No more running away."

Steven's ears flatten and he follows along as if he fears Mercy's disapproval. Neveah keeps up a constant stream of chatter as we walk back to town, all about how exciting it was to hear the tornado sirens and how she wasn't scared even a little, but their younger brother, Malakai, was kind of a crybaby about it.

We've just crossed through the barbed-wire fence when we hear him. "What are you doing out here, pretty pusses?" The barest hint of Oklahoma twang grates on my ears. It's Garrett Remington, my landlord, his features shadowed in the twilight so that his eyes look like dark holes. He's creepy enough that I can believe he really is related to the Remington woman who cursed us all. For a second I think he's going to ask about the rent, but instead he drawls, "Looking for trouble?"

He gives me a grin that sends a shiver of unease down my back. Mom had only a few dates with him. *There's something not right about him*, she'd said. I grab Steven's halter when he starts to surge forward to greet Garrett.

"Catching a runaway dog," Lux answers, her voice sharp. She gives him a full glaring Stone Face, and I'm thankful for it. Anything to distract him from the fact that we haven't paid him yet this month.

Garrett's eyes travel down to the box in my hands. "What have you got there?" he asks, taking a step forward as if to take it from me.

"Girls!"

Garrett jumps, glancing over his shoulder.

"Come on, girls!" It's Mrs. Montoya, Mercy's mom. She's standing with Marisol, who's holding a covered dish, while Letty pets a sad-looking Fluffernut at the end of the road that leads to the Ruiz trailer and mine. Mrs. Montoya must've been worried when her girls weren't home yet and was on her way over to my place when she'd run into Marisol delivering the promised casserole. Mrs. Montoya waves at Garrett and waits as we walk back to the road.

I look back over my shoulder when we join them, and Garrett

is still standing by the fence watching us. He takes off his baseball cap and I can see his eyes, dark and predatory.

Mrs. Montoya, Marisol, and Letty walk with us back into town. Marisol and Letty stop at the trailer to give the casserole to Mom, Steven following the smell of food inside with them. Avoiding questions about the box, I leave it just under the front stoop of our trailer while they go inside. Truthfully, I'm glad to put the box down. There's something about it that's almost magnetic, and I can't decide if it's attracting or repulsing me.

"Five more minutes," Mrs. Montoya tells Mercy as she leads Neveah home. "It's a school night."

We all nod, used to Mrs. Montoya's protectiveness.

"I'll walk you home," Lux tells Mercy. She turns and looks at me. "You coming?"

I'm surprised, because Lux usually wants to go home and call her new girlfriend, Morgan, this time of night.

"Don't you have plans?" I ask.

"I just want to stretch my legs some more." She starts walking toward Mercy's house without looking back to see if we'll catch up.

I wonder if there is something that she wants to tell me, and I follow without asking.

Mercy's house is on the other side of Cottonwood Hollow, about a ten-minute walk on the sidewalks that begin one block over from our dirt road. Living in a town with less than three hundred people, I can tell you the names of almost every family we pass. They wave from front porches as we go, calling hellos and asking after our families, making sure that everyone is safe. Cottonwood trees grow everywhere, their roots jutting out and cracking the sidewalks. We cross Main Street, where the grain silos at the co-op look like tall, dark towers.

The Montoyas' two-story house sits on a wide, shady brick street among other tall, tastefully painted old houses with carefully mowed front yards and little white picket fences. Mercy's dad is waiting for her on the front porch swing, smoking a pipe.

"It's late," he says as Mercy hugs each of us good-bye. "You want me to give you a ride home?"

Lux can't help a smile, amused by his idea of a "late night." She shuts it down as Mr. Montoya looks swiftly away, puffing on his pipe. It makes the men of Cottonwood Hollow nervous when Lux smiles at them.

"We're fine, Mr. Montoya," I tell him. "We can get home on our own."

Mr. Montoya nods, as if all is as it should be. "Be careful," he calls after us as we walk back down the sidewalk and to the street.

"He's actually a pretty nice guy," Lux says quickly, as if making an excuse for the way he'd looked away when she'd smiled at him.

"Don't let it ruin your evening."

"I can smile without putting a spell on someone, you know," she says softly. "I couldn't control it so much when we were younger, and earlier today when that gas-station guy got in my face, I wasn't focusing—"

"You don't need to tell me," I say, nudging her with my elbow. "I know."

Lux nods, but she's quiet, and I sense that she needs this

long, tangled walk to sort something out. Sometimes being a good friend means keeping your distance, even if you're walking side by side.

Lux, her mom, and her stepdad live on the other side of town, so we backtrack and follow Main Street for a while. There are a lot of cars parked along the sidewalks. Most belong to people visiting Flynn's bar, but a few belong to the residents of the old hotel, which was converted into apartments about fifteen years ago. We pause at the gas station, batting away the moths clustered around the glowing soda machines. Usually there would be a handful of Cottonwood Hollow boys hanging around here, drinking stolen whiskey and shooting the breeze, but the storm has scattered them for the night.

I tug the change release button twice on the machine, and quarters come out, enough for two cans of soda. It's been broken for years, and I don't bother to Fix it.

I feed the change back into the machine and buy one strawberry and one cream soda. Lux hums along to the strains of country music drifting from the bar. I hand her the cream soda and we each crack a can open.

Lux takes a drink. "Tastes like summer," she says with a little shiver.

"Only a month until summer vacation," I agree, taking a gulp of my own.

"I wish it wasn't," she says, catching a stray drop of soda on her lip with the back of her hand. She's careful not to smudge her lip gloss. "I don't want to be home all day."

"No more cable?" I tease her. Lux watches reality television shows, the kind where women are auctioned off to bachelors or singing for votes to stay on the island or whatever.

Lux flips me the bird. "Maybe I should read those car manuals you love so much."

We stop at her house, pausing at the end of her driveway. The small bungalow crouches low in the yard, deeply shadowed by massive cottonwood trees and a lone, crooked pine. The television blares loudly through an open window.

I shove my hands in my pockets and wait for her to say whatever's on her mind. Probably it's about how she's figured out there's something behind Mom and me hiding out in the trailer instead of going to the tornado shelter. But maybe it's Morgan, since Lux isn't in any rush to call her tonight.

But I get nothing, and this walk was just to see her home. "See you later," Lux says before she gives me a small wave and disappears inside her house.

I wave back and walk the rest of the way home alone. I wonder if what Lux didn't say tonight was about me or her. I wonder if we could fill a book with all the things we don't say.

The dark doesn't bother me, and I enjoy the quiet of the walk home by myself. I like to look at all the houses I pass, their lit-up, golden windows illuminating tiny squares of other people's lives. Sometimes it's a glimpse of a father watching baseball on the television with his kids, or a young couple dancing to a crackly radio station, other times it's curtains pulled tightly shut so that I'll never know what I'm missing. The streetlights end before they get to the dirt road Mom and I live on, but the storm has pushed the clouds away and there's enough moonlight to see clearly.

When I get back to the trailer, I don't go in. I know Mom will be asleep again, hiding from me and our missing rent money. Besides, this is my moment to finally check on the Mach without disturbance from anyone. I relish this time alone, just me and a problem that can be Fixed with common sense and capable hands.

I get the shop lamp from the rusty metal shed behind the trailer and run an extension cord. I pop the hood of the Mach, propping it up carefully so it doesn't fall and smash my head in. Then I hold up the shop lamp so that it illuminates the underside of each dent. I take a deep breath, my fingers twitching a little. And I push. *Thwunk*. The mound springs back up, flattening out so that the metal is smooth. *Thwunk, thwunk, thwunk*. It's kind of like popping those little packing bubbles. When I've finished the hood, I do the same for the trunk. The roof of the car is a little harder to do through the interior upholstery, but I Fix those dents too.

I still remember the day I found the Mach. Mercy was selling cookies door-to-door for her church fund raiser. We were about two miles down County Road 14, at an old farm owned and run by two ancient women who called themselves the Truett sisters. We didn't know if they had talents like us. They only ever called each other "Sister" in our presence. One was tall, with a thin face and hair she kept hidden beneath a handkerchief, and the other was shorter and wider, with a fat braid she wore hanging over one shoulder.

And then there'd been this *tug*. Toward the barn, which was no surprise. There are always broken things in old barns. Tractors, tillers, old Chevy pickups. But the tug was strong, and Mercy was in the middle of her spiel, so I had nothing better to do.

I snuck into the barn, rolling the door along the track just far enough to squeeze inside. As my eyes adjusted, I was able to make out an old tractor and a baler. But it was the tarp-covered lump near the back of the barn that really pulled at me. I crept around the tractor, careful not to disturb whatever critters might have taken up residence around the equipment.

My hand twitched when I reached out to tug the corner of the tarp.

And there it was. A 1972 Mach 1 Mustang. Faded red paint, a black hood scoop, and racing stripes down the sides. The lettering behind the front wheel well said *MACH 1*. All four tires were flat and the windshield was cracked. I dared to pull the tarp off all the way and found that the interior was home to cracked vinyl seats, dust, and about thirty pounds of mouse shit.

It was beautiful.

And I wanted it to be mine.

At first, the Truett sisters seemed reluctant to even talk about selling the car, but eventually they followed me into the barn, and this time I pulled the barn door open wide enough to spill a swathe of warm, buttery light onto the Mach. I told them I'd saved one thousand and fifty-seven dollars since I'd started working as a dishwasher at the café and I was willing to give them every last penny if they would sell me this car. That's how strongly I felt about it. It was as if I'd found a part of myself in that dusty old barn, and I couldn't leave it there.

Then my hand twitched. Just enough that the short Truett sister noticed it. "You one of them?" she growled between rows of yellowed dentures.

"One of who?" I shot back, already knowing what she meant. One of those Cottonwood Hollow girls. Not the kind of girl who deserved a car like this.

"You a Fixer?"

"Yeah. So?" I waited to see if this was going to help me or hurt me.

"Our mother was a Fixer," the tall Truett sister said, her voice thoughtful.

"She could Fix anything. Kept this farm running, even through the Great Depression," the short sister added.

The tall sister nodded, pursing her mouth in reverence.

"This was my boy's car," the tall sister explained. "He died not long after he bought it. Wasn't in Vietnam more than three weeks before he was shot."

Something in my stomach twisted. The car had been waiting for its owner to come back all these years.

"Since you're a Cottonwood Hollow girl," the tall sister went on, "we'll sell you the car, but only if you Fix it up right. No new parts. Just Fixing."

The short sister raised her eyebrows, just high enough to show she was surprised by the added stipulation.

"*All* Fixing?" I asked, at once irritated and thrilled by the possibility.

"We could teach you a thing or two about cars. And with Fixer talents, it ought to be a breeze."

"I can Fix it," I promised, though it was a lie. I'd never Fixed anything that big or complicated before. It might as well have been a human body, with all its intricate systems and components.

But that tug was strong.

"We'll sell it to you for a thousand dollars," the tall sister told me. "And you Fix it here, before you take it home."

"Deal." I held out my hand to shake on it.

By the time I've Fixed the dents on the Mach, I'm worn out. But when I look over at Mom's little Ford Focus, I can already see a couple of dings on the hood, so I drag my lamp over to her car and start all over. I'm drenched in sweat by the time I finish, and the soreness in my muscles tells me it's time for a hot shower and bed. Fixing things drains me, and the more elaborate the Fix, the more tired I feel by the end of it. But this is a good ache, a good exhaustion, hopefully one that will let me sleep through the questions about Mom and the missing rent money until tomorrow.

The wooden box waits where I left it. It looks harmless there, where the porch light gathers a host of moths and june bugs.

I lean down and pick it up, and the wood is like ice in my hands. I feel that terrible tug again, and it makes the tiny hairs on my arms stand up. It's worse than what I felt when the Mach needed to be Fixed. The pull is harder, fiercer, almost desperate. It sends a fissure of unease down my spine. What is it that so desperately needs to be Fixed?

I'm too tired to find out tonight. I'm not sure why, but I don't think I trust whatever is inside it to be near me while I'm sleeping. Instead, I take the box to the rusty shed and put it on the shelf above the lawn mower, where I keep old pickle jars full of nails and screws.

Just in case.

THREE

IN THE MORNING BEFORE HEADING to school, I pull up in front of Lux's house first. The 351 Cleveland under the hood of the Mach grinds out a low, throaty rumble as I idle, alerting her to my presence. She's outside before I can honk, slinging her backpack over one shoulder. I catch a glimpse of her mother, Tina, at the screen door as it slams shut behind her.

Lux's mother is one of us. Born in Cottonwood Hollow, born with the curse. She is a Healer, though I've only seen her do it a couple times. The first was at our trailer when Lux fell off the front stoop and twisted her ankle when she was ten.

Lux jerks open the passenger door and throws herself inside, her plaid skirt bunching up around her thighs. "Drive away," she commands. "Far, far away."

I look down at the fuel gauge, which is closer to *E* than I would like.

"Mercy's house it is," I chirp brightly, knowing it annoys her.

Lux is not a morning person. I hit the gas harder than I need to, making the engine roar and Lux's head jerk back into the headrest.

"God, I hate you," she mutters, straightening her skirt.

Mercy is waiting on her front porch, framed prettily by the pots of flowers perched on the railing. Her uniform is pressed and neat, from the plaid skirt to the white button-down shirt and little navy-blue jacket. She wears a matching headband and knee socks. Mercy is perhaps the only person I know who likes the Evanston High uniforms. The school district voted to implement them ten years ago, the same time they consolidated Cottonwood Hollow's high school with Evanston's because our enrollment was so low. They'd thought that the uniforms would keep us from noticing that the wealthy Evanston kids had brand-new sports cars, designer backpacks, and spring breaks in places I couldn't pronounce, while most of the Cottonwood Hollow students rode in on a school bus that leaked exhaust fumes through the floorboards.

Spoiler: they did not.

"You could give me shotgun for once," Mercy grumbles as Lux throws the heavy car door open and scoots her seat forward just enough for Mercy to climb into the back. "I can barely fit through here, and I'm tiny, you know."

"Last pickup gets the bitch seat," Lux says.

I look down at the gas gauge again. I don't get paid until Friday, which is four long days from now. Until then, I am totally broke. But Mercy is in the car, so I should be okay for today. Even on E, I know we'll have Enough fuel to get there.

I drive the fifteen miles to Evanston going seventy on a county road, loving the thrill of flying over every hill and around every bend, the freedom of speed and wind and power. Lux fiddles with the knobs on the radio until she finds a station she likes, and then she sings along in her beautiful, silvery voice as she starts handing her makeup to a humming Mercy in the back seat. Mercy's parents don't let her wear makeup to school, so every morning Lux brings her makeup bag and shares with Mercy. And after last period, Mercy washes her face before she goes home.

I let their song sweep over me, a balm to some of those raw places that I haven't told them about. Maybe if I don't tell anyone we don't have the rent money this month, it simply won't be true.

"You could use some of this, too," Lux says, leaning over and applying lip gloss to my mouth.

I swat her hand away. "I'm driving," I grumble. "You're going to kill us all."

"Hold still then. And look at the goddamn road." Lux continues her ministrations.

"Can you please stop swerving around?" Mercy demands from the back seat. "I'm doing my eyeliner right now."

"Blame Lux," I tell her.

Lux laughs. "You can be so ungrateful sometimes."

I swing into the school parking lot and carefully park the Mach in the back row of the lot.

Mercy flicks the back of my head. "Move it, so I'm not late for first period again. Mr. Morris has it out for me, I think."

"He hates all of us," I commiserate, letting Mercy out of the car. It's no secret that most of the residents of Evanston weren't happy when they had to consolidate with the riffraff from Cottonwood Hollow. And it doesn't help that our girls are *peculiar*.

"You'd better run," Lux calls as Mercy throws on her backpack and sprints across the parking lot. "It's a long way from Antarctica to your class!"

"This is not Antarctica," I counter, shutting my car door. "It's just a good, safe parking spot."

"For your baby?" she asks, turning her attention back to me and patting the hood of the Mach with one hand. Her fingernails are painted a startling shade of banana yellow.

"Yes," I agree, rubbing out her prints with the hem of my plaid skirt.

This makes Lux laugh, and we leave the car in relative safety in the back of the lot.

Lux and I have the same first-period class, and we take our time getting there. It's US history with Miss Strong, and she's nearly always late. The school is big, with over a thousand students, and by the time we get our books from our lockers and make our way to the classroom, Miss Strong is still not there.

We usually sit in the back, and while I'm trying to step over the long legs of teenage boys, one of the girls in a middle row refuses to move her backpack out of the way. When I cock my foot back to kick it, she hisses, "*freak*," under her breath. Her words can barely scratch the thick skin I've developed over the years. However, this doesn't stop me from accidentally bumping my backpack into her shoulder as I pass.

Lux lets a chuckle escape as she follows behind me. The girl doesn't bother saying anything nasty to Lux. We slide into our usual seats. Morgan is already there, waiting for us to arrive. Her dark hair is clipped into a stylish angled bob, and she wears the

Evanston High uniform like it's a designer label. She's perhaps the only girl from Evanston who is actually friendly enough to say hello to me. She's said more than hello to Lux, though, and I watch out of the corner of my eye as Lux squeezes Morgan's hand under the desk. I catch a few words, *"so worried, tornado . . . ,"* before I actively try to tune them out and give them some relative privacy. They seem fine, so whatever Lux might have said to me last night when I walked her home, it wasn't about a problem with Morgan.

Lux and Morgan have been out a few times, though Lux's parents have no idea. Every date has ended with Lux sleeping at my place. Over a bowl of popcorn in the comfort of my bed, we dissect the details of every smile they shared, every gesture, every kiss. Lux told her mom and stepdad that she's a lesbian. Her mom, Tina, was cool with it, but her stepdad, Aaron, is convinced that it's just a phase, and that she just needs the right man to "turn her straight."

But in both Evanston and Cottonwood Hollow, Lux has a reputation for being a man-eater, a reputation left over from our freshman and sophomore years, when she was still learning to control her talent. And there was that one algebra teacher that we'd sort of messed with. Okay, we'd really messed with him. But damn, algebra was hard.

Two boys in the front row are talking in low voices, and one with black hair hazards a glance back toward Lux and me. He sees me staring back and winks. This is the first semester I've ever been in a class with him, and all I know about him is he started at Evanston our sophomore year, he's on the baseball team, and everyone calls him Jett. When he grins, white teeth in a coppery-tan face,

I roll my eyes. A couple girls from Cottonwood Hollow got pregnant last year, and now a lot of the Evanston boys think we're easy. I suppose Lux's reputation doesn't help us, either.

Second period I have free, and I spend it at a lonely table in the library up on the mezzanine level. Mercy finds me a few minutes later, and she looks agitated. "I got counted tardy," she hisses. "*Tardy*. Two Evanston girls came in after me and Mr. Morris didn't say anything to them."

"Sorry," I say. "Tomorrow morning we'll leave earlier."

"My parents are going to kill me. That's the third tardy I've had this month."

"When you're a ghost, please don't come back and haunt me," I reply, taking a book off the shelf.

"I know you don't take school as seriously as I do," Mercy whispers furiously, because she's not capable of breaking the silence rule in the library. I'm not a bad student, but the truth is, no one takes school as seriously as Mercy does. Her parents expect straight As, honor rolls, and extracurricular activities. They want Mercy to be the first one in their family to go to college. Mercy's dad is the foreman at the meat-packing plant, and he makes pretty good money. But his heart is set on his little girl going to some fancy college and being a doctor or a lawyer. He orders information packets in the mail for Ivy League colleges, examining them with the same dedication and thoroughness as he does the ground beef at the plant. I don't know what that must feel like, since no one has any expectations regarding my future. Mercy sometimes looks like she might shatter under the weight of those expectations, like tiny fissures are creeping down over her shoulders.

"I take school very seriously," I counter. "After a prestigious academic career, I plan to be the first rocket scientist from Cottonwood Hollow. Your children will study about me in their textbooks. I will be so successful that I will be the face on some kind of money. Probably a five-dollar bill. When I'm forty-five, I'll retire to the Bahamas and live off my bush funds."

"I think you mean 'hedge funds,'" Mercy corrects me, unable to hide a smile.

"No, mine will be bush funds. I'll invent them along with my potato-fueled rockets."

Mercy shares a prim smile, and I know that her panic meter has backed down to an acceptable level again. "Let's leave ten minutes earlier tomorrow, okay?"

"Got it, boss," I tell her, making a salute with the book I'd picked up.

I am famished by lunchtime, but when I dig in my backpack for my emergency lunch money, I remember that I used it last month. I'm standing in the cafeteria line, ready to grab a tray when this revelation occurs. Damn.

The girl behind me clears her throat. *Ahem.* I zip my backpack closed and step out of line. I feel a familiar flush color my cheeks, not because I'm terribly embarrassed, but more because I'm annoyed and maybe a *little* embarrassed.

Lux stands and waves me over to our usual table. She must have been watching me and knows I'm about to make a break for the library before anyone realizes I don't have lunch money.

I slink over to the table, throwing myself on the bench next to her and dropping my bag on the floor by my feet.

"Forget your lunch money?" Lux asks, raising one eyebrow.

"I'm not hungry," I reply.

"Have some of my pizza," she says. "We can share it."

I hate handouts. Hate, hate, hate them.

"You'll never believe it," Mercy says, sitting down next to me with a loaded lunch tray. "The boy in front of me had to leave, so he gave me his pizza and chocolate milk."

I eye the extra pizza and chocolate milk before I can stop myself.

"Do you guys want it?" Mercy asks. "I'd already paid for mine, but it seemed like such a waste for him to throw his away."

Lux's eyes find mine. "It just so happens that Rome forgot her lunch money."

Mercy smiles and tosses her shoulder-length black hair. "Good," she says. "Then it won't go to waste." She hands me the plate with the wedge of pepperoni pizza on it, and follows it with the carton of chocolate milk.

My stomach rumbles in response. Lux grins her catlike smile and mouths the word *Enough*.

"Miss Galveston," a woman's voice calls over the din of clattering plates and conversations. I look over my shoulder and see the school's elderly office assistant standing behind me with a note in her hand. My mind immediately panics, thinking of Mom and Steven.

She thrusts the note into my hand. "In the future," she huffs, "please tell your family that I don't take personal messages for you."

I scramble to unfold the note. *Need somebody for 3–8 at the shop today. Uncle Red.*

Lux reads the note over my shoulder. "*Uncle* Red," she laughs as the assistant walks away. "Remind me to call him that when I see him next time."

Extra shifts mean extra money. I feel a loosening of the tension in my shoulders, the same feeling I get when I've Fixed something that is particularly problematic.

"We can find our own way home," Mercy says, giving my arm a squeeze.

"Yeah, the bus," Lux hisses, narrowing her eyes. "With the *cretins*."

I grin at her, too happy that I'm getting an extra shift to feel bad for her. "Maybe you can share makeup tips with the other passengers," I offer.

"I hope you choke on your pizza and die," Lux returns, taking an elegant sip of her chocolate milk.

She reminds me that I have lunch now, and I eat the pizza with far more enjoyment than the quality deserves. "Thanks," I remember to tell Mercy when I pick the last pepperoni up off the plate and toss it in my mouth.

When the lunch bell rings, I can hardly wait. I am getting an extra shift, and extra money. If I pick up a shift last-minute to help Red out, he always pays me under the table in cash at the end of the night.

Cash. I am going to have cash by the end of the day.

I can buy gas. I can buy lunch tomorrow. I can . . .

I cannot pay the other half of the rent. The reminder nags at me like a hangnail that's been worried until it's pink and sore.

FOUR

WHEN I PULL UP TO Red's shop, four vehicles are waiting in the bay. Red wipes his hands on a greasy rag as he says, "Answer your damn phone next time so I don't have to pretend to be your long-lost uncle. Get your uniform on and let's get to work."

"Aye-aye, Captain," I reply, giving him a sassy salute. I grab my worn blue coveralls from the hook near the door and head to the tiny bathroom to change.

When I emerge, Red is waiting with a verbal list that he counts off on oil-stained fingers. He's close to forty, with a shaved head and some questionable tattoo choices on his forearms. "One of the guys called in sick today so we're running behind. I need an oil change on the minivans, spark plugs and cabin filter on the sedan."

"Got it," I tell him, getting to work. Each mechanic is supposed to bring his own tools, but Red lets me use the odds and ends he's gathered over the years. He even "found" an old black toolbox on wheels that I suspect he actually purchased secondhand somewhere. My name is airbrushed on the back in pink, courtesy of one of the guys who used to work here. Most of the work I do doesn't require any of my talents as a Fixer, just basic mechanical know-how.

I like the rhythm of the garage. I like the smells of grease and metal, the cranking of engines that need new starters or the squeal of an alternator that's going bad. I like the sound of men cursing and tools clattering against the cement floor when something goes awry. Beneath it all, there's the steady beat of country radio, wailing out tunes that Red hums under his breath as he shuffles around the shop with a barely perceptible limp.

At the end of the night, I meet Red at the till in the office and he pulls out fifty bucks. "Here you go, Rome," he growls. "You earned it."

"Thanks, Red," I reply, crumpling up the bills and shoving them into my backpack. I've changed back into my school uniform and am ready to head home. My stomach is growling, and as tempting as it is to take some of this cash and hit a drive-through, I know I should go home and try to talk to Mom.

I am just to the edge of Evanston, about to turn onto the highway instead of taking the county roads home, when the Mach shudders and dies. I ease it off onto the gravel shoulder of the highway, my hands suddenly clammy on the steering wheel.

Damn.

I forgot to get gas, and there's no Mercy in the car to help me make it home.

Two cars whiz past, shaking the windows of the Mach as I sit inside.

This has not been a good day. It has not been a good couple of days, to be honest. A tornado, no rent money, no lunch money, no gas.

I lean forward and put my head on the steering wheel. I close my eyes. I think back to a time when things weren't this hard.

No, wait. Things have always been this hard.

Someone taps on the window, loudly. My head shoots up. I am staring straight into the crotch of some kind of white sports uniform.

"Hey," the owner of the crotch and uniform says. "You okay in there?"

"What?" I shout belligerently as I roll down the window, although I heard him perfectly.

"I said are you okay in there? You need a ride?"

I look up. The crotch and the sports uniform belong to the boy in my first-period class who'd smiled and winked this morning. Jett. *Of course* it's him. This is going to be a fantastic story for Mercy and Lux later.

"No, I'm fine. I just ran out of gas," I reply, opening the door and sliding out of the car. I pull my backpack out with me and sling it over one shoulder. He backs up, giving me room to pass by him and get to my trunk. I'm struck by the immediate largeness of him even as he moves to get out of my space. There's an empty gas can in the back of the Mach, and I pop the trunk and get it out.

"Are you sure?" he asks, eyeing the Mach dubiously. Now that I'm out of the car, I realize that he's wearing a white pinstripe baseball uniform. When he turns around to look at the Mach's front end, I see that the back of his jersey says *Rodriguez 47.*

"I'm sure." His car is parked behind mine, not that I could see it very well out of the rearview mirror. Machs are made for going forward, not for looking back. He's got a late-model Dodge Challenger R/T, a beast of a muscle car with all the bells and whistles, painted bright orange with black racing stripes down the sides.

"Can I take you to the gas station?" he asks, still standing there on the gravel shoulder of the highway with me as I ponder the distance to the nearest gas station. It's at least two miles.

"I can walk," I reply. Getting in cars with strange Evanston boys is a bad idea. If Mercy were here, she would tell me to get back in my car and lock the doors. She would tell me to call her, and then yell at me because I'm out of minutes and can't call anyone anyway.

"It's getting dark. And it's at least a couple miles back to the 7-Eleven."

"I'll be fine." I shrug, moving around him. He's a few inches over six feet tall, and built like you'd expect for an athlete. Big shoulders, muscular thighs, and a tight ass hugged tighter by his baseball pants. He's got black hair and dark eyes. Somehow he seems to be radiating heat, as if he's got a nuclear core.

"Look," he counters. "We have first period together, so it's not like I'm some weird creeper trying to pick you up. It's Rome, isn't it? I'm Jett. Jett Rodriguez."

"Jet like the plane? That's your real name?"

"Like the plane with two *t*'s," he replies with a look that suggests this isn't the first time someone's asked him about his name.

"Can I have your bat?"

"What?"

"Your bat. Since you're obviously some kind of baseball player. Can I have your bat?"

"Why do you want my bat?"

"I'll let you give me a ride to the gas station and back if I can have your bat."

"If you can have my bat?" He echoes the words as if that might make the request understandable.

"Yeah. So if you try anything funny, I can bash your brains in."

He laughs, his eyes crinkling up.

"Okay," he says. "You can *borrow* my bat." He trudges back to the trunk of his car and pulls out a wooden bat. I follow him and he hands it to me, grip first.

"Thanks," I say, taking it in my free hand. I give him the gas can and then take a few practice swings with the bat, once coming closer to his head than I intended.

Jett looks up from the trunk. "You're taking this bashing-my-brains-in thing really seriously," he says.

"Yeah," I agree. "Better to be safe than sorry, right?"

Jett nods, pursing his lips thoughtfully. "I guess so. But you might want to choke up a little on the grip if you want to get in a really good swing that close."

He opens the passenger door for me, which surprises me, and sets me slightly off-kilter.

"Thank you," I say warily as I sit in his passenger seat with the bat between my knees. The car is *nice*. I mean, black-leather-and-working-air-conditioning nice. I flick a careful glance over the sporty gauges and the slick radio. But more than that, it's an R/T model, which means it has a beefy 5.7 liter Hemi under the hood, not far off from the 340s the Challenger had back in the seventies. It could definitely give the Mach a run for its money. I would swoon, if that's what Cottonwood Hollow girls did. But we don't. We hold bats.

"So you're a junior, right?" he asks as he expertly whips a U-turn on the highway so we're heading toward Evanston.

"Yep."

"Me too."

I nod, casting an admiring gaze at the gauges on his dash that I hope he doesn't notice.

"You're from Cottonwood Hollow, aren't you?"

I spear him with a glance, still clutching the bat, waiting to see where he plans to go with that question. "Yep."

"That's cool. I've heard people out there are kind of . . ." His voice trails off.

"If you mean we're not rich, stuck-up assholes, then yeah, we're kind of different."

Jett laughs.

I feel a little guilty, since he is giving me a ride, and decide I could give him slightly better answers in return for his kindness. "I mean, *you're* probably okay. Except for this car and everything."

"What's wrong with my car?" he asks, sounding defensive for the first time.

"It's a rich-boy car. Costs more than the house I live in. Has airbags and stuff."

"I think airbags are pretty standard."

"Depends on the age of the vehicle in question."

"But at least the rest of me is probably okay." He offers me an affable grin. It's too bright, I think. Like he should be in a toothpaste commercial.

"Yeah, I guess so. Tell me about your interesting sportsperson things. What kind of balls do you play with?" I can't resist the chance to needle him a little.

Jett colors a little beneath his coppery skin. "I'm the pitcher for the Evanston baseball team."

"Do people still watch baseball? Is that a thing?"

"Baseball is America's favorite pastime."

"I thought America's favorite pastime was reality TV." I examine the bat more closely. "This is nice."

"Thanks. It was a gift from my dad."

"Did he come to your game tonight?"

"No. He's away on business for his law firm."

"Oh."

"How about your parents?"

"My mom is a waitress." That's probably a lie now.

"And your dad?"

"He's a ghost."

"A ghost?" Jett's eyes leave the road to check my face for signs of humor.

"Yeah. He's been invisible since before I was born." I've been working on that line for years now. Usually it shuts people up, and I'm about ready for this conversation to be over.

"Oh. I'm sorry. Sorry for asking."

"Awkward moments are something I excel at. Go ahead, ask me something else that's really personal."

Jett doesn't take the hint and keeps going. "Why do they call the girls from Cottonwood Hollow freaks?"

I bristle. "We have *talents*."

He raises his eyebrows as if to say, *and?* So I add, "Talents that can shut people up if they ask too many questions."

He pensively quirks his mouth to one side, as if he's considering whether or not I'm screwing with him, and if I might use his bat to remove his head from his body if he keeps asking questions. The 7-Eleven is only a block ahead, the sign shining brightly in the twilight. "I can pitch pretty well," he offers finally, as if that makes us equals.

I actually laugh this time, because I don't think anyone has ever tried to relate to the girls from Cottonwood Hollow. "Our talents are a little different."

We turn into the gas-station lot, and Jett slides the Challenger in next to a pump. He gets out and pops the trunk for me, acting like he's going to put gas in the can.

"Hey," I interrupt him, taking the gas can. "I can do it myself."

He holds his hands up like I'm waving a gun at him. "Got it. I'm going to run in and grab a drink. Do you want anything?"

"No, I'm good," I tell him, which is a lie. I'm starving. And thirsty. I peel off a crumpled five from the wad of cash that I pull out of my bag. I don't want to go into the gas station and smell cooking hot dogs. "Here's for the gas."

He takes the bill and manages not to make a face at its deteriorated state.

47

When he's prepaid inside, I fill up the gas can. It'll be enough to get me home. I can get gas in Cottonwood Hollow in the morning.

I've capped the gas can and put it back in the trunk when Jett comes back. His arms are full of gas-station provisions. He hands me a fountain drink in a giant Styrofoam cup and a package of beef jerky.

"I don't know what Cottonwood Hollow girls eat," he says. "And I didn't want to ask you any more questions. But I bet you could use a snack. I'm starving."

"We drink the blood of virgins, usually, but beef jerky is okay."

Jett's mouth opens a little, like he's warring between being surprised or impressed, as I circle around to the passenger side of the car. He doesn't bother trying to open my door this time, just gets in and wedges his own soda into the cup holder. I put the bat back between my knees, open the bag of beef jerky, and try not to shove a handful in my mouth as he pulls out of the gas-station lot. Instead, I take a big gulp of soda out of the cup he gave me and offer him the first piece of jerky that I pull out of the bag. With his eyes still on the road, he grabs at it carelessly, his fingertips brushing against mine.

Then I shove a discreet handful of jerky into my mouth.

When he's chewed and swallowed a couple of pieces, he forgets we're done with Q&A time and asks, "So were you going home from work?"

"Yep."

"You have a cleaning gig or something?"

48

"No," I answer, annoyed. "I work at Red's Auto. As a mechanic."

"Really?" he asks, unable to hide the surprise in his voice.

"What? Are you surprised that girls can be mechanics?" I've taken a lot of shit from new mechanics for being a teenage girl. Unless it gets nasty, Red usually lets me handle it myself.

"No, I just thought maybe you were cleaning because you've got a smudge of dirt or something on your face."

I flip down the visor to see my face in his mirror. There's a smudge of grease along my jaw. I washed my hands before I left, but I hadn't looked closely at my face in the bathroom mirror. I rub the smudge with my fingers until it fades a little. Then I snap the visor back up, still annoyed.

I change the subject, since Jett is such a chatty fellow. Let him talk about himself for a while. "So you're on your way home?"

"Yeah, we live just a mile outside of Evanston. We used to live in town, over in the Heights neighborhood."

I can barely keep a straight face, because I've seen the Heights and its palatial stone houses with their ivy-covered walls and gated driveways.

Jett continues casually, "But my mom had this big thing where she wanted to live on a few acres and have chickens and goats and stuff, and so we moved out here last semester."

"And do you?" I fiddle with the handle of the bat to keep myself from shoving more beef jerky into my mouth.

"Do I what?"

"Do you have chickens and goats?"

He laughs. "Yeah, we do. No more mowing the yard. The goats keep it pretty well trimmed down."

I recall the jungle of grass growing around our trailer's plywood skirting. I need a goat.

We pull up behind the Mach, and I get out, sad to leave the bag of beef jerky behind in his car. But it would probably be rude to take it. At least, I'm assuming it would be. I stare at it, hesitating a moment before I shut the door and tuck his bat beneath my arm.

Jett pops the trunk and hands me the gas can, educated at least to the point where he knows I want to do this myself. He leaves the headlights on, because it's almost completely dark and I would have to feel along the back of the car to find the fuel cap without them. The gas tanks in these cars are beneath the trunk, which makes it easy when you're at a gas station because you never have to worry about what side the tank is on. You can pull up to any of them, since the tank is square in the middle of the back of the car. I lean the bat against the bumper as I unscrew the gas cap.

"The fuel tanks are back here, huh?" he observes as I fill the tank. "I think I remember reading somewhere that if you got rear-ended in one of these, they'd explode into flames."

"There's kits you can buy to fix that."

"Have you bought one?"

"No. It's on my list of things to do, though. Thanks for reminding me."

I load the empty gas can back into my trunk, shutting the lid with enough force to make sure it latches.

"So you didn't tell me what your talent is," he says.

The highway is strangely dead, and Jett feels strangely close. He still radiates that heat in the cool evening air.

I pick up the bat.

"I don't tell outsiders what my talent is."

He might be blushing, but in the dark it's hard to tell, because his headlights have clicked off.

"Here's your bat," I tell him, handing it to him handle first. "Thanks for the ride."

A car finally rumbles by, its high beams briefly illuminating us both in a shaft of light. Jett smiles. "Sure. See you around," he says as I get in my car. He's not going to get into his until I've pulled away.

I start the engine up, and it growls, appreciative of the added fuel. I roll the window down and stick my head out, shouting, "You know that kind of pulsating feeling you get when you hit your brakes? Your rotors are warped. You need to get that looked at."

I let the roar of the 351 Cleveland drown out any sounds of a response as I hit the gas.

FIVE

I PULL UP IN FRONT of the trailer, and the overgrown yard is dark.
I turn off the car. The only sounds are cicadas and my own scuf-
fling around as I drag out my backpack and slam the door shut.
Mom has forgotten to turn the porch light on and the curtains are
drawn, so I stumble up the front stoop, moving from memory. My
toe hits something on the top step, and I utter a few choice words
that I picked up at Red's shop.

I lean down and feel around for what I kicked as my eyes
adjust to the lack of light. When my palm rubs against the rough
wood of the box from last night, I recoil instantly, that fight-or-
flight instinct telling me to run like hell.

Somehow the box made its way from the shed to the front
steps. But no one goes in my shed. Fear seizes my muscles and
makes it hard for me to move. I slowly look around the dark yard,
as if someone's going to jump out and yell, "Ha! I really got you
good!" But no one is out here. It's just this creepy-ass box and me.

"So you think making me trip and break my leg is going to convince me to open you?" I ask the box, trying to keep my voice steady, but failing miserably. *I am not afraid of a box*, I tell myself.

The box doesn't answer, which is probably good. My hands trembling, I reach down and pick it up, holding it with the tips of my fingers, as if whatever is in it might rub off on me. It's startlingly cold, and that tug comes back, digging deep in my gut. I'm going to get this out of the way tonight. Whatever is in this box needs to shut the hell up and leave me alone. Maybe once I open it, I'll find out how to make it do that.

I open the door and Steven is there to greet me, his nails clicking on the cheap linoleum. "Steven!" I coo. "Were you a good boy? Did you babysit Mommy?"

Mom is sitting on the couch reading, her typical pose if she's not sleeping or working. She's only got one lamp lit next to the couch. The light reflects off yellow wallpaper that is so worn it's got a sheen on it, like it's covered in a layer or two of grease. The rest of the small living room/kitchen/dining room area is cast in shadows.

My eyes find an empty cup of ramen leaning against the foot of the lamp. I sigh, so glad that I skipped the drive-through and abandoned the jerky to come back to a home-cooked meal. Not that either Mom or I ever really cook. Cooking for us is making boxed macaroni and cheese or baking something frozen in the oven. On holidays like Thanksgiving, Mercy's mom usually invites us over. It's like she can feel our lack of turkey or turkey-cooking skills from all the way over on the other side of town. Or maybe Mercy told her.

Mom looks up from the worn paperback she's been reading.

I set my backpack and the box on the kitchen table, shaking my hands and scrubbing them against my skirt as if I can get rid of the cold that's numbed my fingertips. Then I unzip my backpack and pull out the two books I checked out from the library.

First I deal with Mom.

Then the box.

Mom's eyes light up when she sees the reading material. "You want one?" I ask.

Mom nods. "I'm dying for something new to read."

"Then let's talk about the rent."

Mom sighs. "Can we put this conversation on hold for another day or two?"

"I don't know how you think we can avoid it, anyway. You know how Garrett is. He's a *dick*. I'm surprised he isn't here already banging on the door. Rent was due three days ago." I set the books down on the kitchen table and move to stand in front of her. "*Why do you not have your half of the rent money?*"

Mom huffs. "I got laid off."

It's the answer I was beginning to suspect, but it still stings.

Mom continues. "Almost two weeks ago. The café's not making enough money to support a full-time waitress anymore. Jim's keeping on the part-time girl because she's his niece." Mom crosses her arms.

"Two weeks ago? And all this time you thought it'd be okay not to tell me?" My mind reels through memories of Mom getting up in the morning like she was going to work, wearing her little waitress outfit. Up until a few days ago. When she'd just given up the ruse. As if she wanted to get caught once the rent was past due and our problems were starting to get real.

Mom pulls a folded, wrinkled newspaper from between the lumpy couch cushions. It's the classifieds, and she's circled several ads. She holds it out, as if it were some kind of proof. "I thought I would get something new before you found out. And then I'd just tell you that I changed jobs."

"So have you gotten a new job yet?" I ask, snatching the newspaper out of her hands.

"There's no waitressing jobs. A couple fry cooks, but the pay isn't any more than what I made at the café with tips. And let's face it. I wasn't making enough before, either." Her expression gets tighter, harder. The angles and bones of her face are sharp in the lamplight. "There's some office-type jobs. I helped with the books at the café. My math is pretty good and I could file. But you need a résumé and cover letter and all that."

I have these wide swaths of time when I forget that my mom is a thirty-four-year-old with the education of a sixteen-year-old. She reads a lot and can figure out a 15 percent tip at the café or a 40 percent-off discount at the store faster than anyone I know, but some of her adult skills are totally missing. Like the ability to write a résumé, cook a well-balanced meal from scratch, or attend parent-teacher conferences. It hides beneath her skin, like a splinter that only becomes sore when you work at getting it out.

"I can help you," I tell her, knowing I am digging at that splinter.

"I don't need my seventeen-year-old kid writing my god-damned résumé," Mom grinds out, punctuating her statement by picking up one of the pillows next to her and tossing it across the room.

Steven gets up from where he's been sitting and goes to fetch the pillow.

"That was real mature, Mom. Guess what? You *do* need your seventeen-year-old kid writing your résumé," I retort, angry now. Angry because this is our life, and the same problems keep dragging us down, dragging us out to sea, like those riptides in the oceans that I've read about but have never seen myself. "Stop being so damned stubborn. I'm trying to help you."

Steven brings back the pillow. His jowls relax comfortably against the fabric as he places it back on the couch with Mom.

"Good boy, Steven," Mom and I say in unison.

Steven wags his stumpy tail.

"I'll find something," Mom says. "Just give me a little longer. If I don't have anything by the end of the week, we'll go to the library in Evanston and use their computers to type up a résumé."

"Fine," I tell her. "But what are we going to do about the rent?"

Mom shrugs. "I had to use the money you gave me last week to keep the lights on. They were threatening to shut them off if I didn't pay them. Same with the water." Steven rests his big doggy head on Mom's knee, as if commiserating. "We don't even have anything to pawn that's worth a month's rent."

"I get paid on Friday," I offer. "But a week's pay isn't going to be enough." I think about the forty-five dollars left in my pocket. I need gas to get to school. I guess I could ride the school bus for a while. But how would I get a ride home after work? The familiar gears are turning, the money-hungry ones thirsty for grease that creak out *never enough, never enough, never enough*.

"Maybe I can talk to Garrett," Mom suggests, toying with the yellowed pages of her paperback. "Maybe I can convince him to let us catch up next month."

"Good luck with that." I laugh, but it's an empty sound. "Garrett doesn't do anything for free, Mom."

"We'll figure it out," Mom says, and I know this is her attempt at parenting. To make me think that everything is going to be okay. When I was little, I used to believe her, never knowing that some weeks were "ramen weeks" and others were luxurious "Hamburger Helper and canned peas weeks" because of how much she'd made in tips.

"Yeah," I reply automatically, because there's no point in disagreeing. Even if she had gotten a job today, it wouldn't have put the rent money in our pockets right now. "I'm going to bed," I tell her, backing away from the couch. I grab my backpack and the wooden box that seems to be following me around, glad I'm angry enough to make me less afraid of finding out what's inside it.

"Eat something," Mom says. "There's still some ramen in the cupboard. And I think some peanut butter."

"I'm not hungry." I toss the lie over my shoulder as I slink down the dark hallway and back into my room at the end of the trailer.

My bedroom is small. The full-size mattress and box spring that sit on the floor take up nearly half of it. The only other furniture is a dinged-up white dresser with a slightly foggy mirror hanging above it.

I put the box down on top of the dresser, next to various pots and tubes of makeup and a jewelry box that holds mostly cheap jewelry from Lux and Mercy, things like best-friend necklaces and woven friendship bracelets.

"What do you have that is so damn important?" I let the burning anger over the lack of rent money fill me up, push away the fear of some stupid little box.

I wipe at the dirt and grime crusted on the lid, and I can almost make out what looks like a cursive E. Then I scour the top of the dresser until I find a bobby pin and insert it into the lock. It's rusted, but I am a Fixer, and sooner or later, everything works for me. "Awfully damn stubborn for something that wants to be opened," I tell the box.

There's a cold brush against the back of my neck, like in the winter when someone who's been outside touches you just to be a jerk. I whirl around, but no one's there. The anger ebbs and fades, replaced by fear that makes even my Fixer hands tremble a little.

I have to get this done, and then maybe whatever this is will just go away. Maybe all it needs is a Fixer to open it. I jab the bobby pin back in the lock again. I'm tempted to use a screwdriver and pry the damn thing open, because I just want to get this over with, but it goes against my Fixer blood to destroy something when it could be repaired.

Finally, there's a click inside, and the lock has been tumbled. I push the button to release the latch and pull the box open. Rust flecks rain down from the hinges on the back, making an orangey pool on the white paint of my dresser.

Inside is a lump of fabric that is dry and brittle to the touch.

It's a faded floral pattern that reminds me of old curtains. I start to pull on it, but it's wrapped around something. I remove the whole bundle, and carefully, gently, I unwrap it.

A book.

I like books, I tell myself. Maybe this was all in my head. Books are good. The box is just a box. Everything is fine. The trembling in my fingers subsides a little.

The book is slightly smaller than my hand. The cover is made of smooth leather the color of tea and has a cottonwood leaf tooled into it. I cautiously untangle the leather thong tied around it, wincing when it breaks apart in my fingers.

I open the book as gingerly as I can. The pages are yellowed and brittle, and the handwriting inside is a spidery, loopy cursive that is barely visible on the page.

August 10th

Setting up house was so much fun. John showed me the dugout where he had first lived when he settled in Cottonwood Hollow. We spent a beautiful afternoon there. The farmhouse he built for me is spacious and sunny. I know that Father sent the money last fall while we were engaged so that John could build us a proper house before I joined him here. Father has never liked the idea of me moving out west, wishing I would marry into good Boston society like my sister Amelia, but I love the adventure of it all.

Today I unpacked almost all the trunks that I brought with me from Boston, and the new house is much better for it. There's nothing like a woman's touch to make a house into a home.

Little things like tablecloths on the kitchen table and curtains
hanging at the windows. I put the china Mother sent with me
into the hutch and the silver from Grandmother in the drawers.
I don't know when we shall have much cause to entertain, as so
far Cottonwood Hollow boasts only a general store, a saloon,
and a newly built schoolhouse. But John assures me that soon
the community will build a church, and I will meet our neighbors
there.

I am so happy to be Mrs. Emmeline Remington.

I drop the book onto the top of the dresser as if it had burned me. This is Emmeline Remington's diary. The woman who put the curse on the girls of Cottonwood Hollow. Oh, shit. The *E* on the top of the box—of course it was for *Emmeline*. I've got to get rid of it. What have I done? I wish Mercy was here, because maybe she could ask Jesus or somebody to send a lightning bolt and burn the trailer down with the diary inside it. Shit, oh, shit.

The cold touch whispers again at my neck, and I whirl around to face it, my chest heaving as if I've been running for my life. There's no one there. My gut clenches, and it's not the familiar tug of wanting to Fix something; it's hard, visceral fear.

I turn back to the diary again, recalling that Neveah said she saw a lady when she Found it. There's no lady in my room, but I am definitely not alone. I pick up the diary, my steady Fixer hands trembling again. This diary has come to me for a reason, I tell myself. But why? So I could Fix the rusty latch so someone could open it? Was I supposed to be the one to open it, or was I only supposed to Fix the latch?

What if there's no plausible reason at all for me to have it? Maybe the tornado unearthed it with all those other bits of junk from the ruins and the pasture and we just happened to be the unlucky people who stumbled upon it. Maybe *no one* was meant to find it. I look up to see if lightning really *is* going to strike me from above.

I hold the pages upside down, shaking the diary a little to see if anything falls out. But what if the diary *was* meant to come to me? What am I supposed to figure out? That Emmeline Remington was once a happy, normal person before she turned psycho and cursed us all?

I set the book back down on the dresser and begin pulling open drawers to dig out some pajamas. I can handle this. I just have to get back in control of myself. I'm Rome Galveston. This is just a diary. Tomorrow morning, I'll put the book back in the box and bury it out in the pasture. Let someone else deal with it. I've dealt with the curse all my life. I don't have to deal with this diary, too.

I find some comfy sweats and a T-shirt, and begin stripping off my school uniform. I hang it up, knowing if I'm careful I can wear it a couple of times before I have to wash it.

Telling myself that everything is going to be fine, I pull on the sweats and the T-shirt and go to grab my hairbrush off the dresser only to find that the diary is open again. I reach out a trembling hand and slam it shut, as if I can shut back up whatever it is I've released. But the moment I remove my hand, the diary flips open, the pages turning themselves to the same place.

I jump back so far that I stumble into the mattress and fall over, landing on my ass. I scuttle backward against the wall, feeling around on the floor for something to protect myself with, and wishing I had Jett Rodriguez's bat again right now. But there's nothing, so I'm just cowering on the floor, watching the diary and waiting for either the ghost of Emmeline Remington to appear and murder me or for my heart to stop beating like it's about to shatter my rib cage.

Long moments pass, and nothing happens. Maybe I am going to do what the diary wants. And then maybe whatever ghost or spirit or creepy thing it is will leave me alone. "Do you want me to read more?" I ask the room, my voice barely a whisper. The pages of the diary stir. But there's no lightning, so that seems like a good sign.

I get up from the floor and stand at the dresser to read the pages where they lie open.

May 1st

I lost the baby. A daughter. I know it was his fault. I know he was with her again, and it killed me inside. It killed our daughter. I had everything ready for her. I've knit all her little caps and booties, embroidered all her gowns. Mother and Father sent a generous dowry chest for her. Father had promised a gold bar for the birth of his first grandchild, and it was in the chest, along with a set of silver that one day she could have taken to her own house. A christening gown edged with Irish lace. The gown was from Mother, of course. Father is always thinking of money, but Mother knew it would be the gown I treasured most, embroidered by her hands. They sent a letter promising to visit soon.

My daughter was going to be Evangeline Remington, the Queen of Cottonwood Hollow. I had imagined this town growing into a real city with society, like the Boston I loved and left behind. But it's only ever been storms and wind and drought and sunburned farmers looking mournfully over their meager crops. Life on the prairie is hard, and it has made its people harder. I was foolish to come here, foolish to dream that John and I would have a perfect life.

It has cost me my love, my daughter, and soon my life as well. The birthing of my stillborn child has left me weak, and our neighbor, Maisie, who comes to tend me, looks more solemn each time she visits. She wanted to take Evangeline from me already, but I refused. I will hold my daughter into the next life, so that we can go together.

But this is one thing I will wish with my dying breath upon all the daughters of Cottonwood Hollow who follow mine: May they depend on each other; protect each other no matter what the cost, as my sister would have done for me if she were here. May they be blessed with the strength to survive here. I will not, but I know now what I needed. May they possess a clever wit to fill their days with joy, hone the skills to fix what seems beyond repair, find what becomes lost in this vast, open grassland, and heal those who are unwell, like my darling Evangeline. May they have the gift of foresight to avoid the perils that lie around every turn in this unforgiving place, and the ability to read *who is trustworthy and who is not before they make the same mistakes I did with John. May they always find a way to have enough, even when times are hard. And may they be sirens who can draw a man back to them, though I could not. For it is a lonely world without love. And I don't even have the love of my daughter to comfort me now.*

There's a cold ache in my chest. It feels as if I've lost everything. There's no hope, no happiness left in my body. I am strangely weighted, as if grief has taken over my body and made my bones into iron. I feel like I am Emmeline Remington and I have lost everything I ever loved.

I skim through the diary and turn to the last page. The handwriting is shaky, almost erratic, as if Emmeline is losing control of her body. Or maybe her mind.

May 2nd

John took my daughter. Maisie said he buried her. I don't know where, but I will find her, even if I have to claw at the dirt with my fingernails to get her back.

He's leaving with the woman. Maisie saw him going through the house, looking for the silver I brought with me, and the dowry chest Mother and Father sent for Evangeline. He came in here and shouted, saying he needed it. He said I could have the house and the land, though he knows I'm not going to live much longer. He wants to sell it all and go to California to hunt for gold with his new lady love.

Well, the last laugh shall be mine. I've hidden it all—the deed to the land, the gifts from my parents. No one should have that dowry chest or the land but a daughter of Cottonwood Hollow.

The diary slams itself shut.

"Holy shit."

SIX

I CLIMB THROUGH THE OVERGROWN shrubbery in the back of Lux's house. The window is open, and I can hear voices, like maybe she's watching television in her room. When I get close enough, I can see through her parted lavender curtains.

I'm about to hiss, "Lux," through the screen when I realize the voices aren't from a television and I duck down so I'm not seen in case my presence might get Lux in trouble.

"You sure you didn't bait him?" Lux's mother asks.

"I wasn't doing *anything* to Aaron. He's lying."

"Well, that's not what he's saying."

"So you're going to believe him over me?"

"It's not a contest, Lux. And I'm sure it was an accident. He's been under a lot of stress lately since his hours got cut."

I stand up just enough so I can barely peer through the window, trying to see what happened to Lux. Tina lays a hand on

Lux's face, which is red and damp with tears. Tina's Healing her, I realize. I put the pieces together; that son of a bitch Aaron hit Lux.

"Why do you stay with him?" Lux asks, her voice so soft that I have to take a step closer to hear her. "We don't need him. Please, Mom, for once, just listen to me. Make him leave."

"We do need him, Lux," Tina whispers. "He makes good money at the plant. You like those pretty clothes and your cable TV? The new computer we bought you for school last month? All that costs money. Look at Rome and her mama. You want to live like that? Hand-to-mouth in an old trailer out on the edge of town?"

Once when I was eleven, I got into a fight with Roger Wyatt for calling my mom a whore. It was going pretty well for me until he punched me in the solar plexus and it felt like all the air had left my body. Maybe it's the truth of what Tina said that makes her words feel like that fight with Roger Wyatt, but her words hurt no matter what. I clench the diary in my hand, grounding myself in reality, in the here and now.

"Well, nobody's having to Heal Rome, are they?" Lux murmurs when her mom pulls her hand away from Lux's cheek.

"Just stay out of his way. He's not a bad man. And he's a good provider. This is just a rough patch, you'll see. He'll get his full shifts back and things will get better again." Tina pats Lux's leg, but doesn't look her in the eye.

Then Tina leaves Lux alone in her lavender bedroom.

"Lux," I hiss through the screen. "Lux, come here."

Lux's face jerks up from where she's been staring down at the carpet. She rubs her face, wiping away tears with the soft palms of her hands. She takes a swipe or two at her nose before coming to the window and parting the curtains. "How long were you out there?" she asks.

"Long enough. Your douchebag stepdad hit you?"

Lux's face threatens to crumple, her full lower lip trembling slightly. I want to ask her if it's happened before, and if it has, why she never told me. But I suppose it's for the same reason that I never told her that we were behind on the rent, or that I didn't have any lunch money.

I put my hand on the screen, all five fingers spread out. Lux puts her hand against mine, and I see the thin white scar across her palm before the wire netting is between us. Just like the secrets.

"Don't tell Mercy," she whispers. "Or anyone. I don't want them to know. I didn't want *you* to know."

I remember my own secrets. How I have been helping to pay the rent since Mom's shifts got cut nearly a year ago. How we don't have the rent money now. How I wish my life was broken pottery or a rusty hinge, something that could be Fixed.

"I can keep a secret," I reply, hating how the words taste like metal in my mouth. Blood, I think. They taste like blood. But if Lux can have her secrets, then it makes it okay for me to have mine, too.

Lux nods, a curtain of strawberry-blond hair falling over her face.

"Can you come out?" I ask her. "I have something to show you. And Mercy."

Lux withdraws her hand, shakes her hair back from her face with a careless tilt of her chin, as if nothing had just passed between us. No secrets at all. She rolls her eyes. "You know what a pain it's going to be to get her out. It's almost eleven."

"Yeah, but we need to talk. Before school isn't going to be enough for this."

Lux crosses the room back to the door and locks it as soundlessly as she can. Then she comes back to the window and pushes up the screen. "Give me some room," she grunts as she turns her butt toward me and starts poking her long legs out the window. I slog back through the bushes until I get into the grass and brush twigs and leaves from my clothes.

"You look great, by the way," Lux says when she joins me, still dressed in her school uniform.

"I like to be comfortable," I reply, noticing the beginnings of a hole in the knee of my sweat pants.

"So what's this all about?" she asks.

"Let's get Mercy, and I'll tell you both at once."

We walk across town, passing over the main drag and the crowd that's gathered at Flynn's, the local bar. The neon lights cast a soft glow across the wide, raised sidewalk, and the air is thick with the smells of cigarette smoke and frying onions. It makes me wish that I'd bothered to eat something. Wynona, a waitress there, is standing outside smoking a cigarette and talking to Meg Farley. She gives us a friendly wave. We pass the humming soda machines and the grain bins near the co-op, Lux distracting herself by dodging the cracks on the sidewalk as we go.

When we get to Mercy's pretty two-story house, we go straight to the garage. Mr. Montoya keeps a ladder hanging on the back of it, out of sight so that everything looks neat and tidy. Lux and I each grab an end and lift it off the hooks, carrying the ladder between us to the side of the house where Mercy's bedroom is. Carefully, I lean the ladder up against the siding. Lux holds the bottom while I climb up to Mercy's bedroom window. Her parents are in the room directly below hers, so we have to be as quiet as possible, or they'll peer through their blinds to see Lux holding a ladder.

The steps of the wooden ladder are rough and old, and I don't suspect they'll hold long enough for Neveah's friends to sneak her out of her bedroom.

When I get to the top, I don't look down. I've never been a huge fan of heights, but after Lux got splinters in both hands last summer, she's always made me climb. I tap as quietly as possible on the glass of Mercy's window. Of course, it's closed. When she's not reading romances that she smuggles into her house from the library or Mom's dog-eared collection, Mercy reads a lot of true crime novels, which lead her to believe that sleeping with a window open could get her kidnapped and locked in a cellar or chopped into a million bits.

Mercy's curtains part hesitantly, but when she spies me outside she throws open the window. "Are you crazy?" she whisper-shouts. "I thought you were a psycho killer. I was ready to start screaming for my dad."

"Mercy, how many times have we come to your window now? Thirty? Forty? Psycho murderers aren't coming to your window on a fifteen-foot ladder. They're just going to take the stairs like normal people."

Mercy slaps a hand over her mouth before she laughs. "Let me grab my robe," she says, darting back inside the dark cocoon of her bedroom to pull on a pink floral robe over her nightgown. She climbs fearlessly out her window and down the ladder. Mercy is not afraid of heights at all, the ladder having been her idea in the first place.

We scurry into her dad's garage, Mercy finding the light switch in the dark. The bulbs flicker and buzz briefly before turning on all the way. There's a pool table in one back corner and a poker table in the other for when Mr. Montoya's buddies from the meat-packing plant come over every third Friday night to play cards. A 1968 Mustang sits in the middle of the garage, a project car that Mr. Montoya has been working on since we were kids. It's got a 302 in it, and I resist the urge to look under the hood to see what he's done to it lately. Sometimes he asks me my opinion on something like rebuilding the carburetor, and it's all I can do to rein in my enthusiasm and leave him to his weekend tinkering rather than taking over the project myself. He tried to get Mercy or Neveah interested in it, but they're not at all, and Malakai is too little to do much more than hand him wrenches.

Lux takes a seat on the pool table, scooting up on the edge and grabbing the cue ball to send it skiing across the table to crack into the other balls.

Mercy sends Lux a dark look. "Could you *not* make so much noise?"

"Please," Lux scoffs, leaning back. "Your parents won't know we're out here. I've listened to your mom snore. That's the only sound anyone in your house is hearing right now."

I nudge Lux's knee as she swings her legs. "Focus," I tell her. "I have to talk to you both."

"What?" Mercy asks, her expressive brows arching with excitement. "Did you finally get a boyfriend?" Mercy has been waiting for Sam Buford from her Bible study group to notice her for what seems like forever. Until then, she lives vicariously through our romantic endeavors.

I roll my eyes, thinking back briefly to my evening with Jett Rodriguez, baseball pitcher and beef jerky buyer. "No," I answer. "This is about the box that Neveah Found last night after the tornado."

"The box?" Mercy and Lux ask in unison, curiosity piqued.

"I opened it tonight. And this was inside." I hold up Emmeline Remington's diary.

"What is it?" Lux asks, sitting up and taking it from me just as Mercy skims a finger over the leather.

When the three of us touch the diary, a cold wind whips across the pool table, shooting the balls against each other in a great clacking noise and scattering them into the holes, banishing them from the green felt table.

Lux falls off the edge of the pool table, dropping the diary onto it in her haste. "Holy shit! What in the hell was that?" she hisses as she looks around the well-lit garage.

Mercy grabs my arm like she's going to pull me from danger. "Leave it and let's get out of here!" she yelps.

"It's Emmeline Remington's diary," I whisper. The lights flicker.

Mercy tenses, as if she's expecting something else to go flying across the room. When a few moments pass with no further activity, she asks, "Are you sure?" She takes a cautious step forward and picks up the diary with one small, trembling hand. She looks around the room again, waiting to see if something else is going to happen now that she's touched the diary.

"I'm sure. I read some of it before I came over. And the stories are wrong. About almost everything."

Lux picks herself up off the floor. "What do you mean, wrong?" she asks, her eyes darting up to the lights to see if they will flicker again. She lets out a frightened gasp when a june bug lands on her shoulder, leaping away at the scratchy touch and jamming her hip against the table. "Damn it," she curses, rubbing her hip and glaring at the diary as if it had caused her to injure herself.

"Emmeline *was* left by her husband, but she had a baby. A daughter who was stillborn."

Mercy's face falls. "That's so sad. Oh, how awful for her."

"Still not a good reason to curse us, though," Lux points out.

"That's why you have to read this," I tell them. I show them Emmeline's wish for the girls of Cottonwood Hollow.

Mercy traces a finger across the spidery handwriting, reading Emmeline's words.

"I don't know if the tornado woke her up or what, but I think she wants us to know this. She wants us to know that she never meant for our talents to be a curse," I whisper. "They were supposed to be gifts. All of them." I've never thought of my talent for Fixing things as anything but a curse simply because it was such a need. But to see it as a gift changes it, shifting it ever so slightly. How many times had my ability to Fix things been the difference between eating and going hungry? It had certainly helped me get the job at Red's Auto so that I could help pay the rent. And even before that, the very first time I Fixed that microwave so that we could make supper. It wasn't supposed to make me an outcast, an oddity. It was supposed to keep me alive.

Lux looks away. "Being a Siren is a curse if you don't want to keep *any* man around," she mutters. And it's true. Almost any other talent you could see as a gift. But for Lux, being a Siren has never been a good thing.

"It's funny, isn't it?" Mercy asks, looking at Lux and then me. "To think of how differently you could live if you knew you were supposed to be blessed and not cursed. You could just spend all your time walking around doing good for other people, like Emmeline tried to do for us." I can see Mercy filtering things through her belief. Her parents have always seen what their girls have as a gift from God. And maybe it is. Mercy's family has certainly never wanted for anything since she was born, the first Enough in Cottonwood Hollow for nearly thirty years.

Lux shrugs. "I'm cursed and so's my mom. I don't care what the book says." My mind flashes back to Tina standing over Lux, Healing the bruise forming on her daughter's cheek. Who knew that a talent for Healing could be a curse?

Mercy comes closer to Lux and leans her head against Lux's shoulder. Mercy doesn't know why Lux could ever see Healing as a curse, but I do.

But if Mercy knew Aaron hit Lux, she'd be over there in an instant, probably wielding one of Mrs. Montoya's meat tenderizers. Lux's widowed mom marrying Aaron was straight out of a fairy tale. Tina had been widowed while she was pregnant with Lux, and it wasn't until Lux was in the third grade that she remarried.

Suddenly Tina lost that tight, strained look on her face, and Lux had pretty dresses and a Barbie dream house that she reluctantly let me remodel to add a garage for my Matchbox cars. The three of us had been flower girls at the wedding, and even then, Mercy had been in love with romance and knights in shining armor. If Mercy suspected Aaron was less than a prince, she'd be devastated. And maybe Lux and Tina would be, too, if they had to admit that their fairy tale wasn't real after all.

I read the last pages aloud, finishing with Emmeline's final words, "*No one should have that dowry chest or the land but a daughter of Cottonwood Hollow.*"

Lux jolts, jarring Mercy, who'd still been leaning on her. "A treasure?" she squeaks. "Why didn't you lead with that? You're saying Emmeline Remington left a box of treasure for any daughter of Cottonwood Hollow?"

"It sounds like it was a lot of silverware and baby clothes," Mercy says hesitantly, looking at Lux.

"Yeah, *silver* silverware. Like the kind that can be melted down and sold," Lux says. "And a *gold bar.*"

"And the deed to the land. So that's where it is. She left a stipulation in her will, you know. The town pays the taxes on the land so that they can lease out the north forty acres to farm," Mercy says. "The Johnsons and the McGraws farm it. The money from the lease pays for the taxes and makes sure that the homestead is preserved as part of the town's history."

"How do you know all this?" I ask.

"I volunteered for the Cottonwood Hollow Historical Society last summer, remember?"

I sort of remember helping her with a bake sale, but Mercy has so many extracurricular activities and volunteer work that they all sort of blend together.

Lux makes a face. "I don't care about the land. Let's go back to the silver. And the gold bar."

"I don't think we should be selling Emmeline Remington's dowry chest," Mercy says warily. "It sounds like trouble."

"It sounds like she wanted us to have it," Lux shoots back, her green eyes sparking. She fixes them on me, her gaze asking me to know, to understand what this means to her. I think of what her mom said about needing Aaron as a provider. This is Lux's way out. Her way to convince her mom to kick Aaron out.

All I can think about is the rent money. I really, really need that rent money.

Lux is right. Who cares about the gifts? Emmeline is offering us a way to fix everything. I close my eyes briefly, imagine Mom's face if I came home tomorrow or the next day with a wad of cash so that we wouldn't have to worry about Garrett and his stupid rent for a long time.

"We don't even know where it is," Mercy says. "Where would we even start looking?"

"It's got to be somewhere out there in that fenced-off area," Lux says. "The land that Emmeline left for Cottonwood Hollow."

A car drives by with its music turned up and the bass booming loud enough to shake the windows of the garage.

"I need to get back to my bedroom," Mercy whispers as if suddenly someone might be able to hear us. "That could have woken my parents."

I nod. "We'll talk tomorrow." Inside, I'm still buzzing, thinking that maybe we're going to be okay. Maybe this dowry chest is going to change things for us.

Outside the Montoyas' house, Lux holds the bottom of the ladder while Mercy climbs, her pretty pink robe falling in soft folds around her ankles as she ascends. When she's inside, she gives us a wave and an all-clear thumbs-up. Lux and I pull the ladder from the house and carry it to the back of the garage. We hang it gently, careful not to make any more sound than necessary.

The walk back to Lux's house is quiet. She's too wrapped up in plans about that dowry chest, and I'm thinking of the rent, of Aaron, and of Mercy's pretty pink robe and her two-story house with the window boxes as I look down at my sweat pants, the hole in the knee bigger than I remember it being.

"Don't forget," Lux whispers when she's in her room again. She slides the screen back into place.

I nod.

I tuck the diary under my arm and walk back home. Cottonwood Hollow is dark and calm, the entire town asleep, inhaling and exhaling in the same rhythms, gently wafting the clouds over the moon.

When I get back to our trailer, I let myself in quietly through the front door. Then I creep back to my room and change into darker clothes. I leave the diary on top of my dresser and grab my backpack. I listen at Mom's bedroom door and hear both Steven and Mom snoring gently. In the tiny laundry room next to her bedroom, I grab the bottle of bleach from the shelf above the washing machine and stop at the shed outside to put a funnel in my backpack.

The walk back to Lux's house is just as quiet as my walk home earlier. It's only me and the cicadas. The occasional flicker of lightning bugs helps light my way when I pass through the parts of town without street lamps, the sidewalks familiar enough that I can avoid the broken spots, even in the dark. I know who's likely to be smoking out on their porch this time of night or letting the dog out one more time before bed, and I avoid those houses, picking my way up one road, then across and over to the next, not wanting to be seen by anyone.

Lux's front yard is dark. The lights in the house are all off, even the television in the living room that always seems to be on, blaring syndicated dialogue and laugh tracks.

Good.

I hunch over and scuttle up the driveway to Aaron's truck. It's a late-model Ford, a three-quarter ton kitted out with four-wheel drive and leather. Lux said they practically had to mortgage the house to buy it. He's got a personalized license plate on the back of the truck that says AARONS, and when he's not driving it around, he's usually waxing it in the driveway in the shade of the leaning pine.

I tinker with the gas hatch until it pops, even without unlocking the truck and pulling the release switch. One of the perks of being a Fixer, I remind myself. *A gift, not a curse.* I unscrew the gas cap, creeping up slowly to peek over the truck bed and make sure no one in the house is stirring. It's still quiet. Still dark.

I tug the funnel and the bottle of bleach out of my backpack. Fitting the funnel into the gas tank, I unscrew the cap on the bottle of bleach and carefully tilt the bottle up to the funnel.

Glug, glug, glug. I tip the bottle up until all the bleach is in Aaron's gas tank.

When it's empty, I shake errant drops of bleach from the funnel tip, put the lid back on the bottle, and stuff everything back into my bag. I close Aaron's gas tank, shoulder my bag, and leave the same way I came.

Nobody messes with the girls from Cottonwood Hollow.

SEVEN

THE POUNDING ON THE FRONT door wakes me up. "Ugh," I groan, rolling over and accidentally pushing Emmeline Remington's diary off my bed. I'd stayed up almost all night reading it, hoping there'd be more clues about where she'd left this dowry chest that could possibly save us. It's not something I plan on recommending to Lux and Mercy. It was tragic: the tale of a happy young woman from a well-off family who moves out west to be with some guy she met who says he has a prosperous farm in Kansas. Instead of having a happily ever after, she grows sadder and more isolated as her husband begins spending all his time with another woman. He finally leaves her when the child she's carrying, the daughter she desperately wants, *dies*. And then, presumably, so does Emmeline, because the rest of the diary is blank.

The pounding comes again, and I drag myself out of bed as Steven barks at the other end of the trailer, which means Mom is trying to do the same thing from her bedroom. We make it to the front door at the same time, Steven bumping against our thighs to see who's arrived. There's a jangle of keys in the lock.

Mom and I jump. "Shit." She mouths the word and attempts to tug the door open before Garrett Remington pushes it open.

"There you are, girls," Garrett says as he steps into the living room area. His ostrich-leather boots click on the linoleum. "I was starting to think you were avoiding me."

"No," both Mom and I say too loudly.

Garrett smiles, and it's all I can do not to punch him in the face. In the daylight, Garrett looks a lot like an aging Ken doll, unlike the sinister being he'd been when we met him in the pasture after dark. He's wearing a loose jacket with the words *Cottonwood Hollow Rentals* embroidered across his left breast. He's good-looking, somewhere in his mid-forties, with a perpetual tan and that Oklahoma drawl that's out of place because I know he went to high school in Evanston.

"Well, I haven't seen you with this month's rent check. So I thought maybe I'd pop in before you girls left this morning."

"We've hit a bit of a snag, Garrett," Mom says, smiling, as if we're not standing here in our pajamas because he's pushed into our house with his set of landlord's keys.

Garrett grins like he's really enjoying that he's cornered us, and it makes me feel sick inside. "I heard about you getting laid off, honey, and that's just too bad. But you know, I'm a businessman, not a philanthropist. In Evanston, there's places like this lovely home renting for nearly twice what I've been charging you."

"Evanston has a median income of nearly three times Cottonwood Hollow's," I parry.

Mom shoots me a glare that indicates I'm not helping.

Garrett's tongue moves around his mouth like he's trying to use it to pick out something from between his teeth. "Darling," he spits out, "you just get cleverer every time I lay eyes on you. And prettier, too. Just like your mama." His blue eyes flick back to Mom, and he smiles appreciatively. Probably because she's not wearing a bra.

"You know," Garrett says suddenly. "It's been awhile since I've done a walk-through of this place. Seen what needs work. I think I'll do that now. Just in case I need to start bringing prospective tenants out here soon." He surges past us, his hand purposely brushing against my ass even as I attempt to get out of his way. Mom's eyebrows shoot up, her spine going as rigid as iron.

"Garrett," Mom says, "you don't need to—"

"Nonsense, honey," Garrett interrupts her. "It's part of my duties as a landlord. Now why don't you and your little darling go find your pocketbook and get out your rent money?" He goes down the hall toward my room.

Mom's eyes lock on mine, and I realize that I've never noticed how similar they are to my own. That same coppery brown flecked with gold. *Rusty*, Lux had once called them. Like Cottonwood Hollow had oxidized us both. "What are we going to do?" I mouth to Mom, as if she's going to have the answer. I looked it up at the library, and in Kansas, landlords are required to give thirty days' notice before eviction, but that's if you can prove that you're a good tenant—one that's always paid the rent on time. And he can prove that we haven't, thanks to that one episode when I was thirteen.

Mom shrugs helplessly. "I don't even have a check to write him a hot one. We are screwed."

"We have to negotiate," I whisper. "Or stall him somehow." But I have no idea how we are going to do that. I think of Emmeline Remington, and how shitty her life was here. It occurs to me that things in Cottonwood Hollow haven't changed much.

Mom licks her lips, and takes a deep breath like she's about to jump into Truett pond. "Okay," she says. "I know what I have to do."

Garrett bursts back out of my bedroom, his hands in the voluminous pockets of his jacket. He looks at me. "See you did some painting in there, sugar tits. Should've talked to me about that first." It's like he's making a list of all the things we've done wrong in case we get the guts to take him to court. As if we could even afford it.

Mom fists her hands.

"Let's go check your room, shall we?" he says to Mom with a leer. "I seem to remember having some good times back there. Maybe we still can."

Now *I* want to punch him in his face. Garrett Remington is a sick bastard. Mom nods and begins to follow him down the hall, giving me a gesture that says, *Get out*.

There's a sinking ache in my stomach like I've swallowed a thousand ball bearings. This is her new plan, the reason for that deep breath. Mom and I have done a lot of things to get by over the years, but never this.

"Wait!" I shout so loudly that Steven sits, head down and ears pinned back against his skull. I hold up a hand to stop them.

Garrett turns around, and Mom gives me a look that says, *What the hell are you doing?*

"We don't have the rent money," I tell Garrett. He comes back into the living room, that same sick smile on his face. He's getting what he wants. He's making us suffer. Making us beg.

But I won't beg.

"We want to negotiate. My 1972 Mach 1 Mustang for five months' rent." I know he'll never give me that much, but I have to start high or he'll screw me over even worse.

"Three," Garrett says without missing a beat.

"Four," I counter.

"Three because I have to deal with the bother of selling it." He bares his teeth like an animal.

"Fine. Three and we don't see your face here again until the first of August."

"Where's the title?" he asks, rolling his shoulders like this is just another day at the office.

"I'll get it," I reply, my voice hoarse. I go back down the hallway and get the title out of my underwear drawer in the white dresser. I come back out into the living room, and Mom has managed to shuffle Garrett to the front door.

"Here it is," I say, signing over the title with a ballpoint pen I find on the kitchen table and handing it to him.

"And the keys?" Garrett drawls.

I grab them off the kitchen table too and hand them over. When their weight leaves my palm, it feels as if I've ripped off a part of me and given it to him.

"All right, pretty girls," Garrett says, opening the door. "I'll see you in three months." He goes out and slams the door behind him. We stand there still until we hear the sound of the Mach starting up and pulling away, the 351 Cleveland growling. I peek out through the curtains and see he's left his one-ton, gas-guzzling Ram truck parked just off the dirt road to pick up later.

Mom's head swivels toward me. "What were you thinking?" she exclaims, throwing up her hands.

"What was I thinking?" I shout back. "What were *you* thinking? Going back there with him to your bedroom? He's a creep. What if he had wanted *me* to go back there?"

"I would never let him—" Mom slings back, her face contorted with emotion.

"And I wouldn't let *you*, either."

"You shouldn't have given him your car!" Mom shouts back, near tears. "You love that car!"

"Well, we couldn't *live* in it, Mom!"

Steven barks.

"Shut up, Steven!" we both shout.

"You can take my car to school and your job at the shop," Mom says quietly. The fight is gone out of her, and for the first time in my life, I think that she really looks defeated.

"How are you going to look for work without a car?" I snap. I can't keep the edge out of my voice. If she'd had a job, I wouldn't have had to trade the Mach for rent. "You going to walk to Evanston?"

Mom shrugs.

"I'll ride the bus, Mom. And I'll figure out a way home from work." I turn on my heel and stomp back to my side of the trailer.

I'm waiting at the head of the dirt road when the bus comes. I climb on, ignoring the comments and stares from the other Cottonwood Hollow high schoolers not used to seeing me ride the bus. "Get lost," I tell the freshman boy in the farthest seat in the back. He ducks under my arm and scurries up the aisle. I throw myself into the now-vacant seat, bunching my backpack on top of my stomach as I slouch down until I am invisible.

Mercy and Lux get on later, clearly perplexed that I sent a random text from my mom's phone saying I couldn't pick them up this morning. I should have waved them back to me, explained everything that happened this morning on the ride to school. But I can't. I can't make myself sit up, meet their gazes, and spill the truth on the Cottonwood Hollow school bus.

I'd barely been able to pass the empty spot in the front yard where I usually park the Mach without throwing up.

I stay curled up in the back seat until everyone gets off at the high school. Then I pull the emergency lever and jump out the back. The alarm goes off and the bus driver swears at me, but I don't really care.

I skip first period. Not because I don't like history, but because I can't face Lux or Mercy yet. One look from them and I'll crumble inside. Instead I go to the library, climbing up the steps to the small study table on the mezzanine. I dump my books out of my backpack and work on the questions I know Miss Strong will assign at the end of the chapter. I'm not worried about skipping, but I want to keep my brain busy and not think about the Mach or my mom or Garrett.

I plan to duck out before my free period, when I know Mercy will look for me here, but I get absorbed in trying to finish the last question for history and don't notice how late it is until Mercy appears at my elbow.

"Hey," she says. "I thought maybe you weren't coming today."

"I'm here," I say, waving my pencil as if nothing much is going on.

"What happened this morning? You didn't say much in that text from your mom's phone."

"I couldn't drive us."

"Is there something wrong with the Mach?" she asks, frowning. She asks it in the same tone a new mother might use to ask if her baby is sick.

I briefly contemplate lying, but there's no way to hide the fact that the Mach is gone. "I don't have it anymore." The words might as well have been ripped from my vocal cords. That's how painful it is to say them.

"What do you mean?" she asks.

"I sold it. Traded it, I mean. This morning."

"Rome, what did you trade it for?" Mercy turns her small hand over toward me, her white scar barely visible before she closes her hand down over mine.

I'm ashamed that tears are pricking the backs of my eyes. I'm not a little girl, and it's not something to cry over. It's not like I lost my mom, or Steven. It's just an object. Just a car.

"The rent," I squeak out, hating myself for telling her the truth, for letting out just one secret that I'd sworn to keep. But there's no other way to explain that the Mach is gone. "I traded it for three months' rent from Garrett."

"Rome," Mercy admonishes me. "Why didn't you tell us things were that bad?"

I tug my hand out from underneath hers, slamming my history book shut and stuffing it into my backpack. "I have to go," I lie. "I have to meet Miss Strong and tell her why I missed first period."

"Rome," Mercy calls after me as I thunder down the stairs of the mezzanine, causing the librarian to glare.

I hurry down the crowded halls of the massive school, head down, not really sure where I'm going. I bump shoulders with a senior boy who mutters something like "stupid Hollow slut," but I can't find it in me to fight back, or even really be insulted. Eventually I make it outside, and all I can think about when I see the parking lot is getting into my car and hitting the open road. But I don't have the Mach anymore. I can't run away.

So instead I turn left toward the baseball diamond, which is abandoned this time of day. I climb into the stadium bleachers, all the way to the very top. This is the home-team side of the stadium, so the benches are wide and padded. I lie down on the top bench and wait for the sun to bake me into a hard, leathery cadaver that can no longer feel human emotion.

An hour passes. I feel the sun beating down on my eyelids, but I'm comforted by the wall at the back of the bleachers that presses against my arm and keeps me from plunging twenty feet to the ground. Eventually I roll over onto my side and fall asleep.

When I wake up, it's two o'clock. I still have another hour

before it's time to go to work. There's a boys' gym class playing out on the baseball field. They're wearing navy-blue caps and gym shorts, half of them shirtless. As if baseball is a sport that needs a shirts-versus-skins differentiation. But I don't really mind because I spot Jett Rodriguez on the pitcher's mound, perfecting his coppery tan.

I unzip my backpack and catch a whiff of bleach from last night. I dig around until I find the lunch that I'd packed myself this morning. It's the jar of peanut butter and a spoon. I unscrew the lid and dig in. I wince when I encounter a hunk of peanut. I examine the label. Damn it, how many times have I told Mom that I hate chunky peanut butter? Steven loves it, though, and Mom most likely loves Steven more than me. Not that I can blame her. He talks back a lot less than I do.

I want to find it within myself to be angry with Mom for making me trade the Mach for rent, because it's easier to be mad at someone else. But truthfully, Mom hadn't made me do it. I'd done it on my own. And when I think of her walking back to her bedroom with Garrett, I shudder, stabbing my chunky peanut butter with excessive force. I pull one of the books I checked out from the library out of my bag, hoping to distract myself until it's time to walk to Red's shop.

Soon, I hear the scrape of cleats against the bleacher steps. The peanut butter has helped me rally, and I'm ready to sling some pithy remark at an Evanston boy, but it's not just any boy, it's the infamous Jett Rodriguez. Okay, he's not infamous, but I've thought about him and the way his eyes crinkle when he laughs more than a couple of times since he gave me a ride last night.

"Hey," he says. "Is it snack time?"

"Lunchtime," I reply after swallowing a mouthful of peanut butter. I remember the jerky from last night and feel that I should reciprocate in some way. I hold the jar and spoon out to him. "Want some?" I ask.

"Sure," he says, and takes the jar from me. He grabs the spoon, and without wiping it off or anything, digs out a scoop and eats it. He slides the spoon out of his mouth and smiles at me. He has a dimple in his left cheek. I hadn't noticed it in the car last night. But it's oddly endearing, that one dimple. He offers the jar back, and not wanting to appear squeamish, I take a bite without wiping the spoon, either.

He looks like he would laugh at my determination if he could unstick his tongue from the roof of his mouth. Finally, he gets out, "This is crunchy." His face tells me he agrees with my stance on chunky peanut butter.

"I know," I commiserate. My eyes drift lower than his face because he's on the skins team.

He must notice because he asks, "So did you come to watch me?"

I hazard a glance past his well-formed, sweaty pectoral muscles up to his face. "No," I answer honestly. "I was looking for a quiet place to nap."

He does snicker this time, his eyes crinkling up just like yesterday. "You could really kill a guy's ego, you know."

"Turns out it's not that quiet here this time of day. These guys come out and start throwing their balls at each other." He starts to laugh so hard that his broad shoulders shake, and it spurs me on. "But I'm nice, so I don't yell at them to stop or anything. I just get out my lame-ass jar of chunky peanut butter and eat lunch."

When he stops laughing, he asks, "Don't you have class now? Or are you joining the boys' gym class?"

"I usually have psych. But I'm taking a mental health day."

"Oh, I see. I've taken a couple of those myself."

"They're highly underrated." I pass the jar back to him, and he takes another mouthful of peanut butter.

"So what's after lunch?" he asks after a few moments.

"I've got a shift at Red's Auto."

"That's right. The grease smudges." He passes the jar back to me for another bite.

"Yes. The grease." I take a spoonful of peanut butter.

"Well," he says, "maybe look over your schedule, and let me know if there's a time I could take you out for dinner or something."

"I like to eat," I reply, "so I guess that would be okay. Sometime." I'm deliberately vague, and Jett doesn't push me, which I appreciate.

"Or if you prefer, we could get some beef jerky and peanut butter," Jett says, grinning. "I mean technically, it would be a second date."

"How so?" I ask.

"Well, if a date is an activity and then some kind of food, like a movie and pizza or bowling and tacos, or maybe bungee jumping and sushi , then getting gas and eating beef jerky together last night would *technically* have been our first date."

"That's a pretty classy first date. Do you take all the Evanston girls out for beef jerky and gas, or is this just something for Cottonwood Hollow girls?"

"It's just something for you, Rome."

I think I'm blushing, but it could just be the sun shining on my face.

One of the other boys down on the field yells, "Jett! Quit screwing around and get back here! She doesn't want you, bro! Give it up!"

Jett rolls his eyes. "I better go. But I'll probably see you later."

"Yeah, see you later," I echo, still a little unsettled.

It takes longer than I planned to walk across town to Red's Auto. I'm nearly twenty minutes late when I get there, breathless from sprinting the last five blocks in my stupid plaid skirt and school-appropriate black flats.

Red checks his watch when I burst into the shop, my chest ready to explode and my backpack stuck to my back with sweat. "Get lost, Rome?" he asks pointedly.

"Sorry, sorry—" I gasp out. "I had to walk from school today. I didn't know it would take that long. I'll stay late and make up my time."

"Where the hell's your car?" he asks. The fluorescent lighting glares off his shaved skull while he shifts his posture into listening mode. "It's not like you couldn't fix anything on it," he says with a scowl. He's never asked me if I'm a Fixer, but he knows I'm from Cottonwood Hollow, and he's not stupid.

I swipe at my nose, pretending disinterest. "Traded it for something I wanted."

"Traded it. You *traded* that car?" he looks ready to launch an inquisition. Red understands, probably more than anyone else does. The Mach is a part of my identity. He has the same feelings about his Silverado, which he washes and vacuums out nearly three times a week.

"What needs to be done?" I ask, peeling my backpack off my sweaty shirt. I can't look Red in the eye right now. He's always been kind to me, and I'm afraid if he looks at me with that almost parental concern that something inside of me is going to break into a million tiny pieces. Sharp pieces.

Red must sense this because he only says, "Serpentine belt on that Taurus over there. Work with Tim. He's never put a new one on before. I think we'll have a couple oil changes and maybe a set of spark plugs by five. Lots to do." He mercifully lets the subject of the Mach drop.

I hurry to the bathroom and change, grateful for the work and the noise. Maybe if I get all my work done, I can ask one of the guys at the shop to give me a ride home. I could give them some gas money out of the forty-five dollars I have left. Only Tim and Eddie are working tonight, and I'm not a huge fan of either. Tim is fresh out of community college and thinks he knows more than he does. Eddie's just kind of a jerk, but I respect that he at least does his job well.

I skin my knuckles loosening the tensioner to remove the serpentine belt of the Taurus while Tim is still looking over diagrams. He's stocky and always sweaty, the kind of guy who drives a jacked-up truck to compensate for his lack of height. I am taller than him by at least four inches. "How'd you loosen that?" he asks when I've pulled off the belt.

"Leverage, Tim," I grunt out, fishing down for the belt beneath the alternator.

"Let me do that," he whines, looking irritated that I've already pulled the belt out.

"Go for it, champ." I toss him the new belt and leave him to try to fit his fat hands down by the AC compressor.

I take the dry, cracked belt over to the trash, and when I do, I catch sight of the interior of the Taurus. The radio screen is cracked and a little crooked, like somebody tried to steal it but failed. The back seat has two kids' car seats littered with Cheerios and broken crayons.

Somehow, it makes me think of Mom. And the Mach. And of Emmeline, who so desperately wanted her daughter.

Intrigued, I climb in the driver's seat and tinker with the radio while Tim is under the hood muttering to himself. It's not difficult for me to shift the radio back into place, easing the loose wires back into the console. One of the knobs sits in a cup holder. I reattach it, pressing it gently onto the small metal piece where it should be located. And then I rub two fingers over the cracked screen. Gently at first, and the crack seems to fade, like it was really only a scratch. A few more times and it disappears entirely.

I look up to find Tim standing at the passenger door. "What are you doing?" he asks, eyes narrowed.

"Nothing," I answer.

"You're one of *them*, aren't you? I've heard about you Cottonwood Hollow girls. You're all freaks."

"You don't know what you're talking about," I sling back, my temper flaring. "Did you get that belt on all the way yet?"

His mouth puckers. I want to punch it.

"Tim!" Red calls from the office, where he's drowning in a sea of files and receipts that he doesn't quite know where to put. "Run down to AutoZone and get a case of 5W-30. I thought we had a couple in the storeroom, but we're all out."

Tim shoots me a suspicious glare before hurrying away to do Red's bidding.

I finish the serpentine belt myself, and when I reconnect the battery, I lean in the driver's side window and check the radio, as if I didn't already know that it worked now. I spin the dial until I find the same country station that's playing over the shop speakers, until the Taurus' radio sounds like a tinny echo, a song within a song. I sing along, letting the gentle ache of Fixing remind me that I can feel something other than emptiness.

When eight o'clock rolls around, I'm working on the last oil change. Tim and Eddie left before I'd even had a chance to ask for a ride in exchange for gas money.

I hear a car door near the first bay entrance. Red shuffles out, and I wait for him to give the speech, *Sorry, we're closed, but you can leave the car here overnight or bring it back tomorrow.* Every once in a while, it's a desperate person who needs help with a flat or a headlight that's out, and Red will stay open a little later.

I roll out from underneath the car to see if he needs me and realize that he's talking to a woman in a Ford Focus. My mom. Shit. She's come to give me a ride.

Red is grinning goofily at her. If I had my phone right now, I'd snap a picture later to show the other guys in the shop. Mom has gotten out of her yoga pants, clearly dressed for the job hunt in her best and only button-down shirt, a tight black skirt, and heels that are too tall for business, but are the most professional-looking shoes she owns. If she unbuttoned one more button on that top, she could pass for a cocktail waitress. She's smiling back at Red and gestures at me. I can see her mouth the words *my daughter*. When she sees I'm watching, she gives a little wave.

I roll myself back under the car. Let me die here.

Several minutes pass, and the drip pan is full, so I'm forced to roll back out from my hiding place.

I finish the car and slam the hood shut, wiping my hands on a rag from my pocket. I hear Mom *laughing* in the shop office. Red joins in, too. There's nothing for me to do now but hurry into the bathroom and change back into my school uniform and get Mom out of the shop as soon as possible.

In the office, Red is standing with his hands in his pockets, still beaming at Mom. She's leaning over the desk, looking at his books. This gives Red a great view of her cleavage, which she's amped up with a push-up bra today. Clearly, Mom's employing all her best skills on this job hunt.

But if I were to step back and look at this scene like a stranger might see it, Mom is young and pretty, with curly auburn hair and a smile that never fails to get whoever she's looking at to smile back.

It's hard to say who she might have been if she wasn't pregnant with me as a teenager. Maybe she would have owned a business. Maybe she would have been a doctor, or a lawyer. I guess we'll never know.

"This would be more organized if you used the computer," Mom says. "I used to do that at my old job. They taught me how to balance the accounts and make deposits. I can even file."

I can even file.

My mom is killing me.

"Really?" Red says. "I've thought about getting a computer in here, but I don't know a lot about using any of that fancy software. I did fifteen years in the Marines, two tours in the desert. Not a lot of time for college and all that." He looks a little embarrassed by the confession, and I realize that he's not even looking at Mom's cleavage. He's looking at the files. "I've just stuck with the old paper accounting books. I'm not a very organized guy." He gestures at the piles of papers and receipts stacked on the filing cabinets and peeking out of the drawers of the old, scarred desk.

"Well, they say the most intelligent minds are the least organized ones," Mom says, giving him her trademark smile as she stands up. "But let me know if you need any help."

Red is just eating it up, like they all do. Mom's never had a problem getting a boyfriend. It's the quality of the ones she ends up with that's problematic. After about three months, she comes to her senses and realizes that Boyfriend X is actually a complete loser, and she gets rid of him.

"Mom," I interrupt her. "I'm ready to go."

Red looks at me as if he hadn't noticed I was there. "Oh,

Rome. Yeah. You didn't tell me your mom was picking you up tonight."

"I didn't know she was," I return, drumming my fingers impatiently on the desk.

"Of course I am," Mom says, turning her radiant face on me. "It's not like I was going to let you *walk* home."

Red beams at her again. "Rome never talks about you. I had no idea you were so . . ."

"Chatty?" I offer. But I'm really thinking, *young*. There are always questions when people see my mom. *Wait, how old were you when you had Rome?*

Mom actually makes herself blush. She playfully taps Red's forearm. "Oh, you know Rome. She's such a good worker that she doesn't talk about herself on the job. She comes by that naturally, you know. We're both hard workers."

"I bet," Red says, nodding as if every word out of Mom's mouth is the gospel. "I mean, yeah, Rome's a real good worker. She makes the boys from the auto-tech school look like puppies."

"See you tomorrow night," I tell Red.

"Great," Red says. "See you tomorrow." He looks at Mom squarely in the face. "I guess I'll see you too, Stella."

Mom tosses him one of her grins over her shoulder as I drag her away.

I push Mom into the car with probably more force than necessary and throw myself into the driver's seat. "What is wrong with you?" I ask. "Red's my *boss*. Not your future ex-boyfriend."

"Yeah, he's your boss," Mom says. "And he obviously needs an office assistant. Why couldn't it be me?"

I put the car in reverse and back out of the parking spot while Red waves dumbly by the open bay doors. Mom waves back.

"And what was all that crap about using a computer at your old job? The café had paper books just like Red does." I pull out onto the road, making for the highway.

Mom pulls out a book from her purse. The cover reads *Everything You Need to Know about Microsoft Office*. "I got this from the library in Evanston today. On a break from dropping off more applications."

"So you're going to try getting one of those office jobs?" I ask, trying to hide my surprise.

She shrugs. "Maybe. I don't know. I sounded pretty good in there with Red, right? Maybe somebody would hire me."

"Just don't lead with *I can even file*."

EIGHT

WHEN WE PULL INTO THE front yard in Mom's car, I leave the space empty under the cottonwood where I always used to park the Mach. The grass there is dead, and it looks like some kind of morbid memorial. Someone must have come with Garrett to pick up his truck, because it's gone, too. Before I turn off the headlights, I catch sight of Lux and Mercy sitting on the front steps in the dark. Lux is leaning back on her palms, and Mercy sits on the step below her, casually resting her elbow on Lux's knee. Two tote bags sit in the dirt below the bottom step.

It hits me how lucky I am to have them. Obstinate, loud, funny, loyal. They're here, even though I don't want them to be. They're here because I need them to be.

Mercy springs up when we get out of the car. "Hi, Miss Galveston," she chirps.

"You should have let yourselves in," Mom says, putting the

car keys in her bag. "You know the key's under the mat, where it always is."

"I would have, but you know Mercy," Lux replies with a sigh. "She insisted it was rude to bust in and make ourselves at home."

Mercy puts her hands on her hips and shoots Lux a glare.

"You're always welcome," Mom says, trying not to wince when she reaches the steps and Mercy crushes her in a hug.

When Mercy releases Mom, she says, "Oh, I almost forgot. I hope you haven't eaten yet. My mom made way too much lasagna, so she sent some along." She leans down and picks up one of the tote bags, which has what looks like a casserole dish in one of Mrs. Montoya's hand-knit cozies to keep it warm. And a loaf of garlic bread. And a large plastic bowl with a lid that probably has salad to make this a well-balanced meal.

I immediately bridle at the thought of handouts, but Mom takes the bag. "Thank you, Mercy. Be sure to tell your mom that we appreciate it."

Mercy beams, and Lux's eyes threaten to roll back into her head.

When we go inside, Steven jumps joyously at our return, and the arrival of visitors only escalates his enthusiasm. His stump of a tail looks like it will wag right off his butt at any moment. "Steven!" I greet him in the doggy voice he loves. "Were you a good boy? Do you want some lasagna?"

Steven barks what I can only imagine is *yes*.

Mom sets the food down on the kitchen counter and then drifts back to the couch, unsure of what needs to happen next.

Marisol's empty casserole dish from Sunday night is soaking in the sink, waiting to be washed and returned to her.

Thankfully, Mercy takes charge, sliding the lasagna into the oven to heat it back up. She's rummaging through the cupboards next, making *tut-tut* noises as she observes our meager supply of ramen noodles and what looks like a couple cans of SpaghettiOs that she digs out from the back.

"Oh, put those up at the front," I say, my stomach beginning to ache from smelling the lasagna as it heats. "I didn't know we still had those."

Mercy begins sliding out a few other odds and ends from the bag, which must be limitless in its capacity. There are some canned vegetables, a box of cereal, three boxes of macaroni and cheese, a half gallon of milk, and more peanut butter.

"Your mom cleaning out her cupboards?" I ask. I fight back the edge that tinges my voice. I wish I'd never told her the truth. I love Mercy, but I can't be one of her charity projects and still be her best friend.

Mercy puts her hand on her hip again, and even though she's a pixie, she fills the kitchen when she speaks. "Rome Galveston, if you don't stop being a bitch and say thank you, I'm going to kick your ass."

It's exactly what I need right now, and the hot pricks of tears I feel behind my eyes ease a little. "Thanks," I tell her. "I get paid on Friday. I can pay you back."

"Shut your stupid face and get out some bowls for this salad."

I do as I'm told, making faces when Mercy commands me to dig salad from the plastic container and arrange it in the small bowls. Lux wanders in, changed out of her school uniform and into an old T-shirt and shorts.

"You got comfy quick," I tease, because she gave me crap for wearing my pajamas out just last night.

"This is a slumber party, FYI," Lux replies, tossing her long hair over one shoulder. It clouds behind her in a strawberry-blond mass.

"Got it," I answer, picking out what looks like death in the form of a green pepper from my salad bowl. "You staying?" I ask Mercy, who is now rearranging the lonely condiments in our refrigerator to see if she can locate any more of what she considers acceptable food.

"Not on a school night," Mercy calls back from the innards of the fridge. "My parents said I could stay until ten."

"Wow, *ten*," Lux croons. "That's late for you."

Mercy climbs back out of the fridge and shuts the door while holding what might be the only bottle of salad dressing Mom has ever purchased. I think it might have actually been purchased by her last boyfriend, now that I see it more closely. "I'd check the expiration date on that," I tell Mercy.

"It's better than nine, which is what they usually say," Mercy replies haughtily to Lux, ignoring me. "So feel blessed to have my presence for an extra hour."

"We are very blessed," I tell Mercy, knowing that she must have begun negotiations for a ten o'clock curfew at about five to have achieved it. And she must have told her parents my mom and I were in financial trouble and starving in our beat-up trailer. I try not to let that last part sting, but it does, and I push myself away from the counter where I've been leaning and get out a glass for water.

"What about you?" Mercy asks Lux. "What's up with the Tuesday-night sleepover?" She's slicing bread as she talks, comfortable in the kitchen.

Lux licks her lips before answering. "Aaron's truck died on his way to work at the plant this morning, and he's *furious*. He thinks someone did something to it. He swears he's going to find the little shit and beat the crap out of them. Mom thought it would be best if I went somewhere else tonight while he drowns his troubles in baseball and Budweiser."

It's what she doesn't say that sticks with me. Tina wants Lux out of the way so that if Aaron gets mad and hits somebody, it's not Lux. I think back to the other times Lux has randomly popped up at our trailer, and I wonder how many of those times she had been hiding from Aaron. I wonder how often Tina has to hide from Aaron.

"His truck died?" Mercy asks. She looks to me. "Are you going to offer to Fix it?"

"No," both Lux and I say in unison, and with much more force than necessary.

Mercy's eyes widen, her brows shooting up.

"He's having it towed to a shop in Evanston. *Not Red's*," Lux adds, looking at me.

Lux doesn't know that I'm the one who did it, I tell myself. She doesn't know that I put bleach in Aaron's gas tank. It will run again, but the inside of his gas tank is going to be covered in rust, and his fuel system might have to be completely replaced. *It was for you*, I want to tell her. *It was revenge for you.* But it's better if she doesn't know anything about it. Plausible deniability.

"Okay," Mercy says, holding up her hands like we're about to attack, her thin scar visible on her palm, like a white flag of truce. That white scar twists something in my insides, because I know what it means to all of us. She casts one more glance at us both, as if she can tell there's something we're not telling her. We should not have so many secrets. The guilt sits low in my gut, warring with the hunger I feel.

Lux notices her scar, too, and I catch her eye, tilting my head slightly as Mercy turns back to the stove. I want her to end this, to honor the promises we made by ratting out her jerk of a stepdad. But Lux looks away, and I guess I can't blame her, because I have secrets of my own.

When the food is ready, Mercy loads up plates with far too much food and delivers one to Mom and hands the other to me.

Then we go to my room and pile onto my bed. While I eat, I retell the story of what happened today, all except the part about Mom almost going to the bedroom with Garrett.

"You talked to an Evanston boy?" Mercy asks when I tell them about Jett wanting to grab dinner sometime.

"Don't kill me, *Mom*," I reply around a mouthful of garlic bread.

"Good for you," Lux says. "I thought you were naturally man-repellent, but it must not be true. He's cute, too."

I make a face that might repel Lux.

"So are you going to go out with him?" Mercy asks. She's only ever had a crush on Sam Buford, but he doesn't seem to know she exists outside of the holy trinity or holy water or whatever it is that they do at church.

I shrug. "He seems nice, but I don't know. I don't really want to get him involved with all of this." I wave a hand around the room.

"He shouldn't be in your bedroom—" Mercy begins.

"No," Lux spits out, laughing. "She means Cottonwood Hollow." She frowns darkly, probably thinking about her curse. What was meant to be a blessing.

"I mean I don't want to explain to him why I can't meet him somewhere in the Mach. I don't want him to pick me up at this trailer in his fancy car that his daddy bought him."

"You're right," Lux agrees. "It makes much more sense to hate him for the socioeconomic status he was born into."

"Nice use of vocabulary," I retort. "But it is sort of awkward with Jett, isn't it? I mean, they have goats just for the hell of it. People here don't have goats unless they're going to eat them or make cheese in their back shed."

"The Rome *I know* doesn't care about what anybody thinks," Mercy answers, stroking my hair affectionately. "It's one of the things I admire about her."

Lux adds, "And if he does care, kick him to the curb. You're *Rome fucking Galveston*."

With a remarkably straight face, Mercy says, "Don't eat his goats, though. That would be embarrassing for all of us out here in Cottonwood Hollow."

We all laugh, and Steven comes to see what the cackling is all about, pushing open the cracked bedroom door with his jowly face.

"Okay," Lux says, abruptly changing the subject as Steven comes nudging his snout against her legs, waiting for Lux to pet him. "Where the hell is the diary? I looked for it earlier when I came in here to change, and I couldn't find it." She sits up and gives Steven a good petting.

"It should be in my backpack," I recall, heaving myself and the three pounds of lasagna I've just ingested off the bed. On my way to the kitchen, I stop by the couch to pick up Mom's plate and take it with mine to the sink. She's got her nose in the book about using office programs, and she's absolutely fixated. I've never seen her this focused on a goal before. It's almost like she's pulling her head out of the sand and really, actively trying to make things better. But she's also gotten out the emergency box of wine and her glass that says *It's Wine O'clock Somewhere*, which means she's still recovering from Garrett's visit this morning, too.

Mom looks up when I approach and, noticing that I'm alone, says, "I'm glad the girls came over tonight."

"Me too," I agree.

"I'm sorry about this morning," she tells me, closing the book on her index finger to hold her place. She looks serious, and somehow older tonight, like the day's events have aged her. "I want you to know that we're going to get your car back, okay? I'm going to get a good job. A better job. And we'll get it back."

But I know that the best we'll do for a long time is just survive. And that has to be enough for now. This is just like the promises she made when I was little, back when I believed every word that came out of her mouth. But what I know at seventeen that I didn't know at eleven is that sometimes we need those little lies to get by.

We need them to survive, to believe that there's a future beyond just getting by. There's a future beyond just making ends meet.

I nod, because for once I don't want to make some clever quip, some smart remark to tell her I know better. I want her to have what always seems to be missing from this rusting old trailer.

Hope.

I leave the plates in the sink, impressed that Mom has already gone to the trouble of putting away the leftover lasagna and bread. I make a mental note to take a stroll over to Mrs. Montoya's soon and see if she needs anything Fixed.

On the counter on a plastic-wrapped plate is a half-dozen chocolate cupcakes that Mercy somehow produced out of her tote bag. *Enough*, I remind myself. Mercy could have produced all kinds of things from that bag if she tried hard enough. I hazard a peek in the cupboards, and what was once two cans of Spaghet-tiOs is now four. I close the cupboard door, briefly touching my forehead against the cheap wood, which is cool against my skin. *Enough*. That seems more like a gift than a curse to me, too.

I grab my backpack off the kitchen table and go back to my room. Lux is still massaging the many wrinkles of Steven's loose skin, and she and Mercy are arguing about where Emmeline's dowry chest might be. "It could be *anywhere*," Mercy points out. "She may have sent it back home to her family."

"There's got to be more information in the diary," Lux says. "Get it out, Rome. We need to do research. I *need* that dowry chest."

"What do you need it for?" Mercy asks.

"I just want the money, okay? What's wrong with that?" She

can't look Mercy in the eye, but I know exactly what she's thinking. She wants it so that Tina can kick Aaron out. She wants to be financially independent from him.

"Maybe we should donate some of it if we find it," Mercy chatters, smoothing the worn comforter on the bed as she talks, unaware that anything strange is going on with Lux. "Start a fund for girls from Cottonwood Hollow to go to college or something. I mean, it wouldn't have to be that much, but if we *invested* it . . ."

Lux grimaces at the idea of giving the money away. "Just find the damn diary."

I dig around in my backpack, but it's not there. There's the history book, the novel, the notebooks, pens, the mostly eaten jar of peanut butter and the dirty spoon that I shared with Jett. (It's still in there because I haven't taken it out, not because I was saving it like some creepy stalker.) But the diary isn't in there.

"Where is it?" Lux asks, taking the backpack and upending it over my bed. She shakes it out for good measure. A broken pencil and some gum wrappers fall out.

"Maybe I took it out and I don't remember," I mutter, lifting the comforter on the bed like it could be hiding there.

"Do you think it fell out in your mom's car? At school?" Mercy gets up off the bed. "Come on," she says, beckoning us to move. "Let's search the house."

We look all over, even asking Mom if she's seen the leather diary with a cottonwood leaf tooled on the front. She hasn't seen it, of course, which makes me wonder if I left it at school. We reconvene in my bedroom after a thorough search of the car with only the weak, buttery glow of the dome light to illuminate our search.

"Rome," Lux says suddenly, plopping down on my bed. "You said you fell asleep on the bleachers at school. Could someone have gotten into your bag while you were asleep and taken it?"

"Yeah, right, looking for what? Cash?" I scoff. "They're not going to go through a Cottonwood Hollow student's bag looking for that."

"Looking for anything. Pot. Pills. A banged-up-looking diary that could be used to embarrass you."

"Didn't you see Jett there?" Mercy asks, her eyebrows hinting at something dark, something only an *Evanston boy* would think to do.

"You think Jett took the diary out of my bag? I was awake when I saw him, remember?"

"That doesn't mean he didn't take it while you were asleep," Lux says, crossing her arms. "And then come back and be all '*hey, girl*,' laying on the charm later."

"Just ask. Nicely," Mercy adds. "Maybe it fell out of your bag somewhere on the steps and he picked it up. He wouldn't have known it was yours. It's not like it has your name in it."

"Or he went through your bag while you were snoring," Lux teases.

"I don't think he took it," I say airily, as if the possibility doesn't hit every button in me that says liking an Evanston boy is wrong and this is going to be the evidence I need to prove it. Damn him and his baseball bat.

"Well, at least ask him if he's seen it," Lux says.

"We'll look for it at school tomorrow," Mercy adds. "But it's almost ten and if I don't get home on time my parents will slay me."

"Yeah," I say, keeping the tone light despite the gnaw of guilt. I should have kept more careful track of the diary. Lux is dying to find that dowry chest. And so am I. I need more than just the rent money now. I need enough to buy back the Mach before someone else does.

I give Mercy a ride home in Mom's car, and when I return, Lux has changed yet again, this time into a pair of tight jeans and a deep V-neck T-shirt. She's redone her makeup and is fluffing out her hair by hanging her head down between her knees and shaking her head.

"Is it date night?" I ask, flopping myself down on the bed and watching her work. "If so, I'm underdressed."

"Morgan texted while you were out. Do you mind? She said we could go for a drive. Get some ice cream or something."

"Or *something*," I trill, knowing it will annoy her.

Lux stands back up and rolls her eyes. "You're such a perv. But yes, I hope some of *something*."

"I don't mind," I tell Lux as she leans forward toward the mirror above the dresser and checks her lip gloss, using her pinky finger to catch a bit that's smudged too far. *Too far.* How much will it take to push Lux too far? How long until she can't tolerate it here in Cottonwood Hollow anymore?

I sit up when there's a honk out front. "Lux," I say, and this time it's urgent, and there's nothing I can do to stop it. Because it's hit me like a fist in the gut. I reach out and grab her wrist with my hand, and she grimaces a little because I've grabbed her too tightly, and my hands are much stronger than hers. Fixer hands.

I place my other hand to hers, palm to palm, scar to scar.

"You'd tell me, right? If you were going to run again, you'd tell me? You wouldn't just leave without saying good-bye."

Lux's face softens from irritation to melancholy, losing that predatory fierceness that she so often wears. "You know I wouldn't leave without saying good-bye."

"No matter what?"

"No matter what."

NINE

LUX AND I HAVE PLENTY of time before the first bell to find seats in the back of the classroom before either Morgan or Jett show up, since we had to ride the bus. Lux is still moony from her date the night before, and the only cognizant sentences she can come up with this morning start with the name *Morgan* and end with the word *love*. Normally this wouldn't bother me, but I have to wait for Lux to shift back into Stone Face before we can ask Jett if he took the diary.

I spent a lot of time thinking last night, since Lux didn't get back until three in the morning, and I think the diary came to us so that we can find the dowry chest and I can buy back the Mach and Lux and her mom can kick Aaron out for good. Why else would Emmeline deposit the diary right to us if she didn't want to help us out financially? She'd spelled it all out in the diary, *No one should have that dowry chest or the land but a daughter of Cottonwood Hollow.*

But right now, Lux is so giddy that she'll be of no help with the Jett interrogation. She might giggle at Jett if she sees him, and then he'll be following her around for the rest of the day like a lost puppy. And I have to admit that I wouldn't like that. At all.

Lux's gift doesn't work on girls, so it certainly isn't the reason Morgan follows her around all dreamy, smiling when Lux leans over to whisper something into her dark hair. I should mention that to Lux the next time she says she's cursed. At least she'll always know if what she has is real.

"Hi," Jett says when he enters the classroom. I'm looking right at him the moment he's framed in the doorway, as if I was waiting expectantly for his arrival, and he clearly takes this as a sign of encouragement. He talks over the twelve or so other people in the room, and completely bypasses his buddy in the front row. A few people glance at Jett, wondering why he's heading to the back of the classroom where Lux and I had long ago set up dominion.

"Hey," I reply with a shrug. I don't know why I shrug. It's not like he's asked me a question, and yet an Evanston boy calling a Cottonwood Hollow girl out in front of the entire class *is* a question.

"Plan on taking any more naps outside today?" Jett weaves his way between the desks and takes a seat on my left. Lux is on my right, and she barely manages to purse her full lips in time to look annoyed with his familiarity and keep her talent at bay. Morgan's just darkened the doorway with her designer backpack, so Lux can't manage much more than that now, and turns her attention completely away from me and Jett. I guess I'm on my own.

"Not today," I reply to Jett, pulling out one of my Dollar

Tree yellow pencils to take notes. "Too much to do. No time for naps."

"Well, maybe you'll still share your lunch with me," Jett teases, his grin broad enough to pop that dimple in his cheek. He's like sunshine, I realize. There's nothing dark or hungry in him, only light and happiness and laughter. How strange that must be.

"No peanut butter today," I say, forging ahead to more serious matters. I'm doing this for the Mach, I tell myself. And for Lux. I can't be weak now, even if Jett is incredibly attractive. And funny. Steeling myself, I plow on, "Hey, I wanted to ask you if you'd seen a diary from my bag yesterday. If maybe you picked it up."

"A diary?" Jett asks, one dark brow rising theatrically.

"Yes. It's missing from my backpack. And since you're the only person I talked to yesterday other than Mercy at school, I thought you might know where it is."

"Know where it is like I took it?" Jett asks, leaning toward me a little so that I'm caught in that cloud of heat he radiates wherever he goes. His hands are huge, I realize, as he pulls a spiral notebook out of his backpack.

"Yeah, like maybe you picked it up," I agree, though some tiny voice in the back of my head is screaming that I'm going about this all wrong.

"So you want to ask me if I took your diary without telling you."

"Well, if you stole it, I assume you wouldn't tell me. That would make you a pretty crappy thief."

"Oh," Jett says, and his warm, amiable face arranges itself into something resembling granite, the dimple disappearing. "I see. So I'm a *crappy* thief now."

"I didn't say that," I backtrack, hating myself. "Just asking if you saw the diary. If you might know where it is."

"I don't know anything about your diary," Jett says. "And I don't think you know me very well if you think I would take something of yours without asking."

"I'm just saying it's missing. And I thought maybe you might have seen it. Yesterday. At the baseball diamond." I'm speaking in fragments now because apparently my brain has turned to mush.

Jett takes a breath before he answers, his broad shoulders lifting and settling in his Evanston blazer. "I haven't seen your diary, Rome." He stacks his books and pencils together and moves like he's going to get up.

"It's not my diary," I begin lamely. "I just had it . . ."

But it's too late. Jett picks up his things and moves to the front of the classroom to sit next to his teammate before Miss Strong enters. He glances back once, and it's the look of someone who is disappointed. I look over at Lux, but she's got her fingers intertwined with Morgan's under Morgan's desk, and in that moment neither one of them knows I exist.

During my free period, Mercy and I searched the mezzanine in the library, and the diary wasn't there, either. So the three of us spend our lunch break scouring the baseball stadium where I'd fallen asleep. I cringe when we don't leave early enough to avoid Jett's gym class filing out onto the field. I'm still ashamed of the way I treated him, and pretty sure that offer to take me to dinner has been rescinded now.

I watch him as the three of us clamber down the metal steps of the stadium, and he studiously avoids my gaze the entire time, even when one of his buddies points me out and says something about "that peanut butter girl from yesterday." I'd been waiting for him to reveal his true colors, and he did. He's a nice guy. I'm the jerk. Sure, there are some stuck-up, snobby guys at Evanston, but he isn't one of them.

Near the entry to the stadium, while Mercy and Lux argue about what to do next, I watch Jett on the baseball field, wishing that I'd done things differently.

"Let's just give up on the whole diary thing," Lux says. "We don't need it to find the stupid dowry chest. We know it has to be on Remington land somewhere. Unless it's literally buried in a hole in the ground somewhere, it's probably in the house."

Mercy sighs but nods. "I guess we can go out there . . . if you really want to." She looks at me, and I know she's thinking of the last time we were there.

"I've got a late shift at Red's," I tell them. "If we head out there right away, I'll still have enough time to get to work." I'm not looking forward to having Mom take me to and from the shop tonight. It's just another interaction between her and Red that I would prefer to avoid.

When we get off the bus after school, the three of us walk to Lux's house first so that she can drop off her backpack.

While she runs back to her room, Aaron sits in front of the

television, still wearing his coveralls from his early shift at the meat-packing plant and sucking down a bottle of Budweiser while he watches baseball. So what Lux's mom had said was true. If Aaron's got the morning shift now, that's nearly fifteen less hours a week. Tina's not here, and I wonder if she's picking up extra hours at the nursing home to help make up the difference.

When he sees Mercy and me waiting, he snarls, as if he's been waiting for someone to walk in the door so that he can lash out and expend some of his anger, "You're the Fixer girl. Did Lux tell you somebody fucked up my pickup? Guess I should've had you look at it. When I hear from the mechanic about what exactly they did to it, there's going to be hell to pay. You don't fuck with a man's truck like that." Aaron's never been exactly friendly, but there's a raw edge to him now that makes me uneasy.

Mercy edges closer to me.

Aaron takes another swig of his beer. "You heard anything about it?"

"No," I lie without missing a beat. "Sure haven't."

"How about you, *chica*?" he asks Mercy, his features locked in a grimace.

Mercy tenses next to me, and it's all I can do not to step in front of her. But I'm afraid he'll think that makes her look guilty, and that won't help any of us. The mechanic is going to confirm that someone put bleach in Aaron's gas tank, and Aaron's going to start wondering who had a motive. Like maybe the best friend of the stepdaughter he smacked around who knows exactly what to do to his truck to mess it up.

Mercy answers with a grace that I'll never have. That she

shouldn't have to have. "No, Mr. Willard," she says. "Of course not."

"Well, when I find out who did it," he spits, "I'm going to make them pay. Bet your pretty little ass on it." He takes another hard swig from the bottle.

"Come on," Lux says, returning from her bedroom. "Let's go."

Mercy is overly bright when we leave the house, chatting away about whether or not she should volunteer to read to the elderly this summer, like she wants desperately to hide Aaron's nastiness from Lux. So I guess we're all keeping secrets now.

We stop at Mercy's house next, and Mrs. Montoya is in the kitchen when we get there. It's a whole different world from Lux's house. Mrs. Montoya is pulling a baking sheet of chocolate-chip oatmeal cookies from the oven, her face flushed. Her dark hair is pulled back with a clip, and she looks so genuinely pleased to see us I can't even make a joke about her being like some 1950s housewife. Because Mrs. Montoya is happy. The kind of happy I felt when I was driving the Mach with the windows down, soaring over every hill and around every corner. I envy her.

"Hello, Mrs. Montoya," Lux and I greet her in unison. Mrs. Montoya has a bar counter at the edge of the kitchen, and Lux and I each slip onto a stool while Mercy and her mom move around each other like well-fitted cogs, each complementing the other and moving their task along. Mercy slides a few of the cookies off the cooling racks and onto a plate to make room for the fresh batch her mom has just pulled out.

"I wanted to thank you," I tell Mrs. Montoya while she loads up a few more cookies onto the plate Mercy is making for us. "For the dinner you sent over last night." I'm able to tuck my tail between my legs and say thank you for the handout because it's the right thing to do, and because I'm still irritated at myself for handling the conversation with Jett so poorly this morning.

"Oh." Mrs. Montoya waves her potholder at me. The potholder matches the kitchen. Actually, everything in this house matches. "That was nothing. Just some leftovers we had around. I hope Mercy helped you heat everything up?" She looks over at Mercy, knowing I'm inept in the kitchen.

"She did," I confirm. "It was delicious."

"Good," Mrs. Montoya says, and she smiles at me in that way that somehow manages to be kind but not condescending. Very few people can do that, but the Montoyas are one of those families that can.

"Is there anything around that maybe needs to be Fixed?" I ask.

Mrs. Montoya's face softens, and suddenly she resembles Mercy so much that it almost hurts to look at her. "Oh, sweetheart, not right now. But I'll let you know if I need anything, okay?" Mercy's little brother, Malakai, bursts in the front door after the bus drops him off from the elementary school, and Mrs. Montoya gets him a snack and leaves to help him start his homework.

"Where's Neveah?" I ask before shoving a cookie in my mouth.

"She's at a church group function. They're doing charity work after school this week."

"In Evanston?" Lux asks.

"Yeah," Mercy replies, selecting her own cookie. "It was Mrs. Johnson's turn to drive the girls, so she took Neveah and Adele after school. How did the chat with Jett go this morning?"

"Not good," I reply, pretending to be incredibly interested in the cookies. "He responded with a basic 'screw you.'"

"Classy guy," Lux hisses. She'd been too enthralled with Morgan to notice our exchange, and now she's offended on my behalf.

"He didn't actually say that. But it was clear I'd pissed him off and he moved back up to sit with his baseball bro."

"He even came to *sit* with you? You should *definitely* apologize," Mercy says, wiping her lips with a napkin.

"You guys were the ones who told me to ask him if he took it!" I exclaim, irritated. I shove another cookie into my mouth.

"Well, you should have found a nice way to do it," Mercy says. "My guess is you were too blunt, like you always are."

I glare at her while I chew and swallow the cookie. I don't want Mrs. Montoya to catch me speaking with food in my mouth.

"You *are* rude ninety percent of the time," Lux agrees while I'm chewing. She borrows Mercy's napkin to wipe the chocolate off her face.

"You two," I grumble after I swallow the cookie, "are really something. Next time, why don't *you* ask someone if they stole something and see how they take it?"

Mrs. Montoya returns, and Mercy gives her a line about needing to help Lux collect weeds for a natural science lab.

"Are you staying in Cottonwood Hollow?" Mrs. Montoya asks.

"Yes, ma'am," Lux answers, smiling sweetly. If Mrs. Montoya had been a man, she would have begun melting into a pliable, adoring slave.

Mrs. Montoya offers me another cookie from the almost-empty plate. "Well, be careful. I ran into Mrs. Pelter today and she said her son fell and broke his ankle exploring the ruins because he was trying to find a snakeskin for his collection. So the town council has decided just to burn them on Sunday. They say those old trailers are too rusted up and rotting to salvage anything, and after the Pelter boy got hurt, well, they're just too dangerous to have near town. Which reminds me," she adds, holding up a finger, "I offered to make sandwiches for the volunteer firefighters. Let me know if you girls want to help. I could always use an extra hand." She looks more at Lux than me, which makes sense. I'm not much help in the kitchen.

"We won't go near the ruins, Mom," Mercy says. "It's gross over there." She flicks a glance over at me. "And I'm sure Rome and Lux would *love* to help out."

Mrs. Montoya beams at Mercy while Lux and I try to rein in our dismay. "Smart girls. I never have to worry about you." She tugs on Lux's long braid. "Good luck. Let me know if you need anything. I think there are some garden shears and gloves in the garage if you want them."

"Thanks, Mrs. Montoya," Lux says. "You're the best."

"Armando is going to grill burgers. You two are welcome to join us for dinner." Mrs. Montoya gives me a pointed look, as if she knows that I'm likely to skip dinner if she doesn't offer.

"I've got a shift at the shop tonight, Mrs. Montoya, otherwise

I would," I tell her. My heart is somewhere in my throat over Mrs. Montoya and her cookies and dinner invitations. It's one thing to say that you wish someone had a softer life. It's another to do something about it.

Outside, Lux breathes in the afternoon air like she's been starved for oxygen. "Your mom is so . . ." She searches for the right word.

"Perfect," I finish for Lux. It's not hard to be jealous of Mercy's life. Everything seems so smooth, so perfect. I know Mercy feels the weight of their expectations, the strength of their rules, but all I feel in that house is love.

Lux's eyes lock on mine, and I know she is thinking what I am. "Yeah," she says. "She's great."

Mercy's dark hair falls to cover her face when she looks down at her little black ballet flats. "You've known her forever. I don't know why you two act so weird sometimes."

"It's Lux," I reply, needing to feel some lightness in my bones. "She's been sniffing glue again."

Lux rolls her eyes. "I'm going to glue your mouth shut," she replies. "Now let's go out to the homestead. We know Emmeline died there, right? It's not like she hiked across Cottonwood Hollow with this chest to bury it somewhere while she was dying."

"Unless she had her neighbor hide it somewhere," Mercy murmurs. "Maisie. She was the woman who lived there afterward until she was, like, a hundred years old. She was the one who convinced the Cottonwood Historical Society to try to turn it into a museum. Preserve everything just like it was. I need to find the book the society put together. It might have more in it about who she was."

"Which means that it's probably not there," I counter. "Wouldn't someone have found it already?"

"There's all kinds of junk upstairs," Lux says. "I doubt they went through *everything*."

I nod. "If nothing else, maybe we'll pick up other clues," I say. "It can't hurt to look, right?"

"I just don't like that place," Mercy says with a shiver.

"It won't be so bad this time," I say, looking over at Lux. "This time we're all going together."

Lux's face shutters, like she's trying not to think about the last time we were there.

TEN

KANSAS TEMPERATURES HAVE WARMED JUST enough to draw a trickle of sweat between my shoulder blades. It soaks into the white button-down shirt I'm wearing as we stomp through the pasture toward Emmeline Remington's homestead. "We should've changed," Lux grumbles as she pulls a foxtail out of a pleat in her skirt.

"I would have," Mercy mutters as she picks a burr off one of her knee socks, "but you acted like your ass was on fire."

"Stop whining and get moving," I tell them. "I've only got another hour before I have to go to work." I wonder if anyone's made an offer on the Mach yet, or if Garrett's just hot-rodding it around town, enjoying the way people do a double take when they realize it's him driving it and not me.

We're almost to the stand of cottonwoods by the creek, and the Remington homestead is just on the other side. "Has anybody been out here this far since the tornado?" Mercy asks. "Can we still get across the creek?"

"Yeah, like I check it out on a daily basis," Lux retorts. "We'll find out when we get there."

We hear the creek before we see it as we pick our way between the massive cottonwoods. The trees have gorged themselves on water from the creek, their roots digging deep for over a hundred years. A wind stirs the leaves and lifts the ruddy curls off the back of my neck.

"It's still here," Lux says, pointing. The massive cottonwood fell sometime when we were little kids, in a storm a lot like the one we had on Sunday. Bone-white roots stick up into the sky and fan out where they were ripped from the ground. The trunk spans the ravine about fifteen feet above the swollen creek, making it a bridge for the brave only. It's a fall I wouldn't want to take. I look over the edge of the ravine down to the rushing water, which is running high from the storm. Bits of debris float on islands of frothy white stuck around roots growing out of the ravine walls.

"I hate this part," Mercy says, making a face.

The last time we were out here was right after the big algebra-teacher debacle two years ago. One of the students had caught on to the way we'd used Lux's talent as a Siren to get the teacher to believe we'd turned in homework, passed tests. The teacher had been willing to believe anything Lux told him, as long as she would keep smiling at him, keep laughing at his stupid Pythagorean theorem jokes. The principal had called Tina to tell her that

Lux was attempting to have an inappropriate relationship with her teacher, that she was using her *oddity* to get special treatment in the classroom, and that she was going to be suspended for a week and would possibly need to repeat algebra.

Lux ran away while her mom was still on the phone, stopping at my house and using the key under the mat to get in and help herself to a flashlight and a can of ravioli. At the time, Mom was waitressing and I was washing dishes at the café for cash under the table. When Tina stopped by our trailer the next morning to get Lux, she was surprised to find out that Lux hadn't stayed with me the night before. None of us knew where she was.

Mercy and I searched everywhere for Lux, and it was only a fluke that we thought to check the Remington homestead. After all, it was scary and supposedly haunted. We'd even checked the ruins first, hoping she was lounging on some moldy couch in the outermost trailer, eating the stolen can of ravioli. But she hadn't been there, and the homestead was the last place we would check before the bus station in Evanston.

It was near noon when Mercy and I held hands and side-shuffled across the tree bridge. I don't know how Lux did it in the dark by herself the night before.

I barely remember breaking into the homestead. We shimmied through an unlocked window and into the soft darkness of the house as sunlight scratched at dirty windows with dull fingers. We finally found Lux in an upstairs bedroom, curled up in a rocking chair, her cheeks tear-stained and dusty. Her long hair was tangled around her, a cape of strawberry blond keeping her warm as she slept.

She'd screamed when I reached out and softly touched her arm.

But it had been nothing compared to the scolding Mercy gave her. I thought the roof of the house was going to lift off, and afterward there were tears and hugging, Lux choking back sobs that echoed in the dark house.

"Never leave us again," Mercy cried, holding Lux tightly. "Promise me you'll never do anything like this again, Lux." She looked over at me, reaching out to grab my hand. "You either. We have to be strong. We're more than friends. We're sisters. And we'll never keep secrets from one another, and we'll never turn away from each other. Ever. You have to promise. Both of you."

I nodded, my throat tight. The windows must have leaked, because it almost felt like a cold breeze moved through the house.

Lux pulled away from Mercy, dug around in her backpack past the dirty spoon and the empty can of ravioli until she pulled out a sharp metal nail file. "I'll swear it," Lux said. "A blood oath. We'll never keep secrets. And we'll never turn away from each other."

Lux sliced the sharp tip of the nail file across her palm, bright-red blood welling up along the cut. I thought for sure Mercy would say she was crazy, but Mercy took the file from Lux and did the same to her own small palm, wincing only a little. She clasped her palm against Lux's, holding her gaze. "I swear it."

I took the file and cut my palm next, clenching my teeth as I did it.

I clasped my palm to each of theirs in turn, repeated the oath.

And that was it.

We were more than girls from Cottonwood Hollow.

We were blood sisters.

Sworn to never turn away from each other.

Sworn to never keep secrets.

"Well," Lux says, climbing up between the white roots of the fallen cottonwood. "Let's go."

The bark was rubbed off long ago, leaving the trunk smooth and slippery, and I hope that the cheap flats I'm wearing won't send me to my death. They're one of the few types of footwear that is Evanston High approved to go with my uniform.

"Wait," Mercy says, apparently thinking the same thing as she toes off her small ballet flats. "We should all take off our shoes. It'll be safer in bare feet than it will be in these." She peels off her knee socks next and balls them carefully into the toes of her shoes. She tucks each one under an arm. It's not a bad idea, and I do the same, grateful for the contact of skin against the tree when I climb up next to Lux. She's ignored us, still wearing the new shoes Tina found on sale at the mall last week. Morgan has a pair just like them, and they cost more than I make in a day at work, which automatically rules them out as anything I would think to purchase for myself. Mercy climbs up behind me, and we begin side-shuffling after Lux.

Lux is already halfway across the tree bridge when she slips in her pretty shoes. "Shit," she manages to gasp out.

Her arms pinwheel as she leans back over the drop, and the water rushes below, eager to add her to its collection of foam and debris. I snake one arm out and grab her wrist, attempting to anchor her. I throw my other arm out to help keep my balance, and my shoes slip from beneath my arms and plunge into the churning water below. Lux tenses against my grip, but she's not as tiny as Mercy, and the weight of her pulls me toward her. My bare feet slide against the smooth face of the tree trunk, and I yank back as hard as I can without tipping over the other side. Mercy grabs me around the waist, securing me while Lux finds her balance again, Mercy's breath coming in shallow gasps against my back.

"Good thing those were ugly shoes," Lux shouts over the rush of the water as her green eyes find mine. She laughs, and I feel Mercy exhale a sigh of relief.

"I can't believe you sometimes." I catch sight of one of my shoes floating down the creek. We begin shuffling across again. Lux reaches solid ground first and leaps between the branches. She holds out a hand for me, and then Mercy, and we jump down.

Mercy punches Lux in the shoulder. "You stupid jerk, next time listen to me," she says. "You could've killed us all. Not to mention Rome's poor shoes are gone."

"Yeah, my poor shoes," I echo indignantly. "What am I going to wear to school tomorrow?"

"Rain boots?" Lux suggests with a grin. "Don't act so beat up about it, Rome. I'll find you a pair when we get back. I'm sure I've got another pair in the back of my closet."

"Those were barely a month old," I grumble.

"All right," Mercy says, using her no-nonsense voice. "Let's focus here. We need to get to the farmhouse and look for this dowry chest. It's already almost five, and I promised Mom I would be home for dinner."

"*Home for dinner*," Lux mimics in a high-pitched voice.

"You were invited, so stop being rude." Mercy shakes her finger at Lux. Then she tosses her hair and stomps off between the tall cottonwoods that shield the homestead from view.

"*You were invited!*" I echo Mercy silently, mouthing the words and pointing at Lux before stomping off after Mercy in my bare feet. The fact that Mercy still considers manners to be paramount when we're hunting for a dowry chest hidden by a dead woman over a hundred years ago cracks me up, and I can use all the laughs I can get right now.

Lux snickers as she follows me.

The Remington homestead is a large, gray, weather-beaten farmhouse in remarkable shape for its age. I know the Cottonwood Hollow Historical Society tried to maintain it, but my guess is its preservation has more to do with the curse. Or gift, as Emmeline thought of it. A tangle of roses snakes up the west wall, thorns finding purchase in the soft, porous wood siding. The front door is padlocked shut, the lock rusted. But there's a window around the side, the same one Mercy and I wiggled through two years ago. Beneath the window, I get down on one knee, the grass tickling the underside of my bare thigh. Mercy climbs up to the window, using my knee as a step. She struggles with the swollen wood for a moment, jiggling the window back and forth until it loosens and gradually slides up. She pulls herself through, muttering quietly to herself all the while.

When I hear a soft thud, I stand up, brushing the grass from my skirt. Lux pulls herself up to the window and goes through it next. I follow last, tumbling to the floor as slowly and softly as I can. Lux and Mercy are brushing each other off as I stand up from where I've landed on the dirty floor.

We're in the parlor. Dusty chairs shrouded in the remains of gossamer-thin doilies frame each side of a big fireplace. We move through the parlor into the kitchen, where the hand-hewn cupboards have been pulled open, as if someone left in the middle of making dinner. The floor creaks beneath my bare feet. I look down at the kitchen table. There are four smears in the dust, and I reach out to place a finger in each one, laying my thumb just at the edge of the table.

Lux's gaze falls on my hand, and we both look down and notice the footprints in the dust. "Someone's been here," she breathes.

"Do you think whoever it is might still be here?" Mercy asks, and the question makes me go rigid. We all freeze, waiting, listening for any hint of a creaking footstep or a closing door.

"I think we're alone," Lux says finally.

The words are barely out of her mouth before an icy wind surges through the room, pressing my skirt against my thighs and blowing my hair into my face. Lux reaches down and grabs my hand, her palm clammy, eyes frightened. This is one presence that even a Siren can't tame. Mercy glues herself to my side, and I can feel her heart battering against my arm.

And just as quickly, the room stills.

"Do you think it's her again? Like with the diary?" Mercy breathes. "Is it Emmeline?"

There's no doubt in my mind that the wind is Emmeline, and

even though I don't think she means to harm us, I don't think that her presence means she's happy, either.

I try to keep my voice steady as I answer her. "I think it is," I say quietly, as if rationally speaking aloud could strangle my fear. "But I don't think Emmeline could leave prints," I whisper, sliding my fingertips out of the dust. "Someone else has been here."

"Do you think she's mad at us for coming?" Mercy asks, looking around the room as if there's going to be some message written in the dust that says GET OUT NOW.

"Maybe she doesn't like that someone else was here," Lux suggests in a whisper, looking up the staircase in the corner of the room. "Maybe she only wants the girls from Cottonwood Hollow in her house."

For the first time, I begin to wonder if someone else is looking for the dowry chest, too. Maybe Emmeline is mad because that someone else is not a daughter of Cottonwood Hollow.

"Was she here before?" Mercy asks as we climb the stairs, all of us holding hands and moving at a glacial pace, as if Emmeline herself might appear at any moment.

"Not like this," Lux answers in a whisper. The stairs creak loudly, and her words are almost completely drowned out. "It's like Rome reading her diary woke her up."

Upstairs, there's a narrow hall and three bedrooms. The first bedroom is empty, but in the center of the second sits an empty cradle. My chest constricts, and all I can think about is Emmeline's spidery handwriting in the journal spelling out the name *Evangeline. Evangeline. Evangeline.* The air in the room cools considerably, as if Emmeline can read my thoughts. I can barely keep my hands from shaking when the three of us back out of the empty nursery.

The last bedroom is the one where we found Lux. The rocking chair is still pulled next to the windows, as if the occupant of the room enjoyed the view. There's a four-poster bed and a vanity table with a low stool. The vanity's mirror is covered in a cloth that might have once been black but is now a dusty gray. Someone pulled out all the drawers and dumped them upside down. The dust is smeared, as if whoever was here was searching for something and was desperate to leave no crevice unexamined.

Mercy's need for order and cleanliness overcomes her fear of whatever spirit is in the house with us, and she kneels and picks up each drawer, sliding them carefully back into their grooves until they're flush with the front of the vanity. She scoops up handfuls of what look like strings of beads and a brush and comb and places them on top of the vanity table.

"Look," Lux says, her voice rising in pitch. "It's still here. The chest."

I feel a surge of hope. Maybe Emmeline will save the Mach and Lux in one fell swoop. There's a wooden chest at the end of the bed, big enough to hold everything Emmeline had described in her diary. The lock is scratched, the wood around it scarred with grooves. Someone's been trying to open it. My heart falls somewhere down in my stomach.

"Don't you think the historical society probably looked through this already?" Mercy asks gently.

Logic tells me Mercy is right, but I don't want to believe it. I just want everything to work out for once in my life.

"Maybe we should hurry," Lux says, ignoring her. "What if whoever was here comes back?" She drops to her knees and frantically pulls at the lid, but it's still locked. Whoever was in here didn't get it open. Mercy reaches down into her bra and pulls out a bobby pin.

"What?" she asks Lux when Lux raises an eyebrow. "I like to clip my hair back when I'm reading." Mercy looks at me. "If nothing else, maybe there's another diary in it. Or some letters or something that someone missed."

The three of us kneel in front of the chest, and I take the bobby pin, which is still warm from her skin. It may be the only warm thing in this room, because I swear the temperature has dropped another twenty degrees. Using the bobby pin, I lean over and begin to jimmy the lock. It's old and stiff, the mechanisms I need to tumble long set in their ways. I work until the lock begins to blur before my eyes and my hands are cramping, but I am a Fixer. Eventually, the lock tumbles for me.

The latch releases, and Lux and Mercy push open the lid. There's a cloud of dust, and then it's as if the sun has gone out. There's not even the faint glow coming from the dirty windows. It's black. The floor shakes, the furniture vibrating. Lux grabs my hand, and Mercy hugs herself against my waist. Their bodies are rigid with fear against mine, and I open my mouth to shout or scream, but no sound comes out. It's an earthquake or a tornado, or maybe just the end. The mirror in the vanity shatters, the shards tinkling against the floor as the wind roars. The air presses against us. The house groans, and I think I can hear the glass of every window in the world cracking in the scream of a woman.

And then silence. The air pressure drops, and the house breathes a sigh of relief. Perhaps of acceptance. Mercy lets out a strangled gasp, and Lux coughs. The light returns, slowly illuminating the room again. We're surrounded by a halo of shattered mirror, a perfect circle of dirty glass.

"It didn't touch us," Mercy whispers as she releases me. She crosses herself, as if this has been an act of God and not Emmeline Remington.

Lux presses her forehead against my shoulder, shuddering in quiet relief. I close my eyes and lean my cheek on the top of her head, willing myself to stop shaking, to be strong for her and Mercy. Whatever else, I am the rock for my friends.

"Are you okay?" Mercy finally gasps out, running her small, nimble fingers over my face and neck, looking for any sign of blood. She lurches across me to check Lux. "Are you hurt?" she asks again.

"I'm okay." I cough, lifting my cheek from Lux's head. "Are you all right?"

Mercy nods, her dark eyes welling with what might be tears of fear or relief or perhaps just disbelief.

"Lux," I say, nudging her with my shoulder. "Are you okay?"

Lux lifts her head from my shoulder, and her eyes are unmistakably wet. "I thought that was the end," she whispers.

Mercy leans across me and grabs Lux in a fierce hug. "You're okay, Lux," she murmurs. "You're safe."

Lux pulls away from Mercy, steeling herself to face us again. "I'm fine," she says, swiping at her eyes. She leans over the open chest, her hand trembling as she holds it over the contents. "It's things for the baby," she breathes. "Things for Evangeline."

The room is briefly shattered with light, bursting three times before it goes back to the gloomy glow.

"Is that a yes?" Lux asks, looking around the room warily, as if the crazy earthquake-tornado might start up again.

I feel Mercy's body tense against mine.

Nothing happens, and Mercy relaxes. I start to breathe again. "She was a lucky girl," Mercy says softly to the house. "She was lucky to be so loved by you."

The room warms a few degrees.

Lux begins cautiously inspecting the chest, doing her best not to anger Emmeline's ghost with any carelessness for the intrusion, but I know without looking that it's not the dowry chest. There are baby gowns and blankets, bibs and quilts. There's a framed picture that looks to be hand drawn. There's even a lacy christening gown. But there's no silver. No gold. This is just a chest meant to welcome Evangeline. The daughter who didn't survive to be loved.

"I'm sorry," Mercy says, a tear trickling down from one eye.

Mercy is the best of us.

"I'm sorry that you didn't get to live a long life with Evangeline," Mercy continues. "But your legacy lives on. You've given talents to all of the daughters of Cottonwood Hollow."

Lux shudders. She still believes she is cursed.

"We're looking for the dowry chest," Lux tells Emmeline's icy presence. She can't hide the edge of desperation in her voice. "We need help. We need *your* help."

The sunlight coming through the windows seems to bend and shake.

The floor beneath our knees vibrates.

"We are the daughters of Cottonwood Hollow," I whisper, pushing away the cold fingers of fear moving up my spine, and the shaking ceases. The dust motes still in the air, as if time has stopped.

Nothing else happens. No light, no wind, no darkness. Just calm, as if the house and Emmeline decided we didn't mean any harm to her. While Mercy gently folds each item of clothing or blanket that came out of the chest, placing them carefully back inside with her small hands, Lux grows more despondent.

"We should lock it back up," I say, putting my hand on the lid of the chest. I move to close it, but notice that we've left the framed picture out. I pick it up, looking at it more closely.

"It's just a picture of the town," Mercy says. "There's one like that in the book we put together for the Cottonwood Hollow Historical Society. It's probably the same one."

It's sketched in pencil, a miniature of the town of Cottonwood Hollow and the Remington land. It's clearly an amateur's work, the houses sketched with little flowers around them. There are a few words written in the same spidery script from Emmeline's diary.

"It's a map," Lux says. "Look." She points at the hills on the eastern edge of Remington land. "That's where the ruins are now." She traces the wavy lines of the creek and the tiny fishes jumping out of them. "And here's the creek and the homestead." Little roses are drawn around the homestead.

"I don't see any big 'X marks the spot,'" I say, looking over the map. "But let's take it with us. Maybe if we look it over we'll see something." I try not to think about another day lost looking for the chest. Another day that might be the one when Garrett Remington sells my Mach to someone else.

Lux sighs. "So this is a bust. This house has already been gone through and we have no idea where the chest could be. It could literally be in any hole dug on eighty acres."

I shrug, feeling more hopeless than I want to admit right now.

Lux is quiet when we leave the homestead. I carry the picture carefully, noting that the frame is a little loose and the glass front slips around. It needs to be Fixed, but I'm not going to do it out here when I need to get to work.

When we've crossed back over the tree bridge, Mercy says, trying to cheer us up, "Well, at least we know the chest isn't in any of the rooms we searched today."

"But *someone* was," Lux follows, putting her new shoes back on her feet now that we've crossed the tree bridge.

"Someone was," I agree, "and they were looking for something. Maybe the same thing we're looking for."

"They couldn't know about the diary," Mercy counters.

"What if whoever took it read it and found out all about the dowry chest?" Lux asks, picking the head off a foxtail and throwing it to the ground. "What if they already found it, and *that's* why Emmeline is pissed and making mini tornadoes in her house. Maybe she's mad because it wasn't a daughter of Cottonwood Hollow like she wanted."

"We don't even know if the diary was taken," I counter, frustrated that this all comes back to me losing the diary. "I mean, look at all the weird shit Emmeline did in that house. What if she just made the diary disappear? What if we were never meant to have it more than one night?"

"And that was the only night we could have found the dowry chest?" Lux follows my line of thought. She kicks furiously at the grass.

"I don't see what the big deal is," Mercy says quietly to Lux. "Why do you need this money all of a sudden? What's the big push?"

"Shopping," Lux lies. "I want to go shopping."

Mercy rolls her eyes. "If this is about you trying to fit in with those rich Evanston girls, and your Evanston *girlfriend*—"

"This isn't about Morgan!" Lux retorts. "This is about what *I* want."

"And if we did find money, Lux, don't you think it should all go to Rome? She just had to trade her car for the rent!"

Lux's face falls. For her, that dowry chest is a way out. Even if it's not a realistic one. Even if it will never be enough to make her financially independent from her stepfather. Even if it was never enough to make her mom kick him out on his ass. I want her to just tell Mercy what's going on, to stop with the secrets. But I can't make her tell, because I'd be a hypocrite. There are secrets I keep from them. About paying half of the rent. About Mom almost sleeping with Garrett to pay it. About ruining the fuel system in Aaron's truck. About being so afraid of being hurt or abandoned that I push away anyone who's not them.

"Rome—" Lux begins an apology. Her green eyes find mine, and I know she's hurting, that she doesn't want to keep secrets any more than I do. But she's afraid. Afraid of what's on the other side of that door if she pushes it open, if she admits that what's happening in her house isn't right.

I shrug her off. "It's fine," I say.

"What is it?" Mercy asks, crossing her arms. She's on the verge of blowing up, just like she did in the Remington homestead two years ago. "What are you two keeping from me?"

"Nothing," Lux slings back, and I know she's getting angry.

She's ashamed, I realize. She's ashamed to tell Mercy.

"I hate it when you do this. I hate it. We promised. We swore that we wouldn't keep secrets. That we wouldn't turn away from each other." And for the first time in our friendship, Mercy evokes the blood oath on purpose, holding out her hand so that we can see the thin white scar. She points at it with one small, slim finger. "Don't do this to me. We're supposed to be friends. We're supposed to be sisters."

"You wouldn't understand, okay? So just drop it!" Lux says.

Mercy's in a full-on rage now. "Try me. I'm not a baby. You two treat me like I'm made of glass. Just tell me what the hell is going on!"

"Oh, Mercy, you *are* a baby," Lux shoots back. "You with your perfect life and your perfect family and the perfect grades and the perfect scholarship you're going to get to some fancy college. You don't know what it's like to be Rome or me. Things have never been hard for you. Nobody's ever looked down on you because you live in a trailer or you're a slut or you're repeating algebra. It's different for you. Everything is. You're going to leave here some-day. You're going to go on with your perfect life and do amazing, wonderful things and we'll still be *here*."

The words sting when she says them, and I wonder if they're true. Maybe Lux and I have always been preparing for this. Pro-tecting Mercy, keeping her safe until her wings were strong enough for her to fly away. Maybe because we thought she was the only one of the three of us who would ever really fly.

Mercy steps back, as if Lux has slapped her.

Lux knows she's winning, and she delivers the final blow. The one that Mercy won't think to question. "Not everyone is as perfect as you, okay? Maybe I just want that money because I do. Isn't that enough for you? Aaron's hours were cut. He's not the foreman, like *your* dad. Who do you think cut his hours, anyway? *Your dad. The foreman.*"

Mercy's mouth falls open, and her eyes are wet with tears.

"I didn't know," she whispers. "I'm so sorry, Lux. I'm so sorry." She looks at me like I should have stopped her midrant.

"It doesn't matter," Lux murmurs. "We'll probably never find the chest anyway. It's just a stupid pipe dream like everything else." There's a shadow of guilt that obscures her features, and she looks away from Mercy. "I'm sorry about what I said to you," Lux says. She can't even look Mercy in the eyes when she says it, which tells me that all these secrets are eating Lux up, too.

"Wait," Mercy says, wiping her eyes. She looks at me, and for a brief second it's like we're reading each other's minds. "Find it. We need to *Find* it," Mercy says.

"And we have a Finder," I finish.

Lux stops and turns around. She actually smiles. "God, we have a Finder. How could no one have thought of that before? Neveah! Your little sister is a *Finder*, Mercy." She hugs Mercy, and Mercy holds her so tightly that I think she might crack Lux's bones.

Mercy feels guilty.

That's what we've done to her. Lux has fed her half-truths, and I'm just standing here as an accomplice, wondering why I never realized this strange facet of our friendship. Mercy is going to leave us, and we're just waiting for it.

"Neveah's got that church service project after school all week," Mercy says, letting go of Lux and looking grimly determined to make things right. "But she could come along on Saturday. We'll look then. Bright and early."

"Here," Lux says, holding out her hand to take the framed map from me. "Give that to me. I'll stay for dinner at Mercy's house, and while I'm there we can dig up the book from the historical society and see if we can find anything out about Maisie, if she was the last person with Emmeline."

As we walk back to Cottonwood Hollow, Lux looks as if she could fly, too, the tips of her ballet flats barely touching the ground. But I feel like I'm made of lead.

ELEVEN

An hour later, I'm underneath the chassis of a Buick when I see the sleek Dodge Challenger roll into the last shop bay door. "Shit," I mutter to myself. It's Jett Rodriguez in his stupid car with its stupid warped rotors. We managed to avoid each other for the rest of the day at school because he'd left. He was probably at the dentist getting his perfect white teeth looked at. I stick my tongue into one of my back molars, wondering how long it's been since I've been to the dentist.

"Rome!" Red shouts. "Get the keys from the Dodge Challenger. He's got an appointment to have his brakes looked at."

I wait a beat, taking a deep breath before I roll out from under the car. Sitting up, I grab a grease rag from the pocket of my coveralls and wipe my hands. Then I stand up and walk over to him in my work boots, the only pair of shoes I actually own thanks to Lux this afternoon.

"Hey," I say as Jett gets out of his car. "Can I get your

keys?" I feel Red's eyes boring holes into me from the office window, where he's shuffling through papers, making sure I'm being polite to the customers. He's not one to talk. He has less patience with other humans than I do.

"I wondered if I'd see you here," Jett says, pulling his key fob out of the pocket of his jeans.

I'm not good at apologies, but I know that I need to give him one now. I wipe my hands on my coveralls, because they're starting to sweat. "Look, I'm sorry about how I came off this morning. I don't think you took the diary. I mean I didn't really think you did. I was just asking because it was lost. And sometimes things come out of my mouth the wrong way. I wasn't trying to be a jerk. My friends say sometimes I'm a jerk."

Jett makes kind of a half smile, like he's trying not to laugh. "Yeah, it was kind of an awkward moment."

I nod, looking down at the floor of the shop while I give my face a chance to cool down from the embarrassment of apologizing. Tim and Eddie are trying to listen in on the conversation from where they're clustered around the engine of a Toyota Tundra. I look over my shoulder and see that Red's figured out Jett and I know each other, and he's giving Jett the stink eye.

"Did you find it? The diary?" Jett asks.

"No. It's still lost."

"Did you write anything good in it?" he asks, that big stupid grin back on his face. "Anything about me?" His dimple pops.

I roll my eyes.

"Is that your boss?" Jett must have finally noticed Red.

"Yeah."

"He looks angry. At me."

"He hates everyone on principle. Don't take it personally."

"You guys must really get along well."

"Touché. We do. We're a lot alike."

"So how about getting that pizza tomorrow night? Or tacos. Or whatever sounds good."

"I have work. Until eight."

"I've got practice, so eightish works for me. If you want to go." He hurriedly adds that last part, stumbling a little.

My stomach growls. "Yeah, that would be good. I could go get pizza or tacos or whatever."

"Should I pick you up here or at your house?"

"Um, here, I guess."

"Sounds good. Well, I guess I'll go. My friend's waiting outside to give me a ride back to practice. I'll see you later." He glances back over at Red, who's now holding a tire iron. "Give me a heads-up if your boss charges me while my back is turned." He hands me the key fob.

"Will do." I can barely manage to suppress a grin.

As soon as Jett leaves, Tim starts in. "Rome's got a date with a guy? I didn't even know you liked guys, Rome. I thought maybe you were one of those—"

"Shut your face if you want to keep your job, dipshit," Red growls, setting down the tire iron he's carrying on the top of my toolbox. I didn't see him walk over here, but he stands behind me now. "And it's your turn to clean the bathroom, Tim. Why don't you go get on that?"

Tim grimaces, but he needs this job, so he skulks off. Eddie follows, wanting to get out of blasting range in case Red is pissed for a while.

"You okay?" Red asks, crossing his arms. "You want me to get rid of Tim?"

"You mean like in a 'hide the body' kind of way?"

"Like I cut the little shit's shifts until he quits kind of way."

"He's a jerk, but I can deal with him."

"What about the other guy? Challenger guy?"

"Jett?"

"His name is Jett? Jesus Christ. It's no wonder kids today are so fucked up. Was he bothering you? He was over here a long time. You know him from school?"

"Yeah, he's an Evanston boy."

"Thought you had a rule about no Evanston boys."

"Well, you know how they say rules are meant to be broken."

"Just be careful, okay?"

"I can take care of myself," I tell Red, crossing my arms. I look over at him and realize he's standing the same way.

"I know you can. I see you do it all the time." He takes a deep breath. "So how are other things?"

"What other things?" I ask.

"Like your Mach. What happened?"

"I sold it. Time for something different." I don't like to lie to Red, but I don't want him to feel sorry for me, either.

"Huh. Well, I didn't see that coming. Must be getting old." He smiles at me, and there's nothing behind it, no motives or pity, and for a second I almost spill everything.

Red has always respected me, always treated me like an

equal, and I don't want to lose that. So I laugh, "Yeah. Or it could be all those exhaust fumes getting to your brain."

"Whatever, grease monkey." He starts to turn away, but before he does he says, "Let me know if you need some extra shifts. I've got the money if you've got the time."

There's something warm in my chest, but it's probably just the smell of gasoline. I look over at Tim, who's still cleaning the bathroom, and Eddie, who's admiring the Challenger and not paying any attention to us, so I do something I never thought I'd do. I dart in and give Red a quick hug.

He's so surprised that he doesn't say anything. He just pats my back with his big, grease-stained hands.

And then I pull away, confident that neither of us will ever feel the need to speak of it again. We understand each other that way.

Red deals with Jett when he comes back to get his car just before closing time. I wanted to say hello again, but Red told me he's been working on the electrical system of this car for three mornings now, and he can't seem to figure it out. I can't shake what he said about the extra shifts and how much it meant to me that he offered them without prying, without strings. He knows that I won't take a handout, but I'm willing to take on any honest work. So instead of getting another few minutes with Jett outside of school, I'm lying half under the front of a 1987 Chevy Cavalier, dodging the mouse shit falling from the wiring beneath the dashboard above me.

I prop myself up against the driver's seat just far enough to watch Red explaining what Tim and Eddie did to the rotors. My arms ache from holding them above my head for so long, and I'm about to give up and just Fix the wiring rather than doing it the old-fashioned way. I don't care if I'm exhausted afterward. I'm ready to get out from under this storm of mouse pellets. I like Red a lot, but there's only so much poop that can fall in my face before I'm done.

Not long after Tim and Eddie leave for the night, Mom's car pulls up to the garage. She's carrying something, and Red practically sprints across the shop to greet her. I've never seen him greet anyone that way, and it makes me uneasy. Mom is beaming, wearing that same little black skirt from yesterday, this time with a shiny red top that is more date appropriate than job-hunting appropriate.

I drag myself out from underneath the dash of the Cavalier, finally having Fixed the wiring problem. My body is stiff and sore, and I spend a few moments just rolling my shoulders and bending my taxed joints. I wash up and change in the bathroom, which is newly cleaned thanks to Tim. I slip on Lux's borrowed flats that we'd stopped to get after our adventure at the homestead. They are soft and supple and don't rub my toes and heels the way my lost ones did. Damn Lux and her fancy shoes. I'm not giving them back.

When I get to the office, Red is leaning against the desk while Mom is waving around a stack of paper. "So I just printed all these up today and I don't even need them!" she laughs.

"What's that?" I ask, wiping my damp hands on my skirt.

"Résumés I made at the library. But Red, I mean, *Mr. Montgomery*, offered me a job running the office here. Can you imagine?" she gushes. "We'll be working together!"

"You can call me Red," he says, still grinning.

There are no words to express exactly how I feel about this development. "That's really something," is all I can manage to utter. I want to scream at Mom, but I don't want to do it in front of Red. I am terrified that she's going to mess this up for me. I admire Red. I respect him. I don't want her to hook him like she's hooked so many other men just to dump him in a few months. He hasn't dated anyone that I know of since I started working for him, probably because he's always here, making sure everything is running smoothly. Someone to manage his office and his paperwork would carve out more time for him. I'm stuck in the middle. I want Mom to get a good job, and I want Red to be able to have more time outside of the shop, or at least out of the office. But I don't want Mom to break his heart, or disappoint him when he realizes that she has no idea how to run an office.

"Yep, he took one look at my résumé and realized how qualified I am."

"It'll be a big help having someone full time in here. I've needed to do it for a while. It'll give me a chance to get back to working in the shop." Red looks pleased with the development.

"Well," Mom babbles, "I guess we should go so you can close up. But I'll see you tomorrow morning at eight a.m. sharp. I am so excited! I'm going to do such a good job, Mr. Montgomery."

Her excitement twists something in my gut. She really wants to do this. She wants to make a better life with a better job.

"Really, Stella, just call me Red."

"*Red*," Mom says with a bright smile.

"Or you know, we could go grab a bite or something to celebrate," Red offers.

Mom purses her lips, and I see the excuse ready for delivery. We don't have the money to go out to dinner. And I've seen that look a hundred times before. *Wouldn't you know? We've already eaten. Maybe next time.*

Red doesn't falter, "My treat." Maybe he read the look. Or maybe it's just a coincidence.

"You know what?" Mom says, as if the next words were going to be her answer all along. "I'm starving. How about you, Rome?"

"I'm fine," I answer, hoping to avoid the situation altogether.

Mom laughs. "Oh, Rome. You just kill me sometimes."

I would like to kill her right now, actually.

"Great," Red says. "What sounds good? Pizza?"

"I've always wanted to try Martinello's on Sixth," Mom says. It's not Pizza Hut. It's a pricier Italian restaurant that sells wood-fired pizza and food with Italian names I can't pronounce. I've never gone in, but I've seen the menu posted at the door. This is a test. *Warning, Red Montgomery. Fasten your seat belt and prepare for impact.*

Red doesn't flinch at all. "Sounds great. I'll close up and we'll head over."

In the car, I examine Mom's résumé. It's printed on the cheap paper that's available for five cents per page at the library. "This is what you showed him?" I ask. "This says you have an associate's degree in secretarial sciences. That's not even a thing, Mom. They don't even call them *secretaries* anymore. They're administrative assistants. And besides, you haven't even finished *high school*."

Mom sighs. "I knew you'd be a buzzkill."

"Mom, this says you type one hundred words per minute and are proficient in Word, Excel, PowerPoint, Adobe Photoshop, and *the Google*. Do you even know what any of these are?"

"I got that book at the library, remember? And I used Word to type up this fancy résumé in their computer lab. Did you know that they have templates you can use and everything?"

"Mom, did you show this to Red? Does he really think you can do all these things?"

"Yes, I showed it to him. How was I supposed to get a job if I didn't show the résumé to anyone?"

"You *lied* to get the job, Mom! He's going to figure it out when he needs you to actually do this stuff." I try to swallow, but my throat is tight. "Please, Mom. I really like him. And I like this job. Please don't mess this up for me."

"I don't know why you're so panicked, Rome. I can keep books. I did it some at the café last year. And I'll figure out the computer stuff as I go along. He doesn't even have a computer yet, anyway. He says he has to get one."

"What if he fires us both when he figures out that you have no idea what you're doing?"

Mom's features tighten, and she rips the résumé from my hand. "I am doing the best I can, Rome. I am trying to make a better life for you. For both of us. You're right. I don't have that high-school diploma. I certainly don't have some stupid college degree or any real fucking job skills, because I have been too busy

152

just fucking surviving for the last seventeen years, okay? You sold your car. Now I'm writing fake résumés. We're both doing the best we can."

I look away from her because I know that everything she said is true, but my next request is selfish. "Just please don't make him another ex-boyfriend. I really like him."

"It's just dinner, Rome. We're both hungry. And I don't know about you, but I'm broke."

Red gives us a wave from the door of his Silverado as he gets in. Mom hands me the keys and I start the car to follow him.

The restaurant isn't packed. We manage to get a table within minutes, and the waitress is friendly and chatty, thinking we're some happy family out to grab a bite to eat. I watch Red as he pulls out Mom's chair for her. He's wearing The Collared Shirt. The one that hangs in his office like he's going to change into it after work, but he never does. It's plaid and has pearlized buttons, but for a guy who usually wears coveralls, it's the equivalent of wearing a suit. Even if he's a free dinner to Mom, he thinks this is a date, or something close to it. He's going all out. He's taking us both to dinner.

Truthfully, out of all the guys Mom's dated, he'd be one of the best, if not the king of them all. He's got a job, he doesn't do drugs, and he doesn't stare at me in a way that makes me uncomfortable. Mom's had a steady trail of ex-boyfriends, averaging a couple per year. I think she gets lonely, and sometimes she thinks I need a father figure in my life. But the moment they show the slightest hint that they might be losers, she gives them the heave-ho. When I was younger and actually liked some of the guys she dumped, I thought it was because she was the loser, but then I realized there had been good reasons. Carl partied too much and couldn't hold down a job. Stefano stared at me whenever Mom left the room. Eliot wanted Mom to change her hair and her clothes and read the *New York Times* instead of her beloved paperbacks. And he wanted to get rid of Steven altogether, which was obviously a deal breaker.

I guess the gist of it is maybe I didn't realize how many of her decisions were made for me and not for her.

Red surprises me by ordering a bottle of red wine rather than a beer. Mom is clearly unsettled by this as well, because I had seen her finger running through the list of beers that she thought would make her seem fun and flirty to a guy like Red. Her candy-apple-red nail had been hovering between a PBR and a Bud Light. I order a soda because it's unlikely Red supports underage drinking.

"So this is cozy, isn't it?" Mom says, looking around.

"Nice place," Red says. "I came here once a couple years ago when my buddy from the corps was in town."

"That's right! You were in the Marines!" Mom exclaims. "That's so interesting. You must have traveled and seen *so* many things!"

Like war, I think to myself, but Mom manages to put a positive spin on just about anything related to a man buying her dinner.

Red goes on about his two tours of duty, telling only the light, funny parts and nothing about the scars I noticed on his left leg that time I saw him in shorts. As Red chats with Mom, my stomach churns. Mom got that job by lying to Red, one of the few decent human beings I know. And I'm just sitting here, watching her play him as the pizza comes.

Red refills her glass of wine while they're talking, and I barely notice through the haze of guilt that Mom has said something to me. She's my mom, I tell myself. She needs this. Let her feel like she's finally moving up in the world. Her words echo in my brain, *I certainly don't have some stupid college degree or any real fucking job skills, because I have been too busy just fucking surviving for the last seventeen years, okay?* She's right. Every move she's made since I've been born has been about surviving.

Mom repeats herself, "The ladies' room?"

"I'm good," I mumble, and Mom's face falls a little because she'd been hoping I'd join in her middate strategizing session. *Does he seem interested? Should we press for dessert?* We've been on these kinds of dates before, where the guy tries to impress Mom by taking us both out. The difference here is that Red is genuinely nice and those other guys had just been hoping for an invitation to come home with Mom.

Red stands when she gets up and leaves the table.

What little food I managed to eat is hardening into a stone in my gut.

"I have to talk to you," I whisper.

Red sits back down. "What?" he asks around a mouthful of pizza. Mom's left, and he feels comfortable enough to stuff his face around me.

"You have to know the truth about my mom." I'm sure Mercy's God is going to spear me right now with some kind of electric bolt for this betrayal.

"What? She seems nice."

"Everything on that résumé is a lie. She's been a waitress her whole life. She doesn't have a degree in anything. And she's only been using a computer for about three days now." I grab Mom's wine glass and take a couple of swigs to steady my nerves. I might as well go down completely in flames.

Red sighs. "Rome, I'm a lot of things, but I'm not stupid." He takes a gulp of his own wine.

"You *knew* she lied?"

"Even I know there's no such thing as a degree in secretarial science or whatever she put on there. But here's the thing. She's trying. And you're a good kid. A good mechanic. Let's give her a chance. If it works out, great. If not, she gets some work experience that will look good on a real résumé." He takes a moment to refill Mom's wine glass so she won't be able to tell I was drinking out of it. "I don't know what I would've done with a kid at seventeen or however the hell old she was. But you turned out okay. So, let's give her a shot."

I am momentarily dumbfounded. But Mom's traipsing back across the dining room, and suddenly I think of Lux's mom, Tina, and how much of a fairy tale it had been when she married Aaron, and she and Lux and Aaron had become this big happy family, or at least it seemed that way to me until recently. But the point is, I'd never dreamed of that for Mom and me.

So I grind out, "If this is a date, and not really a work dinner, then you should know that I like you, but if you hurt her, I will gut you."

He chokes on his wine, coughing into his hand as Mom sits down. "Goodness," she says, patting him on the back.

Red waves her off and begins breathing again.

The ride home is jubilant. Mom cranks the radio, singing along at the top of her lungs. During commercial breaks she revisits the dinner with me, commenting on how Red knew how to pronounce the name of the fancy red wine, and how interesting it is that he has tattoos on both arms. And did I know that he built that business all on his own? That he used to run it all by himself and live in the little apartment above it? And that the business kept growing and now he has five mechanics working for him?

Normally I would have shut her down, made some comment about how his shaved head reminds me of a shiny cue ball. But Red is a genuinely good guy, and if he was interested in my mom, it would be really selfish and petty of me to ruin it for her. So I smile and nod, and take secret joy from the fact that Red Montgomery knows her game. He knows her game and he's letting us stick around anyway.

By the time we get to Cottonwood Hollow, Mom's Focus is running on fumes. "Got any cash?" Mom asks as we pull into town. She hands me her purse. "I've got about three bucks in quarters."

When I was little, this was a game. *How much money can we find?* We'd search the couch cushions, the seats of the car, the booths of the café, and the pockets and wallet of whatever boyfriend she had at the time. I still have forty-five dollars left of the money Red paid me under the table on Monday, and I'm sure as hell not going to give it all to Mom.

"I've got ten bucks," I tell her. It's enough to get her to work and back for a while, but not enough to make her think I'm hoarding it. I still need to put minutes on my phone. And maybe buy ramen for next week.

"Great," Mom says. "Eight in gas and two for M&M's?" It's another one of our traditions. *Twenty percent tip*, Mom always called it when I was kid. If we had twenty bucks, we'd blow four of it on something stupid. But it was those stupid things that I remember the most. The nail polish or the movie rental culled out of a wrinkled twenty-dollar bill. Not the frozen burritos or the gasoline.

Mom looks so happy from her successful date with Red that I don't want to shoot her down. I want those M&M's and the look on her face when she thinks we're going to make a comeback after a particularly rough bout in the ring of life. She's fighting her hardest, harder than I've ever seen. She's learning new things, taking risks, and it's starting to pay off.

"Sure thing," I reply. I don't pull the money out of my backpack while we're in the car because I don't want her to see the cash I really have.

We turn into the gas station, and I pull up to the first pump, ignoring a group of five or six Cottonwood Hollow boys hanging out by the door. They're drinking from Styrofoam cups that most likely contain soda and cheap alcohol stolen from someone's parents' liquor cabinet. The few boys I've dated from Cottonwood Hollow were mostly interested in me helping them Fix their trucks, but after Lux and the teacher scandal, they became more interested in what I was willing to do in their back seats.

Sam is there, the boy who Mercy has had a crush on since she was fourteen. "Hey, Rome," he calls as I'm putting the eight bucks into the fuel tank. I take a deep breath, because I've always loved the smell of gasoline, even though it's not good for my brain cells. I guess we all love things that are bad for us.

"Hey, Sam," I reply. He's a pretty nice guy as far as Cottonwood Hollow guys go, even if he's too dumb to realize that Mercy is crazy for him. He's got curly blond hair and light-blue eyes.

"Need any help?" He leaves his buddies by the door and comes over to the Focus.

"I think I've got it covered," I reply. A Cottonwood Hollow boy asking a Fixer if she needs help with a car is ridiculous. Only Mercy's interest in him makes me respond without adding any creative language.

"I'll wash the windshield," he offers, picking up the squeegee from the bucket of wash water near the pump.

"Go for it," I murmur as the gas pump ticks.

He pulls the squeegee out of the bucket and begins washing the windshield. Mom doesn't even notice because she's already reading a paperback that she's produced from the depths of her purse. Any blank space that she can fill with fiction, she usually does.

"So how's school?" he asks, as if we don't both go to Evanston.

"Super. How's things for you?" This gas pump has to be the slowest one known to mankind. The numbers inch slowly up in the machine. *$5.98. $5.99. $6.00* . . .

"Pretty good." He scrubs at some particularly persistent bug guts, like he's working his way up to his next question. "I heard you were hanging out with Jett Rodriguez. The pitcher."

"Yeah?" I prompt. I'm actually surprised that news about Jett has already made the rounds, but I try not to let on.

"Just be careful around him. You know how those Evanston guys are. They think our girls are weird. He might be just messing with you."

"What do you think?" I ask, relieved when I can stop the pump at eight dollars exactly and exit this conversation. I pull out the pump, stopping to tap the tip on the edge of the tank, not wanting to waste a drop. I hang the pump up in the stand.

"About Jett? Well—"

"No, I mean about Cottonwood Hollow girls. Do *you* think we're weird?"

"No!" Sam exclaims. "That's not what I meant."

"I never see you talking with Mercy. And supposedly you all study your Bibles together every week."

Sam's eyes widen. "Mercy? Well, she's a real nice girl. But I don't think her parents let her date."

"You could ask." Mercy would kill me right now if she knew I was talking to Sam about her. "I'm sure her parents would let her go out with an upstanding young man like you."

"I'd rather ask you," Sam says, offering me a pretty smile. He crosses to my side of the car and drops the squeegee back in the bucket. I'm careful to keep my face neutral. This is not the response I anticipated, and all I can think about is how heartbroken Mercy would be if she were here.

"You're barking up the wrong tree, Sam," I reply. "A girl like me would eat you alive."

Sam opens his mouth to offer some response, but I hold up a hand to stop him.

"Go on back to your buddies," I tell him. "We'll forget this conversation happened." Because I can't tell Mercy he asked me out. Ever. *Ever*. And whatever comes after *ever*.

I walk past them and pull open the door, which squeaks. The hinges creak and the latch hasn't worked right for the last six months. Every time I come in here, it tugs at me, makes my fingers twitch to Fix it.

I head back to the candy aisle, the smells of dusty shelves and old hot dogs searing on rollers familiar to me. They have a special on a hot-dog-and-soda combo on Friday nights that only costs a dollar fifty, which Mom and I consider to be a bargain because there's no limit on how many condiment packets we can take. While I'm picking up two bags of M&M's beneath the glare of the fake security camera, I hear the unmistakable rumble of a 351 Cleveland pulling up outside.

I look out the window, but I don't need to. I already know who's out there. It's Garrett, driving my Mach. He's got a For Sale sign in the back window, which is dumb because you can barely see out the rear window of a Mach to begin with. I wonder again if anyone has made an offer on it yet. He pulls up right in front of Mom, backing in until the rear bumper of the Mach is a couple feet away from the front bumper of her Focus.

I clench the M&M's tight in my fist as I watch him fill up, my breath caught somewhere in my chest. He fiddles with the gas cap for a while because he's a jerk and he can't figure out how to open it. Then he stares at Mom while he pumps the gas, and even she can't pretend that she's reading beneath his intrusive gaze.

The Cottonwood Hollow boys near the front of the gas station are now watching with interest. They're undoubtedly discussing why Garrett Remington is driving Rome Galveston's car, while she's inside paying for gas for her mom's Ford Focus. I've always been known for that car, from the time I bought it with my dishwashing money at the age of fourteen, when I was too young to even drive it legally. I force myself to breathe, stretching out my lungs and gulping air as if it might save me now.

I walk stiffly to the cashier. I pay for the gas and the M&M's, then walk outside, determined not to let this moment ruin me, cave me in like a fist around an aluminum can.

"Hey, Rome," Garrett says when I get near the gas pumps where he's standing. "Where's your pretty girlfriends? The man-eater and the little Finder girl?" He must be too stupid to realize that Mercy and Neveah are two different girls, or he's got their talents confused. His eyes rove over me, and I wonder if this is how Lux feels all the time. No wonder she feels cursed.

I lift my chin up just a little to make me strong enough not to reply.

And that's when I hear the thud. Mom's Focus rams into the rear end of the Mach. Of course the Mach is made of metal, so the impact leaves only a small ding, but the plastic front bumper of the Focus is cracked. Mom, having climbed over into the driver's seat at some point in time, wears a look of surprise on her pretty face as she rolls down the window.

"Whoops!" she calls out. The high-school boys are elbowing

each other and pointing. "Sorry, Garrett! You know how women drivers are!"

Garrett's mouth is hanging open, but I just climb in the passenger seat. Mom backs up, then squeals around the Mach, barely missing hitting it a second time.

"Sorry about that," Mom says when we're on our way home.

"I can Fix it," I reply, handing her one of the bags of M&M's. But I'm grinning and thinking of how Mercy and Mrs. Montoya had worked around each other in the kitchen, like two cogs that fit together perfectly. That's me and Mom tonight. In perfect sync.

TWELVE

WHEN I GET HOME, I take a shower, as if I could wash off Garrett's gaze. I put on my old sweats and a T-shirt and crawl into bed. Not even Steven's cold nose on my cheek can make me feel better when he settles in beside me instead of hanging out with Mom. Dogs know when you need them.

I did the right thing trading the Mach for rent. Okay, maybe not the right thing, but the only thing.

I'd kept my deal with the Truett sisters when I found the Mach and restored it using only my talent as a Fixer. It had taken almost six months to finish. I Fixed the car in their barn, and they taught me everything they knew about being a mechanic, which turned out to be a lot. The tall Truett sister, Abigail, had run the farm, a Strong Back who could toss a square bale of hay on the bed of their Apache pickup as if it were a toy. The shorter Truett sister, Bernadette, was a Reader, which explained how she'd easily identified me as a Fixer. She'd helped their mom with the farm machinery back in the day, and even though she wasn't really a Fixer, she had a knack for turning the complex gears and pulleys of any machine into simple parts that were easy to understand.

Sometimes I still drive by their farm just to remember how I'd felt when I was there. Like the world was full of possibilities, if only I tried hard enough. And it didn't matter if I was one of those strange Cottonwood Hollow girls, or if Mom was in the process of creating another ex-boyfriend, or if we lived in a trailer that had seen better days.

All that mattered was that I could Fix that car.

And now that car is gone.

My eyes feel suspiciously hot and wet, and I finally do what I've wanted to do since I sold the car. I cry, my face pressed against Steven's fur, until we both fall asleep.

Someone taps on my bedroom window. Steven gives a low growl, punctuated by a soft "woof." I sit up, wiping at my face in case there's any evidence of my earlier weakness. I yank the mini blinds away from the window. It's Lux and Mercy.

Lux motions for me to come outside.

I look at the clock. It's almost midnight. What the hell are Lux and Mercy doing here at this time of night? My heart pounds. What if something's wrong? I hurry through the dark trailer, Steven trotting behind me. His nails click on the linoleum when we get to the kitchen. By the front door, I stop and slide on Lux's borrowed shoes.

"Stay, Steven," I tell him.

Steven whines, but for once does what he's told.

"What are you doing here?" I ask Lux and Mercy.

"I found something," Mercy says. They're both dressed in regular clothes, and I'm still wearing an old T-shirt and the sweats I sleep in. "So I texted Lux, but your phone's not working yet, so . . ."

"I'll put minutes on it tomorrow," I tell her. "What did you find?"

"It's Maisie," Lux says. "Mercy found her book from the historical society and it turns out Maisie was a *Truett*."

"And?" Familial relations in a town this small aren't that big of a surprise.

"What if Maisie hid the chest for Emmeline?" Mercy says. "She might have hidden it on Truett land. That stone barn out there is definitely old enough to have been around back then."

Excitement makes me draw a breath. The Truett sisters' old barn was full of junk. Maybe the dowry chest is out there, just waiting for us to find it. "You want to go *now?*" I ask, surprised that Mercy's sneaking out to go on what could very well be a wild goose chase.

Mercy shoots a guilty glance at Lux. "I thought maybe we could just take a look around. Just in case. Some family from Texas bought the farm, and Mom said they'll be moving in any day now."

Of all the places to go poke around right now, the Truett farm isn't the one that I'd pick. I'll just be thinking about the Mach and how Abigail and Bernadette would be shaking their heads at me now if they knew that I'd traded it off. I know Mercy is only doing this because she feels guilty about her dad cutting Aaron's shifts, and I want to tell her that she shouldn't feel any sympathy for that bastard at all.

Lux says, "Mercy said her mom went to an estate sale there. They sold off all the furniture and things in the house. She didn't remember seeing any trunks or anything. So we think if it's around, maybe it's in the barn."

I think back to where I'd uncovered the Mach, which seemed like a treasure to me then. Excitement about possibly finding the dowry chest out there makes me push away the guilt I feel for trading off the car the Truett sisters sold me.

"So let's go take a look around," Lux cajoles. "Maybe we'll find it tonight. It could happen, couldn't it?" She looks up at the stars like she's flinging a desperate wish into the darkness, and there's a recklessness in her eyes that makes me uneasy.

"All right," I say. "We can go look around. How are we going to get there? I don't think Mom will be okay with me stealing her car for a midnight joyride."

Lux points at the bikes lying in the grass.

"Bikes?" I ask, putting my hands on my hips. "What are we, twelve?"

"It didn't seem like a good time to wake up my parents and ask to use the minivan, either," Mercy says.

"Fine. Bikes it is."

Lux rides Mercy's old turquoise bike with the streamers on the handlebars, which is far too small and makes her legs stick out at funny angles. I pedal Mrs. Montoya's bike with the basket on the front. Mercy sits on the front handlebars above the basket, holding her legs out as we coast down the county road in the dark. The farm is only two miles from town, and we pass Truett pond and the old windmill.

"Remember how we used to skinny-dip out there?" Lux laughs as we pass. The closer we get to the Truett farm and the possibility of finding the dowry chest, the more excited she gets.

I laugh, remembering our skinny-dipping days when our biggest worry was whether or not the pond water would wash out the spray-on glittery, neon hair color we all put on before Mercy had to go home. We'd screamed with laughter in the dark, sang our favorite songs at the top of our lungs, just the three of us and the wide expanse of pasture and starlight.

When we top the next hill, the Truett sisters' house and massive stone barn come into view, and we turn down their driveway. The farmyard is dark, but Mercy has two flashlights in the basket of her mom's bike. She turns them on and hands one to me so we can find our way to the barn. We lay our bikes on the ground.

The grass is tall and thick, and there are no cars around, which tells me the new owners of the farmhouse haven't moved in yet. I slide the barn door open just a crack, and it groans loudly in the dark.

Mercy jumps. "Shh!"

"No one's out here," Lux says. "We can be as loud as we want."

Mercy looks hesitantly toward the road. "Someone might drive by."

"Well, they'd see the flashlights before they'd hear us," I say practically.

Mercy shuts her light off.

Lux rolls her eyes. "No one's going to see us, Mercy."

When I tug the door far enough for us to squeeze through, I go in first. My nose is filled with the smells of dust and dirt and old hay and manure. "Turn your light back on," I tell Mercy when she and Lux enter behind me. "Shine it on the floor. Make sure you don't trip on anything."

I cast my light around the barn. It looks like I remember it. The first floor has an old tractor and a planter attachment parked next to it. Abigail Truett's rusty Apache pickup is parked next to the planter. I put my hand on the hood, recalling driving out to the fields with her to check on the beans or on some cow she thought was going to calf soon. A small part of me thinks Abigail wouldn't mind if I borrowed it, but the family from Texas that bought the farm and equipment might.

"It wouldn't be down here," I tell Lux and Mercy. "This is all farm equipment. If the chest was here, it would be in the loft."

I shine my light over at the ladder. "Be careful," I tell them. "There are some weak places in the floor up there." It wasn't great to navigate the loft in the daylight, let alone in the dark with only a couple of flashlights to guide us.

I climb the ladder first, Mercy and Lux behind me.

The hayloft is stacked with cardboard boxes and baskets of junk. Three heavy, wooden chests rest in one back corner.

"Look!" Lux says when the light falls on them. "One of those could be the dowry chest!" She pushes past Mercy, following the glowing beam.

"Wait!" I shout.

Mercy darts out a quick hand and grabs Lux by the hem of her shirt.

Lux stops, turning to glare at Mercy. "Hey! Morgan got me this shirt."

I shine a light down on the floor, illuminating the large gap between the floorboards and the black space below. "That's a good twenty-foot drop," I tell Lux. "Worth stretching out your shirt a little."

We edge around the hole, making our way over to the corner.

A shuffling sound comes from the dark behind us, and cold fingers of fear creep up my spine.

We're not alone.

"What was that?" Mercy whispers, her flashlight beam frantically darting back and forth behind us in an attempt to locate the culprit.

One of the baskets falls over, and Lux lets out a yelp of fear as I change my grip on the flashlight so that I can swing it like a club.

Small green eyes flicker, first one pair and then another.

"Barn cats," I say, relieved. "It's just barn cats."

Two fluffy ginger cats trot over, one darting between Lux's legs and the other sniffing hesitantly at her shoes. "Go on," Lux tells them. "I don't want your hair all over me."

"Why didn't anyone take the Truett sisters' cats after they died?" Mercy asks, clearly worried about their fate.

"They're barn cats," I tell her. "They eat the rats out here. They wouldn't be happy in somebody's house. They're half wild."

Mercy reaches down to pet one, and it actually lets her.

Leave it to Mercy to charm a feral cat. "Aren't you a pretty one?" Mercy coos.

"Let's focus here," Lux says. "The trunks. What's in them?"

Looking around at the dusty piles, I feel my excitement ebbing away. What had seemed like an obvious connection between the Truetts and Emmeline didn't look so sure now that we were in the barn. "I don't remember the sisters ever talking about Emmeline."

"Well, maybe it's because you never asked," Lux replies. "Or maybe the chest was up here and they didn't know it."

"We'll see," I say, hoping to placate Lux. I want to find the chest as much as she does if it means I can get the Mach back again. But somehow, looking around this barn that was once so familiar to me, I don't believe this is where we'll find the chest. There are only memories here, and most of them bittersweet. Lux and Mercy hadn't quite understood my attachment to the Truett sisters. The whole town had turned out at their funerals out of respect when they died within hours of each other, but I'd been there out of more than that. I'd brought a handful of the sunflowers that they loved, casting them over the freshly dug graves after everyone had left, and knowing that wherever those cranky old women were, it wasn't in the ground.

We open all three chests. There are old quilts, tablecloths, a set of chipped crockery, a mantelpiece clock, some letters from the son who died in Vietnam. There are a few photographs of two little girls standing outside the old stone barn—Abigail and Bernadette when they were little.

Lux sits back on her heels. "Nothing," she sighs, frustrated. "Nothing again."

Mercy places a gentle hand on Lux's shoulder. "Don't worry," she says. "Saturday morning we'll go out and look with Neveah. We'll Find it."

But Lux's face shutters and she pulls away from Mercy, keeping that distance between them. I wish Lux would just tell Mercy what's going on. More than that, I wish I could Fix things for her, but I know I can't. Fixing only works on things, not people.

Mercy opens her mouth to say something, but a pair of headlights cut through the open windows of the barn.

"Shit!" I hiss. "Get down! Turn the flashlight off!"

Mercy and Lux obey instantly, ducking down.

I shut off my flashlight, crawling to the front of the barn to peer out the window.

"Who is it?" Lux whispers from the corner where she and Mercy are cowering.

"I can't tell," I tell them. "It's too dark. It's definitely a truck. Big. Maybe a three-quarter or a ton. Gas engine, not diesel, from the sound of it. But I can't tell what color or make." The truck creeps around the front driveway of the Truett farm, as if whoever's driving is looking for something. Or someone.

Mercy and Lux follow me, crawling to the window. The truck idles for a few minutes in front of the Truett sisters' farmhouse.

"Do you think it's the same person who was in the homestead?" Lux whispers.

"Probably," I reply, shivering. "It's someone who read the diary. Someone who knows what we know."

"You think someone else found it after you lost it?" Mercy whispers.

"They must have. They're looking at all the same places we are."

I feel Lux tense next to me. "We have to hurry," she says, her voice urgent. "We can't let them find the dowry chest before we do." Her hand touches mine in the dark.

After a few minutes, the driver puts the truck in gear and pulls out of the farmyard, back down the driveway toward the road. Maybe whoever it was decided it was safer to look around in the daylight.

"Do you think they saw the bikes?" Mercy asks.

"No," I reply. "The grass is too tall."

Lux looks over at me, her green eyes wary in the dark.

"Still," I say. "Let's cut through the pasture. Let's not take the road."

Mercy and Lux nod in unison.

We climb down the ladder and grab the bikes, walking them across the Truett pasture that borders Emmeline Remington's land. Everyone is quiet, disappointed that once again we've found nothing.

When we get near Truett pond, I have an idea.

I drop the bicycle and cut straight to the pond. Mercy lets out a small squeak of surprise when the bike falls next to her, but I leave them behind, running to the water. When I get to the dock, I shimmy out of my sweat pants and kick them away with one foot. My shirt goes next, and when I'm completely naked I take two bounding steps and leap into the darkness.

I plunge down into the inky depths, letting the cold water take me far away from Cottonwood Hollow. Far away from the secrets we're keeping from each other. I know I'm near the bottom of the pond, and I kick harder, even though my lungs are tight and burning, as if making it all the way down would somehow prove something. Maybe that I'm worthy of a better hand than the one I've been dealt. My lungs are aching, searing, near to bursting. I kick once more, reaching out, my fingertips grazing the pondweed growing in the bowels of the pool. Almost there.

But no. I am not enough.

I turn back and kick, letting the water slide around me until I see moonlight. When I break the surface, I gulp in air, let the songs of the cicadas fill my ears.

"I was starting to think you weren't coming back up," Lux says from somewhere in the darkness. The heels of her shoes tap out a lonely beat on the dock as she approaches the end.

"Does the fact that you're still up there mean you're going to chicken out?" I ask her, still gasping.

"We're not kids anymore," Lux says darkly. "Maybe you two are, but I haven't been for a long time." I feel her pulling away from me, and it worries me.

"Chicken," I goad her, narrowing my eyes, knowing she can never resist a dare. I make a clucking sound.

The dark look on Lux's face cracks with a laugh. "Never," she says. "I've never been a chicken in my life."

There's a scurry of light footsteps, and I know Mercy has joined her on the dock. "What are you doing?" Mercy huffs out. "What if we get caught? We're not flat-chested ten-year-olds any-more."

"What if you stopped worrying, just for tonight?" I ask.

Mercy removes her shirt, folding it neatly and setting it on top of her shoes, as if the sun-bleached wood of the dock might mar it. Lux shrugs off her clothes, her outline haloed in silver as the clouds drift away from the moon. Then she leaps off the edge of the dock, her body a pale blur before she hits the water.

Mercy sighs and begins removing her pants. "I cannot believe we're doing this."

"Prude," I tease, kicking around until I'm facing the pasture and the dark silhouette of the old windmill against the starry sky.

Lux surfaces next to me, gasping like she's about to die. "Jesus, Rome, you didn't tell me it was freezing in here."

"Why ruin a good surprise?" I ask, grinning.

Even Mercy's splash is tiny when her small, compact body hits the water. Lux floats on her back, her strawberry-blond hair making a dark halo around her head.

Mercy surfaces near me with a gasp, her hair in flat curtains on each side of her face. "Oh!" she gasps, but she's smiling, too. "It's so, so c-cold!"

I kick away, diving down again and coming back up to swim across the pond in smooth, even strokes. As she floats on the other side of the pond, Mercy begins to hum the tune to an old song we loved when we were thirteen, a haunting melody about a girl who runs away. It's not long before I'm humming along, and then Lux's silvery voice joins us in the darkness, and before I know it, we're singing like when we were little girls again, not caring who might hear us out here. The moon lowers a little to get a closer listen, and the stars sway softly along with the refrain. When we sing there are no secrets between us, just days and months and years of moments like this one. When we finish the last refrain, I'm laughing, and so is Lux, and Mercy begins a rendition of a bawdy tune that we learned at Flynn's bar, and song after song keeps us in this moment until we run out of breath and voice and the cows in the distance are mooing their disappointment that the concert is over.

When we're all exhausted, we make our way back to the dock and climb the old rusty ladder attached to the side. As I emerge from the dark water, my body feels heavy and slow.

"That was so much fun," Mercy laughs, her voice hoarse as she pulls her clothes back on. "Like when we were kids."

Lux reaches out and pushes a black, damp strand of hair that sticks to Mercy's face, her face softer, less worried than before. Maybe all we needed was a trip down memory lane, the three of us doing something together only because it was stupid and fun.

Later, I crawl into bed with Steven, my hair and skin still smelling of pond water, playing our songs over again in my head.

THIRTEEN

THE NEXT MORNING I DRIVE into Evanston with Mom, who is visibly nervous about her first day at the shop. So nervous, in fact, that we arrive at the shop thirty minutes early. While we wait for Red, she pelts me with questions about the day-to-day operations. She was confident last night, but the early light of day shines brightly into the pits and crevices of her fears. She wanted to wear the little black skirt again with some open-toed heels, but I convinced her that with all the tools and grease, open-toed heels and hand-wash clothing were not a good idea. So I let her borrow my nicest pair of jeans and a button-down shirt.

She wore the heels anyway.

"Maybe the IHOP is hiring now," she babbles when we park in front of Red's Auto. "I could waitress there. I'm good at it. Not everyone is good at it, you know."

"Mom, you did this. You got this job. There's no going back. You're not a waitress anymore. You're an office manager."

Mom turns to me from the passenger seat, where she grips the same faux-leather purse she's been carrying for eight years. "I can do this," she says, her rusty-brown eyes finding mine.

"You can do this." And then I do something I never do. I hug my mom. I don't know what's coming over me lately. Maybe Mercy is rubbing off on me. It's a quick hug, just a squeeze, and it makes Mom laugh. "God, Rome. I'm so scared. Thank you."

"You're going to be great."

"What if I have a question? Can I text you?" The edge of panic is back in her voice.

"Yeah," I tell her. "I'll put money back on my phone when I get to school."

"Oh, shit, *shit*, you need to be dropped off at school. I forgot." She looks around at the car like it has somehow betrayed her.

"I'm dropping *you* off," I tell her. "You're not going to need the car today. You'll be at your job, remember?"

Mom nods, swallowing hard.

"You pack a lunch?" I ask, watching as Mom produces a peanut butter sandwich and a worn paperback from the depths of her purse. "Okay, then you're good. I'll be back after school for my shift."

Mom nods again, and I have this strange feeling that must be what she felt when she left me at kindergarten for the first time.

Red pulls up in the parking stall next to us in his shiny Silverado. He waxes the truck with enough frequency that it gleams like onyx in the sun. He gives Mom a goofy wave, and somehow it's enough to give Mom back the confidence she had last night.

"See you later," I tell Mom as she climbs out of the car. She smooths down her shirt and adjusts her purse on her arm, making sure that her paperback isn't sticking out. Mom wants to make a good impression, and that strangely makes me proud of her. Sort of that kindergarten feeling again.

"Bye!" she squeaks before she shuts the door and gives Red her megawatt smile.

At school, I meet Mercy by her locker and give her twenty bucks. She hands me her credit card, and I hurry down to the computer lab to buy phone minutes before class starts.

When I'm finished, I put Mercy's card in my backpack for safekeeping. Checking the clock, I see I've got five more minutes before class starts, and I search online at the usual auto sale sites to see if Garrett's listed the Mach anywhere. Nothing so far. My throat feels tight. I hope we can find the dowry chest in time.

I glance at the clock again. I'm going to have to run. While I'm jogging down the hall, I power up my phone, wincing as it pings shrilly, alerting me to missed messages from Lux, Mercy, Mom, and Red. The school counselor yells at me to stop running, but I've already turned the corner and made it to Miss Strong's class.

As usual, Miss Strong is late. Lux is whispering to Morgan in the back row, and Jett isn't here yet. I put my phone on silent before I send off one text to Lux and Mercy, *Back in business.*

Lux reads the message and texts back, *Is it Saturday yet?*

I reply, *Can't come soon enough. We need time travel.*

Jett sneaks in right behind Miss Strong when she enters. My stomach does a little flip when I see that he's had his hair cut and it looks like he's wearing a new shirt beneath his school blazer. I'd packed a pair of jeans and a T-shirt in my bag to wear on our date. *Shit, shit, shit.*

"Lux," I whisper as Miss Strong begins writing the homework on the board.

"What?" she asks, shooting daggers at me with her eyes since I've interrupted her flirt session with Morgan.

"Do you have anything I could wear on a date?"

"Like, on me right now?" she asks, holding out her hands incredulously.

"Like at school? In your gym locker or something?"

"Wait, did you say date?" she asks, her interest piqued. "On a Thursday night? With who?"

"Jett. I thought we were just super-casually grabbing something to eat after I finish work and he finished practice, but it looks like he's wearing a new shirt under his blazer. And he got his *hair cut.* Can you help me out?"

"What, you don't want to wear your mechanic's coveralls?"

I shoot her an irritated look. "You talk big for someone who's unemployed."

"I'll see what I can do, okay?" she replies with a grin.

But then my phone vibrates. It's a text from Mom:

I ANSWERED THE PHONE! NOTHING EXPLODED OR ANYTHING!

After class, Lux stops me by our lockers. This is normally the time I shuffle off to the library and she sprints across the school to her Family and Consumer Science class so that she's not late, so I know something is wrong.

"Mom just texted me. She's says Aaron's *pissed*. Even more than before. He wasn't wrong about somebody messing with his truck. The mechanic called and it looks like someone put *bleach* in his gas tank."

"Bleach?" I ask as innocently as possible.

"I guess they're going to have to flush out the whole fuel system. The tank is all rusty. Aaron is beyond furious now. He thinks . . . he thinks maybe one of us had something to do with it."

"That's stupid," I reply. "You don't know the first thing about cars."

"Yeah, Rome. But *you* do. Did you do it? Did you screw up his truck?"

I look away from Lux, because even though her Siren talents don't work on me, she's still one of my two best friends, and when she looks at me like that, I have a hard time lying to her. "No, of course not. Must have been some punk kid who did it as a prank."

"Rome, this is *exactly* like something you would do. Especially after . . ." Lux lets her voice trail off, and I know without her saying it that she means the night I found out Aaron hit her. "You can't just go around deciding to get revenge on whoever pisses you off. This is my life. Not yours."

"There's no proof that I did it, is there?" I ask, my voice higher in pitch than I would like. "Aaron's got no proof that it was you. Or me or Mercy."

"Mom says maybe I should stay somewhere else tonight."

"Why should *you* have to stay somewhere else?" I ask. "Your mom should kick him out. This is complete crap that you have to hide from him."

Lux's temper flares. "She's doing what she can, Rome. Not all of us are *Stella*, dropping men left and right."

"*My* mom may not be perfect, but she's not afraid to get rid of a man who's a jerk. And she'd never let one of them lay a hand on me."

"Not everyone wants to live in a tin can on the edge of town, Rome. Some of us have higher aspirations." Her words might as well have been dipped in acid. She knows all of my soft spots, those tender hollows beneath my armor.

"So you let him use you as a punching bag as long as he brings home enough money for you to have your stupid fancy shoes? You know what? I don't even like these," I add, pointing down at the ballet flats I'm still borrowing from her. I'd like to take them off and throw them at her, but I need them too much, which infuriates me even more. "*I think they're ugly.*" I throw in that last part just to piss her off.

Lux's face flushes bright red. "I'd make you give them back right here and now, but I'm not sure you could hobble down barefoot to the Dollar Tree to buy new ones."

I slam my locker door shut before I turn on my heel and leave her standing in the hallway alone. Crowds of students press around us, creating distance and noise, unaware that we're drifting apart anyway.

The mezzanine isn't much better. I'm still furious at Lux, and when Mercy arrives, I lash out without thinking. "What are you doing here?" I ask. "Shouldn't you be studying for Yale or some shit?" Lux's words from yesterday by the creek echo in my brain. Mercy will leave us one day. We've always been preparing for that.

Mercy recoils, her dark eyebrows somewhere in the stratosphere.

But she's not my friend for nothing and she's far stronger than she looks. "Yeah, maybe I should be. And then when you remember how to act like a decent human being, you can talk to me again."

She manages to pull me back to logic and reason. "I'm sorry," I sputter. "I shouldn't have said that to you. It's Lux. We had a fight, and I'm still mad."

"Well, don't take it out on me. I'm just here to see if you want to study for chemistry."

"I want to light chemistry on fire."

"So is that a no?" she asks, barely containing her smile. She sits down next to me at the table, and I know that she's ready to listen.

I unload my tale about my date with Jett tonight and then about Lux and me fighting. I spill that Lux thinks maybe I'm the one who put the bleach in Aaron's gas tank. I tell Mercy I'm angry at Lux, too, because she made me lose my shoes yesterday, which is really only a tiny part of it all. But I don't tell Mercy everything that's happened between Lux and me lately. I don't break my promises, even when I'm angry.

"Why would you do anything to his truck?" Mercy asks. "Just because you're a mechanic doesn't mean you'd mess up his truck."

I shrug.

"I mean, he was *very* rude when we stopped by yesterday, but his truck was vandalized before that."

"Maybe he crossed the wrong person," I answer cryptically. "Maybe he deserved it."

Mercy sighs. "I feel like you two are hiding things from me. More than just the stuff about Aaron's shifts getting cut. I know you think that I don't understand what you go through, but at least let me try, Rome."

I ignore the curl of guilt that coils itself in my chest. "You should still be angry at us, anyway. Especially after what Lux said yesterday."

"About me leaving you to go to some fancy college?" Mercy asks. "We don't know that for sure, Rome. And it's not like I'm the only one of the three of us who could go to college. You and Lux talk like everything's already decided, and you're going to keep on going forever like you are now."

I shrug. I guess I thought we would. Lux and I would always be in Cottonwood Hollow. I'd keep being a mechanic, and Lux would . . . well, she'd watch her reality TV shows and get her nails done every Saturday afternoon with Tina.

"Don't close doors before you get to them. You could go to college and get a job designing Mustangs for Ford. You could own your own auto shop. You could do anything you want, Rome."

By the end of the school day, it's Mercy and not Lux who helps me out of my date dilemma. She meets me by Mom's car in the parking lot, and she's carrying a halter top and Lux's makeup bag.

"How'd you get this?" I ask her.

"Lux," she sighs. "She borrowed the top from Morgan, who had it in her locker. And of course the makeup is Lux's."

"Did you tell her it was for *me*?" I ask.

"Of course I did. You two may be mad at each other, but you're just alike. Neither one of you wants to wound the other permanently. Just *temporarily*."

"Well, you can tell her I said thank you," I announce. "But I'm not ready to apologize today."

"I'm not going to be the go-between for you two. Tomorrow you'll bring this all back and you'll offer to Fix Aaron's truck if he hasn't had it done already. Even if you didn't mess it up, it's the right thing to do. It will help Lux's family, and it'll show her you care about her."

As if I would ever consider Fixing Aaron's truck. I'd die before I did it.

"I can't Fix it," I mutter darkly, taking the top and makeup from Mercy.

Mercy sighs. "*Try*, Rome. Try for me and Lux. And she texted again about Saturday. We're going to meet at my house at nine in the morning. She said to tell you because she's not speaking to you, either."

We've fought before, but never over secrets like these.

FOURTEEN

At eight o'clock, I scurry out from under the Toyota I'm work-ing on at the shop and lock myself in the bathroom. I change into the black halter top and shimmy into my old jeans. I wash my hands and check my face for grease smudges before I use Lux's makeup bag to add a little liner, eye shadow, and lip gloss. Damn it, Lux has nice makeup. I pull out my ponytail and fluff up my curls before I leave the bathroom. There's a mini body spray that I use to help mask the smell of grease and metal.

Unfortunately, Mom and Red are still in the office. She did really well on her first day, and she's practically glowing with pride. They've already closed down and locked the bay doors. The only way out is through the office, so there's no escaping them now.

Red asks, "Is that what you wore to school today?"

"She's going on a *date*," Mom answers for him. She's grin-ning slyly because she already knows it's not a Cottonwood Hollow boy, or she would have heard it around town already.

"I'm going out," I confirm, looking at Mom.

"Who is he?" Red asks, frowning.

"The Challenger guy," I answer, knowing he's more likely to remember a car than a name.

"*Helicopter?*" he asks.

"Jett," I correct, but I can't suppress my smile.

"Is he coming here to pick you up?" Mom asks, practically dancing with excitement.

"Yes, but don't talk to him. Or look at him. Or *anything*," I warn her.

"Well, we should at least get to say *hello*," Mom says. "I'm your mother, you know."

"Where is he taking you?" Red asks, still frowning. "When will you be back?"

"He's taking me out to dinner, *Dad*," I drawl, just so he knows how out of line he is. I don't smile, even though I want to. It's actually kind of nice that he cares so much.

When I go outside, I find Jett is already in the parking lot. He gets out of the car and calls out a friendly hello.

"Hey," I reply, looking over my shoulder. Waiting inside and giving me some privacy is probably something that never occurred to Mom and Red. Instead, they're locking the office door slowly, shooting glances our way and whispering back and forth.

"Do you need to say good-bye or anything?" Jett asks when he catches sight of them. He's wearing the new button-down shirt that was under his blazer this morning, nice jeans, and is obviously freshly showered after practice.

"They're fine."

"Rome, honey, do you need anything?" Mom calls as she crosses the parking lot in her too-tall heels. "Money or something?"

I want to laugh inside because I know that Mom has maybe a handful of change to her name. And it's probably change that she's scrounged from Red's office. Red is known to leave it in little bowls and cans here and there from when he uses the soda machine at the gas station across the street.

"I'm good, Mom," I answer.

"Aren't you going to introduce us?" Mom asks when she stops next to me. We're nearly identical; Mom is me with an added seventeen years. I wait for Jett to state the obvious, that my mom is so *young*.

Jett stands a little straighter. "Hi, Mrs. Galveston," he says to Mom, holding out his big, tan hand.

Mom reaches out and takes it. "Oh, it's *Miss* Galveston," she purrs. "But you can call me Stella."

"Stella," Jett corrects himself. "I'm Jett Rodriguez."

"Jett," Mom says as if she likes the taste of the word in her mouth. "That's a nice name. Very unique."

"Rome is kind of a unique name, too," Jett offers.

"I named her after the city," Mom says. "I always wanted to visit Rome."

She has never told me this. Ever. Suddenly I have this image of Mom as a seventeen-year-old yearning to see the world.

"It's a beautiful place," Jett responds, somehow crushing the air out of my lungs. "You should visit someday. My family went there a few summers ago."

He might as well have announced that he's an alien from outer space. How can I ever go out on a date with a boy who's been to Rome? I haven't even crossed state lines. How ironic that my name is made up of two places and I've never been anywhere.

Mom doesn't miss a beat. "When I go, I'll ask you about the best places to visit so that Rome and I don't miss a thing." She gives me a brilliant smile, one she usually reserves for future ex-boyfriends.

Jett doesn't know it, but her smile is a caution to me. A plea. *Don't throw this away. Don't throw this away because you're afraid.*

"You need any cash, Rome?" Red asks as he joins us. He's stuffing his keys in the pocket of his jeans, and I notice that he's put on The Collared Shirt again and is attempting to look more professional man than mechanic. "Tomorrow's payday, you know." His eyes bore into mine as if begging me to take some money from him.

"I'm fine, Red. Thanks," I reply, agitated that he's offering as much as I'm honored by it. He's a good guy. A really good guy. I wish somehow that Mom wasn't working here, and I wasn't working here, and he was just some guy that she'd met on the street. Because Red is probably one of the kindest human beings I know beneath the cranky, oil-stained, and tattooed exterior.

Red's gaze is fixed on Jett now. "You be good to Rome, you hear?" he says. "Or I know some guys who can cut your brakes and make it look like an accident. Fuck, I *am* that guy."

"Yes, sir," Jett replies, taking it in stride.

"*Jesus Christ, Red,*" I swear, rolling my eyes. "I think we're ready to go." I grab Jett by the elbow and lead him back toward his car.

"Have fun, honey!" Mom yells after us. "Live your best life!"

I swear, I'm going to die right here in the Red's Auto parking lot.

In the car on the way to a restaurant, Jett finally manages to speak. "So your mom seems nice."

"She's kind of crazy. And so is Red. Sorry about that. He's my boss, but sometimes he thinks he's got to watch out for me."

"It's fine. I mean, that says a lot about you that so many people want to look out for you. It means they really like you, you know? Even if Red is a little intense."

"Yeah, he can be scary. But thanks. For saying that," I add. "And for not responding with any sudden movements that could've gotten you shot or something."

Jett laughs, and I do too.

"I'm just kidding about the shooting part. I mean, I think I am. Red could be packing heat at any time. It's usually hard to tell in his mechanic's coveralls."

Jett manages to suppress a grin. "Speaking of," he begins, "you look great. Not that you didn't look nice in *your* coveralls the other night."

"Well, I make most things look good. It's just who I am." I don't add that I'm flattered, or that I borrowed the shirt from Mercy who borrowed it from Lux, who borrowed it from Morgan because it's a brand none of us could ever afford. The jeans are from Walmart, and the only reason they look so good is that I inherited my ass from my mom.

"So are tacos okay?" he asks. "Or would you rather do pizza? Or Chinese? I think Chen's is open."

"I did pizza last night, actually, and I'm not exactly a chopsticks aficionado, so I'm going to say tacos."

"Puerto Blanco it is, then."

We pull into the parking lot of a little Mexican place on the west side of town. It's pretty busy for a Thursday night, and we wait a few moments at the entryway before the hostess sees us and takes Jett's name. After that, it's fifteen minutes of standing around and commenting on the wallpaper and the other patrons and ignoring the small twitch in my hand because the hostess's podium is leaning and needs just a *tiny* shim to set it back to rights. Finally, Jett's name is called.

"Fancy," I remark nervously as they seat us at a tiny table in the back. There's a candle in the middle of the table, flickering in a red glass bowl.

"If you don't like this, we can see if they can seat us somewhere else," Jett says hesitantly.

"Nope. I don't mean it like that. I mean that the candle is nice." My cheeks heat a little when he stares at me. Damn.

"Oh," Jett falters. "Good. Let's sit." He pulls out the chair for me. I make a mental note to tell this all to Mercy, who will die from the many acts of chivalry Jett has displayed since I met him on the side of the road earlier this week.

"Thanks," I say when I sit down. Jett sits down on the other seat, and we both pick up the menus that the hostess left.

"So do you work tomorrow?" Jett asks.

"No," I reply. "I'm actually off tomorrow. Although it's payday, so I'll be stopping by there. It's like I can't stay away."

"Payday is good," Jett replies.

"Do you have a job?" I ask, even though I expect the answer will be no.

"Not during the school year. In the spring, baseball takes up most of my free time. I worked painting houses last summer. Got on with the same crew to do it again this summer."

I'm a little surprised that he works at all, given that his previous address was in the Heights neighborhood, and I nod because I don't know what to say. *Whoa, dude, that's adorable.* But I don't want to think less of him because his life is different from mine, even if it's an automatic tic that I have to force myself to shut off. It's no better than when people do that to me for being a girl from Cottonwood Hollow.

"I worked in Haiti building houses the summer before that," Jett adds to the conversation, filling the hole I'd left gaping.

"Haiti?" I ask. "Why Haiti?"

"Well, technically, it was a missionary trip. When I was a freshman, I got arrested for theft, so my parents shipped me off for a summer to set me straight."

"You got arrested for *stealing* something?" I ask, my interest immediately piqued. Finally, Jett Rodriguez is not 100 percent perfect. And it explains the way he'd reacted when I asked if he had stolen the diary from my backpack.

"Don't laugh," Jett says, though he looks like he's about to do it himself. "But I got arrested for stealing baseball cards."

I can't help it. A small snicker leaks out of my carefully glossed lips.

Jett rolls his eyes. "Okay, it's a little funny. But remember that I was *fourteen*, and sometimes guys at that age make stupid decisions."

"Guys at any age make stupid decisions," I reply before I can stop myself.

He laughs, his eyes crinkling up as the waitress returns to take our orders and drop off chips and salsa. She's young and cute and her eyes spend far too long roving over Jett's broad shoulders.

"What about you?" Jett asks. "I know you like all the hard awkward questions. So what's the worst thing you've ever done?"

There are a million answers, and none of them are appropriate for a first date, especially not a first date with an Evanston boy. But I don't want to lie to him, even if it would be easy for me. So I pick the most recent, if not the worst, of my transgressions. "I put bleach in somebody's gas tank," I offer.

Jett grins, even as he looks surprised. "You're even more of a badass than I had imagined."

"Well, you know us Cottonwood Hollow girls," I reply before I can stop myself. I'd wanted to keep Cottonwood Hollow out of our date if I could help it.

"You're all kind of a mystery, really. I've only heard rumors."

"Well, most of it is probably true. So I won't bother to tell you not to believe it."

"Can you cast spells over unsuspecting men?"

I remember Lux and the algebra teacher. "No," I say. "*I* can't, anyway. That's not a talent that I have."

"But there are some Cottonwood Hollow girls who can."

"Some can. Most don't want to. A lot of people don't realize that just because you have a talent doesn't mean you can always use it *well*. It's no different from you striking out in one inning when you'd hit a home run the inning before."

"You and Mercy and Lux seem pretty tight."

"We are."

"Have you guys been friends a long time?"

"Basically since we were born. Cottonwood Hollow girls tend to stick together."

"Are you ever going to tell me what your talent is?"

"No."

"Can I guess?

"You can guess."

"Your talent is knitting. You are a knitter."

I nearly spit out my soda. "No."

"You can juggle. No, wait. You can make papier-mâché masks that resemble Hollywood stars. You can read people's minds. You can read people's *auras*."

"None of those are right. Keep guessing. But plan on ordering dessert later, because at this rate we'll be here all night."

"Maybe I don't want to guess," Jett says, serious now. "Maybe I just want to wait until you're ready to tell me."

I'm a little taken aback by this, because everyone who knows a Cottonwood Hollow girl wants to know what her talent is. Jett is still watching me thoughtfully with his dark eyes.

"All right," I reply. "I'll tell you my talent when I'm ready. When I think you deserve to know."

"Sounds good," he replies, digging for another chip.

The rest of the date is too easy. He's funny, he reads books, and he has an embarrassing collection of baseball cards and action figures still in their boxes from his childhood. He's the perfect combination of funny, awkward, and handsome.

I also notice when he gets up to use the bathroom that his jeans are almost as flattering as his tight baseball pants.

When the waitress brings the check, I make a move to get cash out of my wallet.

Jett holds up a hand. "When I ask a girl out on a date, I pay for it."

"Do you ask a lot of girls out?" I ask, realizing it's rude right after the words fall out of my mouth.

Jett grins, as if he finds my response refreshing rather than insulting. "Not a lot," he says. "But if you want, I can start keeping a tally. Rome Galveston, one. Maybe I can make notches on my bat or something." He picks up the black folder with the bill and slips in a card. I can't tell if it's a bank card or a credit card. Not that it matters. But I've never had a bank account because my experience with Mom's is that it gets overdrawn a lot and you get charged a lot of money for bounced checks.

"I'm sorry," I reply. "As you can see, I haven't been out on a ton of dates. At least not *nice* dates. More like the let-me-drive-you-around-in-my-pickup-truck kind." I pause for a beat. "And I have a habit of being too blunt. Mercy says I lack a filter."

"I kind of like the lack of filter."

"Well, then you're in for a treat. Half of what comes out of my mouth is completely undiluted."

"I can hardly wait," Jett says as the waitress picks up his tab. "So it's almost ten. Do you have a curfew?"

"Yeah, it's whenever I get home."

"I've got to be in by eleven on a school night. So I guess after this I'll take you back to the shop? Where's your car parked?"

If I could, I would light the restaurant on fire using eye lasers. Just to distract him so that I don't have to answer his question. Also, eye lasers would have been a much cooler talent than being a Fixer. "I don't have the Mach anymore," I reply as the words slice me into ribbons. I realize that in my haste of sending Mom home and giving her little information about this date, I also screwed myself out of a ride back to Cottonwood Hollow.

"What do you mean?" Jett asks. "Did you sell your car?"

"Yes," I reply because it's easier than explaining that technically I traded it.

"Going to get something else?" he asks. "Maybe something that won't blow up if you're rear-ended?" he jokes. The waitress returns with his card and receipt.

"I'll have you know that the Mach was *a tank*. A beautiful, fast tank."

"I'll drive you home."

"I can call my mom and she can pick me up at the shop."

"It's no trouble." He smiles affably. "I'll take you home. And if you ever need a ride to school or home or wherever, just let me know. We can get food and do an activity and call it a date," he adds with a teasing note.

There's no way I can refuse now without seeming like a jerk, so I just nod. We leave the restaurant and walk to his car.

I get in, taking in the smell of leather seats and the cologne he put on for our date.

Jett gets in the driver's seat, and we head toward Cottonwood Hollow.

"So how are the goats?" I ask Jett as we speed down the highway. I wipe my hands on my jeans. I wish I'd told Mom to meet me at the shop. I wish I hadn't agreed to let Jett drive me home.

"The goats are good. So are the chickens."

"Does your mom plan on purchasing any more farm animals anytime soon? Or maybe some kind of guard dog. Maybe an alligator."

Jett grins. "No alligators, I think. She only likes them if they make up a purse. But now she's into painting. Lots of painting. She took over my dad's office because she swears that it is the only room with *light*."

"What's your dad do?" I ask, even though I'm fairly sure he mentioned it the last time I was in his car.

"He's a lawyer. Partner in a big firm. Lots of suits. Ties. Stuff like that."

"So you're *set* if you commit a murder." I think about the trailer, and how it's going to look to this son of a lawyer. Small, old, sad. Pitiable, even.

"Yeah, having a lawyer in the family is pretty convenient," Jett agrees placidly. A few moments pass, filled with the soft crooning of the radio. "I thought for a minute when we met your mom that you had an older sister."

I nearly laugh, and it's enough to distract me from our destination for a minute. "Do not *ever* say that to her. She will die from happiness." I shake my head. "Actually, just try not to talk to her ever, if you can help it."

We pass the Welcome to Cottonwood Hollow sign.

As we drive down the main drag, I try to see Cottonwood Hollow as Jett must see it. Fading facades of old buildings, a bar that seems to be doing pretty good business. Raised, cracked sidewalks torn asunder by the roots of massive cottonwoods that grow all over the town. A crowd of boys wearing cowboy boots or worn-out sneakers and dusty jeans hanging around the gas station.

"Which way?" he asks.

I have a brief fantasy of telling him to turn toward the wide, shady streets where Mercy is probably reading a smuggled romance novel right now, and pretending that I live in her pretty house with its flowers and white picket fence. That's the kind of house that a boy like Jett should drop a girl off at. The kind where he'd walk her to her door and kiss her good night while both parents slept soundly upstairs and the scent of petunias wafted on the air around them.

But that is not my life, and to pretend that it was would be cowardly, and weak.

I'm not weak.

So instead, I swallow my pride, wipe my hands on my jeans again. "Take a right." We cruise down Elm and I direct him toward the dirt road that leads toward our trailer.

I tell myself that I want to do this. I want him to see where I live. I want him to look at the trailer and the weedy yard and the plywood skirting and the front stoop that I'm always shimming up to make it steady. I want him to see all of that and still want me.

We get to the head of the dirt road that leads to the row of trailers. This is my last chance. I could tell him to stop here, but I won't.

The Challenger crawls slowly down the dirt road, passing two trailers until we get to ours.

"That's it," I say, pointing toward the small, narrow, single-wide trailer. It's got faded cream siding, with a toffee-colored stripe around the middle. The front stoop is illuminated by the porch light that Mom has left on for me.

Jett doesn't say anything; there's no condescension or disdain. He just unbuckles and gets out of the car. He walks around to my door, and I try to think of something witty to say.

He opens the door and I get out.

I pause for some comment about the trailer, hugging my arms across my chest, waiting to see what it will be.

Jett offers me his hand. I take it. His hand is big and just a little rough. Radiating heat like all the rest of him.

He smiles at me.

We stand in the ambient glow of the porch light, cicadas chirping around us.

"I had a good time," Jett says.

That's it.

There's no surprise, no pity. No disgust. Just a boy standing in a front yard with a girl, probably wondering whether or not we are going to kiss, just like he would have if we were really that imaginary boy and girl standing in front of Mercy's house.

I find my voice. "Me too."

"This may sound really lame, but I like you. And tomorrow I've got a game and there's going to be a party afterward with the team at Clay's house. Is there any chance you'd want to come with me?" His last words come out in a nervous rush.

"You want to take me to an Evanston party?" I ask. I hope when I say the word *Evanston* it doesn't sound synonymous with the word *shit*, but it probably does.

"Yes."

"As your mechanic or your date?" I tease.

Jett manfully attempts to keep a straight face. "My brakes are great, by the way. I'm surprised you didn't ask. Seems like something a responsible mechanic would do."

"So would this date include me in the baseball stands, cheering for you or something? Would I need to wear an Evanston Eagles shirt? Or have pom-poms?"

"It would be awesome if it included that. But if baseball doesn't thrill you, we could meet up after."

"I think I could probably make it to a game," I say with a shrug. "I'll have to find where your parents are sitting, though, so I can ask your mom about her goats. *And* the chickens. And whether or not it's too soon to call her *Mom*."

He laughs, his eyes crinkling up in that way that makes something light and quick jolt in my stomach.

I kiss him.

I can tell he's a little surprised, because he stiffens at first before settling his big, warm hands around my waist. He goes for a second kiss, and then a third.

"I like you, too," I tell him when we both pull away.

FIFTEEN

I STAND ON THE FRONT porch, waving at Jett as he drives away. When his taillights fade, I look down at my feet and see Lux's stupid ballet flats. And then I remember our fight. And how it had all started when she told me that her mom had warned her to stay out tonight because Aaron is pissed about his truck and thinks we had something to do with it. I was angry with her, and we'd each hurt each other over the secrets we've kept.

I stare at my palm, at that thin white scar slicing across it, remembering everything that we'd sworn to each other, me and Lux and Mercy. But I broke that promise. I turned away. I turned away from Lux when she needed me because I was angry. The air around me grows cool, as if Emmeline Remington didn't disappear with her diary. And I realize now how wrong I've been. I thought that I was meant to find Emmeline's diary so that we could find the dowry chest and I could buy back the Mach and Lux and her mom could kick Aaron out.

But that wasn't it at all. Emmeline wanted us to know that she hadn't cursed us. She'd meant everything to be a gift, not just the talents, but the strength of our bond, the lengths to which we will go for each other. And that's why I was supposed to find the diary, to remind me of what Lux and Mercy and I truly are to each other. *But this is one thing I will wish with my dying breath upon all the daughters of Cottonwood Hollow who follow mine: May they depend on each other; protect each other no matter what the cost, as my sister would have done for me if she were here.*

I have to do the one thing that only a true sister could do for Lux.

I have to protect her.

Even if the cost is our friendship.

I don't even bother to go inside the trailer. I know where Lux is, and I know she needs me. I start running, not a jog, but a flat-out sprint that blurs the world around me, streaks of houses and cottonwoods and the pounding of my feet on the road in those beautiful, fragile shoes.

When I get to Lux's house, all the lights are on, turning the small bungalow into a beacon. The neighbors have come to stand out on their porches, and a few more peek from behind drawn curtains. Their faces are conflicted, the look of people unsure about whether or not they should act, if what happens behind closed doors should be left there.

Only Tina's car is parked in the drive.

I open the screen door and jiggle the handle of the front door. It's locked, but I know where the spare key is. I almost stumble when I feel that familiar tug from the other side of the door, like many broken things are waiting for me to Fix them. I put my hand on the door to steady myself when I hear the muffled sound of someone crying inside.

I've got to do it now, before I lose my nerve. I have to do what Emmeline wanted me to do. Protect Lux, no matter the cost. Even if I know she'll never forgive me. I dial Rick Ruiz's number on my phone. He's the sheriff's deputy, and my neighbor, and he owes me one for Fixing his electricity last Sunday.

My hands shake like I'm eighty years old. I don't know what I'll find when I open this door. But I've known Rick since I was a kid, and I've babysat Letty loads of times. I know Rick will answer when he sees my number, even though it's late.

He picks up on the second ring. "Hello?" he answers, his voice slurred with sleep.

"Rick, I need help."

"Rome, what's wrong?" he says, more awake now.

"Come to Lux's house quick," I say in a low voice. "I think she and her mom are in trouble. Get one of the local EMTs to come, too."

My fingers are still trembling when I lean down and grab the key out from under the ceramic toad on the front stoop. These are Fixer hands, and they have been steady all my life. But they are not steady now. I scrape the key around the keyhole twice before I'm able to jam it in and twist.

Then I push open the front door, briefly confused by the resistance I meet, as if someone is leaning on the other side. There's no one there, but the little table where Tina and Aaron drop their keys when they come home is knocked over. I shove the door with my shoulder, wincing at the noise as the table scrapes across the wood floor.

I'm not fully prepared for what I find in the living room.

At first I can only process the big things, and then the smaller ones come into focus. The recliner is turned over on its side; the television has been knocked off the stand. Then it's a bottle of Budweiser leaking on the couch, a lone ballet flat by the radiator. The hand-drawn map of Cottonwood Hollow, the glass broken out. Fragments of the vase Mom and I gave Tina as a wedding gift. Debris litters the floor, shattered dishes and what looks like drops of blood, and it takes me a few moments more before I find the people in all the mess.

Lux is lying on her side, curled up near the fallen TV, its screen cracked and splintered. Her nose is bleeding, smearing red over her lips and chin, and her left eye is nearly swollen shut beneath the smudge of her eye shadow. Her school uniform top is ripped at the shoulder and hanging nearly completely open, exposing pink, flushed skin and part of the polka-dotted bra she's wearing.

Tina is collapsed against the wall near the kitchen, her face purplish and almost unrecognizable. She doesn't even notice I'm here. It's hard to tell if her eyes are barely open or swollen shut.

I rush to Lux and drop to my knees, desperate to see how badly she's hurt. I wouldn't even know she was alive if it weren't for the occasional shudder of her body. Dried tears have left salty tracks down her cheeks.

My hands hover above her, unsure of what to do first. I should have listened to Lux when she said she shouldn't go home.

I shouldn't have fought with her. I shouldn't have put bleach in Aaron's gas tank. Oh, shit, shit, shit. This is my fault.

Lux's strawberry-blond hair is coming out of its bun, trailing limp, pale strands around her neck and pooling in gentle whorls on the floor. I cautiously stroke the hair away from her face and neck. Tears make it damp against my hands. She opens her eyes, the puffy one barely a slit.

"What happened?" I ask, even though I know.

"He said it was my fault," Lux whispers.

I continue to stroke her hair back off her face, exposing more swelling as I do.

The bleach. Aaron must have decided for sure that we put the bleach in his gas tank to get revenge for him hitting Lux. My chest is tight and cold and it's hard to breathe, because I've never hurt this much in my life. But I am not prepared for her next words.

"He said I use my curse on him. That I tried to seduce him. That I *make* him do those things. But I don't, Rome. I swear I don't."

I feel vomit rising in my throat. I have to force the words past my tongue when I ask, "Did he try to *touch* you?" All the pieces are coming together now. This isn't about Aaron's truck, and Lux's fear of Aaron was never just about him hitting her.

"He kissed me, even though I told him to leave me alone. He grabbed me," she says, her lower lip trembling as she moves her hands to wipe his touch away. "I *begged him not to*, Rome. It's not the first time. I always tell him no, Rome. You have to believe me. I don't ever use my curse on him. I never did. *I swear it*. Please, please believe me." She reaches out and her bloody fingers wrap around my wrists.

I look her straight in the eyes. "I believe you, Lux." I clench my fists, wishing he were here so I could smash his face in. Aaron was trying to touch her, to force her to do things she didn't want to do, all the while blaming it on her and her talent as a Siren. Of course she said it was a curse. Who would believe Lux if she told them that she wasn't doing it? After the algebra teacher in Evanston, would anyone believe her if she said it wasn't her fault?

Lux struggles to sit up, looking around the room like she's not sure where she is. I reach out and try to steady her.

When she speaks, her voice is crackly, distorted. Maybe she had screamed for help for too long. "He tore my shirt when I tried to get away from him. And then Mom came home early. And she just flew at him. And he hit her. And he kept hitting her." She looks around for Tina, sees her slumped against the wall. Lux's chest heaves like she's beginning to hyperventilate. "Is she breathing?"

"Let me check on her. We have to call an ambulance, Lux," I tell her, hoping that she'll see reason. Hoping that she won't hate me forever for calling Rick. I feel her fear when I touch her, see the panic rising in her again. "We have to get help."

"No," she hisses, looking frantically around her, as if someone might hear us. "We'll be all right. Mom can Heal us. She'll wake up. She has to wake up. We can't tell anyone what happened. This is why I made you promise, Rome. No one will believe it's not my fault. They'll think I used my curse to seduce him. To lead him on."

"No, Lux," I whisper gently. "It's not your fault. It was never your fault." I hate myself for not having listened more closely. For not poking and prodding and making her tell me everything.

That's what friends, no, *sisters*, are supposed to do. And I've failed her.

"Remember, you promised." Lux pulls away from me and finds her feet, stumbling drunkenly over to her mom.

Rick shouts as he enters the house in his deputy uniform, pushing his way in against the debris as I had before, "Hello? Rome? Lux? Tina? Where are you?" His hand hovers over his holstered gun as he surveys the scene.

Our eyes meet, his dark with understanding.

An EMT comes in with a black bag, looking around the room with a placid expression, as if he's seen this kind of thing before. When he spots Tina, he immediately hurries over to her.

I pull Lux away from her mom to give the EMT some room to work. He's trying to talk to Tina, touching her face and lifting her eyelids to shine a small flashlight in her eyes.

Something must have dissipated the fog of fear and panic in Lux's brain, because she realizes now that Rick and the EMT are here. "The police," she whispers, turning around in my arms to face me. Her hands grab my shirt. "Someone called the police. They're going to find out. They're going to think I did what Aaron said."

And I realize what a complete betrayal this will be when Lux realizes that it was me who revealed her secret. Her curse will be in the spotlight again. There will be people who believe Aaron. People who believe she somehow did all this to herself by being too pretty, too young, too flirtatious. People who believe she was asking for it all along, this beautiful Siren from Cottonwood Hollow.

"No, Lux," I tell her, grabbing her wrists in my strong hands.

Fixer hands. I wish I could Fix us now. "You didn't do anything wrong. Rick and the EMT are here to help. We're all here to help."

"It was *you*," she hisses as she puts all the pieces together. She tries to pull away.

"It was me," I admit, because I can't lie to her, not now. I did the one thing I could do. What I should have done from the very beginning, what Emmeline was trying to tell me all along. Protect my sister, no matter the cost.

"No," Lux sobs. "Not *you*, Rome. Mrs. Montoya or the neighbors, but *not you*."

We are both crying now, hot tears spilling down my cheeks. "I'm sorry," I whisper. "I'm sorry," this time louder. "But I can't let him hurt you again, Lux."

"That was *never* your call, Rome. That was never your decision. You *promised me* that you wouldn't tell." Her face is mottled and red, tears barely escaping the eye that's nearly swollen shut.

"I know. And I'm sorry. But this is bigger than us, Lux."

She cries, her beautiful, battered face crumpling before my eyes, breaking beneath my betrayal. "I trusted you, Rome. You were my sister. My blood sister."

"I know, Lux. That's why I did it." I'm still holding on to her, refusing to let go. As if I can just hold on long enough, she'll forgive me.

Mom enters the living room, her lips pursed and her eyes wide as she surveys the damage. I don't know if Rick called her, or if some maternal instinct in her signaled that I was in trouble. "Rome," she says. "We need to get out of the way and let them work." She's right. Two new EMTs bring in a stretcher to move

Tina, and I hear the wail of an ambulance heading toward us.

"I won't leave you," I tell Lux, wishing her hold on our friendship was stronger than my broken promise. "I'll go with you to the hospital. I'll come with you to talk to the police, whatever you need to do. We'll do this together."

"Get away from me! I never want to see you again!" she screams, ripping out of my grasp and shoving me away. Her hair falls completely down, tangling around her in thick ropes.

"Lux, honey, we'll come to the hospital with you—" Mom begins, trying to make peace between us.

But Lux can't see or hear anyone but me now. Her green eyes slice across me in a way that cuts me to the bone. "I'm sorry," I whisper. Everything in me aches, like I've been hit by a truck. "I'm sorry, Lux."

"Don't," she hisses. "Don't pretend you ever cared about me."

Mom and I stand outside in the yard and watch as the paramedics roll the gurney carrying Tina into the ambulance. Lux comes next, and she's fighting all the way, screaming at Rick that she's fine, that everybody's fine.

I'm holding the broken picture, the hand-drawn map of Cottonwood Hollow. I can't stop crying. It shakes my shoulders, shakes my whole body, wrenching loose screws and bolts that have held me together for so long. I cry for Lux. I cry for Tina. I cry for broken promises. And then I cry just for me.

SIXTEEN

I MANAGE TO DRAG MYSELF to school the next morning. Mom would have let me stay home and hide forever in my bedroom if that was what I really wanted. She'd done the same when she lost her job at the café. But that isn't who I am. At least, I don't think it is. I can't believe I failed so spectacularly. All I had to do was be Lux's sister, her best friend, and really look into what was going on in her life.

I slink into first period, finding my seat in the back next to Lux's empty one. Of course she's not here. Mom said they released Tina early this morning, but Lux had never been admitted to the hospital, instead refusing any treatment other than what she'd gotten from the paramedics. Even if Tina had been conscious, she still might not have been able to Heal herself, Mom had told me in a whisper. Even Healers can't mend broken bones. She looked at me with careful eyes that suggested she'd figured out what was going on in that house, too.

Aaron still hasn't been found.

In first period, Morgan stares at the empty seat between us, looking uncomfortable. "Do you know where Lux is?" she asks, her blue eyes locking on mine. "She's not answering her phone. I've left a million voice mails, texts. Did she say anything to you?"

I shrug. I'd tried texting Lux this morning, too.

I'm sorry. I had to do it. Please let me come over to talk.

I'm so sorry. Let me know if you want me to skip school and help you clean up.

Lux, please don't let go.

Dammit, Lux. Answer your goddamned phone.

"Well, can you at least tell me if she's okay?" Morgan asks, her slim, pretty hands clutching the edge of her desk as if it is the only solid thing in her ephemeral world.

"I can't tell you anything," I reply. "You'll have to talk to Lux." I've done enough damage to our friendship without getting involved in her relationship with Morgan.

"Is she breaking up with me?" Morgan asks, her blue eyes tearing up. "Is that what this is? She can't even do it to my face?"

"Oh, Jesus Christ, Morgan, not everything is about you, okay?" I say, spearing her with a glare.

Morgan sniffs, looking down so that her bobbed hair slips forward and covers her face.

"I'm sorry," I say quickly, my voice low. "It's not anything that you did. Something happened with her stepdad."

Morgan looks up, immediately alarmed. "What happened?" she asks.

"I can't tell you everything. But I know Lux loves you. And

212

that she needs you. Don't stop texting her. Just keep trying. It can take time to get through to her." I wish that Lux would answer my texts, tell me I hadn't broken everything apart. But since she won't, I have to take solace in knowing that she has Morgan to comfort her.

Morgan nods. "Thanks," she says. "I'll keep texting."

My throat is too tight to say anything else.

Jett strolls in with his backpack on one shoulder, looking like he just walked off the set of a men's-wear commercial, with his perfect hair and his slightly windblown blazer and button-down shirt. He gives me his big grin and I can barely manage to twitch my lips in response.

I'm angry, and hurt, and lost without Lux. And Mercy is going to kill me when she hears this. She won't cut me out completely like Lux, but she'll freeze me out for a while nonetheless. And it will never be the same between us now that Lux and I have broken apart. I have betrayed them both in different ways. Lux by not keeping a promise, and Mercy by keeping a secret from her.

And Jett just grins like the happiest guy in the world with his buddy in the front row and his baseball team and his fancy car and his mom who has goats.

I really hate everyone right now.

I manage to squeeze out of the room after class while Miss Strong asks Jett and his friend about their baseball game tonight, and dodge Morgan, who's summoned the courage to start pelting me with questions about Lux again.

But it's not a complete escape. Mercy finds me on the mezzanine in the library.

Her eyebrows are arched to a knife-sharp angle, and her dark eyes lock on me.

"What happened to Lux?" she hisses, seizing my arm in what feels like an iron vise grip. "Mrs. Levinson just asked me if I would collect Lux's homework assignments for her because she *might be gone for a while*."

She's strong for someone so small.

Mercy grabs the other chair at the little table and scoots it next to mine, bashing into my legs in the process.

I wince but take the pain, because it feels like all I deserve right now. And it's better than feeling nothing, anyway. Mercy slams herself down into the chair and repeats, "*What happened to Lux?*"

"Her stepdad beat her up. And Tina. Last night."

"Wait, were you *there*?" Mercy asks, leaning forward in her seat.

"I found them . . . afterward."

"Is this the first time?" Mercy asks, but she's already calculating the days, the moments that we shared. "The sleepover on a school night." Mercy's face changes slightly. "The dowry chest." I watch her expression shift as she puts all the pieces of the puzzle together. She knows Lux as well as I do, and there were so many telling signs that we'd missed. "That's why she wanted it. She wanted her mom to kick him out, but they were worried about money. It was never just about my dad cutting his hours."

I nod miserably. Why hadn't I read the signs that were everywhere?

Drive away, she had commanded. *Far, far away.*

I can smile without putting a spell on someone, you know, she had said softly. *I couldn't control it so much when we were younger . . .*

I don't want to be home all day, she had whispered.

I'm cursed and so's my mom, I don't care what the book says, she had said.

Mercy pulls me back to reality. "You did put the bleach in his tank, didn't you? That's why you were so weird and saying maybe Aaron deserved it. *You knew* he'd hurt her and you didn't tell me." Mercy's eyes are shiny with tears, and I need to find the words to make her understand, but I don't know if they will be enough.

"She made me *promise*, Mercy." A promise is sacred for us. The girls from Cottonwood Hollow don't have much, but we've always had our word.

"She made you promise not to tell *me?*"

"She made me promise not to tell *anyone*."

But I haven't even told Mercy the worst part yet. I try to get it out fast, as if maybe it will make me less guilty. "But that's not everything. I guess Aaron was trying to . . . force himself on her. I didn't know until last night." The words make me gag. "She was afraid the police would think she was using her talent as a Siren on him. That's what he kept telling her. He told her that it was her fault. That she was making him touch her."

Mercy's mouth falls open, and for a second I think that she's going to be physically ill. After a few shallow breaths, finally, she can form words. "That fucking sicko. I'm going to find him and kill him myself. Why did you only put bleach in his gas tank? Why didn't you light his stupid truck on fire?"

"I didn't know about everything. Otherwise I would've." That's probably the truth.

"Well, there's still time," Mercy says, looking like she's ready to form a search party right now. "We can probably find him around Evanston somewhere." I've never seen her so angry.

"Mom talked to Rick early this morning and he said they can't find Aaron. I guess Aaron did get his truck repaired, and that's how he was gone last night before I got there."

"Do you think they'll believe him? That Lux used her Siren talent to lure him?" Mercy asks, and I know she's thinking about the algebra teacher, too.

"I hope not," I say, my voice nearly breaking. "But look around you. If Lux and her mom press charges, the county seat is in Evanston, and this is where they'd have a trial. And this town isn't exactly sympathetic toward girls from Cottonwood Hollow. Aaron's from Evanston, too. It's hard to say who he knows or has connections to." The logical part of my brain knows that Aaron is the one at fault for what happened last night. But I wish I'd told Lux's secret long before—anything to have kept her from getting hurt like she did. Even if it's the knife that severs our friendship forever.

"I just can't believe this, Rome. Maybe you didn't know about everything, but you knew Aaron *hurt* her. Why would you ever keep a secret like that?"

"Because she wanted me to." My voice breaks. "And I thought if she could keep her secrets, then it would be okay to keep mine, too."

"What are you talking about? The bleach in Aaron's gas tank?"

"Not just that. I mean everything." The truth comes spilling out, everything I'd sworn to myself that I'd never tell. "I've been helping Mom pay the rent for a year now. Things have been so hard, Mercy. That's why I needed all the hours at the shop. Selling the Mach was just a last resort, to keep my mom from offering other things to keep Garrett from kicking us out. . . ." I can't even put into words what she had almost done to keep a roof over our heads. "But I couldn't tell you. I didn't want to be some charity project that you had to feel sorry for."

"If that's what you think, Rome, then you aren't my best friend. And definitely not my sister. You can't just go through life never asking for help because you think it makes you weak. Do you know what weak is? It's keeping secrets like Lux's when you know she's in danger." She looks away, and I don't know that I've ever felt so ashamed.

Tears sting my eyes. "Lux is never going to forgive me for this."

Mercy just gets up and walks away, and then I realize that she might not either.

Oh, Emmeline. Maybe it was a curse after all.

SEVENTEEN

I STAY IN THE LIBRARY for the next two class periods. I find the book Mercy had at home with the information about the Remingtons and Maisie Truett, the one written up by the Cottonwood Hollow Historical Society. It's regular copy paper bound with one of those plastic spines, the front covered in clear plastic. I'm surprised the school even has a copy. It must have been donated by Cottonwood Hollow.

I flip through the pages, and when I get to the story about Emmeline, I notice that it simply says she and her husband built the Remington homestead. There's nothing else in it about John Remington. Nothing about where he was born or if he had any family around. Nothing about the small dugout he'd lived in before he traveled back East and married into Emmeline's money. There's not even mention of when he purchased the land. But the diary had made it seem like he had some sort of past. Was he planning to give up farming? What was his motive for finding a wealthy bride?

I turn the pages until I find the map Mercy said would be here. The book says it was hand drawn by Emmeline. It does look like an exact copy of the one we found in the chest in the homestead. All the little flowers are there around the houses. Cottonwoods stand near where our trailer is now. The eighty-acre Remington plot is demarcated with small hatch marks. The creek. The homestead. But no hills. The land where the ruins are now is completely empty, save for a small cluster of flowers where the hills should have been, as if Emmeline was planning to fill in that area with something else.

Why would she leave the hills off one map but draw them on another? And why doesn't the book include information about John Remington's life before he married Emmeline?

"This is the first time anyone has ever checked this book out," the librarian informs me at the front desk as I stuff the book into my bag.

All I can think is that I want to tell Mercy and Lux about what I've found, and neither of them is speaking to me.

I move my body around the school purely by muscle memory. Everything I see here reminds me of Lux and Mercy, and the other students are starting to whisper when I walk by, like news of what happened to Lux has made its way to Evanston.

At lunch, I run into Jett just outside of the cafeteria. "Hey," he says, giving me his big grin. "Can't wait to see you tonight. Do you want to ride to the party with me after the game, or were you planning on having your own ride?"

"My own ride?" I ask dumbly. It's as if all the cogs in my

brain are rusted and slow.

"I mean, are you going to drive yourself? I didn't know if you were planning on bringing your friends. Lux and Mercy. Did you know Mercy goes to the same church as my mom? Yeah, Mom's other latest thing is religion. The goats are getting old, I guess."

Lux and Mercy's names trip a trigger that might as well be a nuclear bomb. I should have told Mercy the truth, and I never should have fought with Lux so that she felt she had nowhere to turn from Aaron.

But he doesn't know any of that, this handsome, wealthy boy from Evanston who is worlds apart from me.

"No," I reply, my mouth moving in ways that seem strange to the rest of my body.

"No, you're not riding with your friends?" Jett asks, his dark eyes wide and innocent.

"No, I'm not going." I know it's not Jett's fault, but I can't stop myself. Suddenly he is every Evanston boy, every person who's ever pointed their finger at Lux or me or Mercy and called us names. The words tumble out like spilled ball bearings, rolling faster and faster as I go. "I'm not going to your stupid ball game. Or anything that has to do with this stupid school. The Evanston students hate us. They've always hated the girls from Cottonwood Hollow. They think we're weird. They call us freaks. Sluts. Why should I go to your stupid game so they can hate me there? I get enough as it is."

Jett's face is a storm of confusion, and I don't even care enough to clarify things for him because nothing's going to change the fact that he's an Evanston boy, and I'm one of the peculiar girls from Cottonwood Hollow. We were never meant to be together in the first place. I thought that if I gave him a chance, a real chance, we could make things work between us. I showed him my job at the shop and my high-school dropout mom and our ancient, narrow trailer on the edge of town. I gave him every reason to turn away with my sharp words. And it seemed like he was going to pass every test, jump every hurdle.

But it was me. All this time it was really me. I'm the one who can't clear the hurdles. I can't accept that he's different, and I can't get over who I am and where I come from.

I leave him there, walking away from lunch and class. I walk straight out to the parking lot, get in Mom's Ford Focus, and drive to Red's Auto. I just want to hide underneath the hood of a car and feel only metal and grease. I want to Fix things until my body is so tired and heavy that it drowns out everything else. I enter the office, where Mom and Red are taking their lunch break together.

"Rome?" Mom says, surprised to see me as she holds her peanut butter sandwich made with the heels of the loaf.

"I need to work," I say, my voice quavering.

Red stands up. "Is everything okay? Aren't you supposed to be at school?"

"Please. I just need . . ." I don't know how to finish. I don't know how to explain what I need right now. I am a Fixer, but there's no way that I can Fix this.

"Why don't you take the car and go home? You're tired. I'll meet you there after work," Mom says.

I open my mouth to argue that she can't come home if I have the only car between the two of us, but Red answers for her, "I'll give your mom a ride home. I know you had a rough time of it last night, Rome. Get some sleep. You got a shift tomorrow."

And strangely, his kindness almost breaks me.

"I'll send your paycheck home with your mom," Red says when I don't ask about it.

I drive the county roads home to Cottonwood Hollow at seventy, waiting for the speed to make me feel alive like it always did when I drove the Mach. Instead I'm chugging around the curves and over the hills, cursing the stupid four-cylinder engine. This car doesn't fly like the Mach. It doesn't sing around corners or burst up over hills. It's just a big, dumb hunk of metal and plastic and rubber.

I park the car in front of Lux's house. She still hasn't answered any of my texts. I stomp up to the front stoop, fists clenched like I'm going into battle. I swing open the screen door and try the door handle. It's locked. I check under the ceramic toad for the spare key, but it's gone. I knock on the door, hard enough to bruise my knuckles before changing to the flat of my fist.

"Lux!" I call through the door. "I know you're in there! Let me in!" There are no sounds. I imagine her on the other side, her cheek pressed against the door.

"Damn it, Lux! Let me in! Please! Don't do this!" I sound pathetic, even to me, but I don't care.

I pull away from the front door and scurry around the house to Lux's bedroom window. I push through the shrubs, the branches scratching my bare legs and snagging my skirt, but I'm too frantic now to care.

When I peer through the lavender curtains, I see exactly what

I feared. All of Lux's dresser drawers have been pulled open. One is pulled all the way out and thrown next to the bed. It's empty. All the pictures taped to her vanity mirror are missing. There's a pair of old jeans on the floor still folded, as if at the last minute Lux decided she couldn't fit them in her suitcase.

I put my hand against the screen like we did that night we promised to keep her secret between us. But she's gone.

EIGHTEEN

I'M TOO SCARED TO BE alone, wondering what happened to Lux. Did she leave with her mom? Did she go on her own?

I park the Focus in front of Flynn's. Inside, it's smoky and dark. I find a stool at the bar. Wynona sees me, struts over with her wide hips swinging. "No school today, sweets?" she asks, giving me a wink.

"No," I tell her. Wynona is a Strong Back, and once I saw her pick up a guy twice her size and toss him out into the street. She waitresses here for Flynn when her trucker husband's not in town.

"How about some lunch?" she asks.

"Can I get some onion rings and a Dr Pepper?" I ask.

"Sure thing." She whirls around and fills a glass with ice and soda, slides it across the scarred wooden bar, and then disappears back into the kitchen.

I look around. It's mostly old farmers having lunch here.

The stage where Flynn has bands on Friday and Saturday nights is empty. Country music plays low over the speakers.

Flynn emerges from the apartment above the bar. He's got a daughter a year younger than me. Vidalia. A Sight.

"Rome," he says. "What are you doing here?" He's big, even bigger than Jett, with a flannel shirt and a beard that makes him look like a lumberjack. But now I'm thinking about Jett, and how guilty I feel for telling him off in the middle of the hallway at school. I was angry about what I did to Lux and Mercy. Jett was just an easy target.

I'm supposed to be a Fixer, but it seems like everything I touch lately breaks to pieces.

"Just having some lunch," I say.

"Saw your Mach," Flynn says, leaning against the bar. "Garrett was driving it around. He was bragging that he'd got it off you in some steal of a trade."

I take a drink, letting the clink of the ice be my response.

"Well, with any luck you'll be able to buy it back at auction," Flynn says. "He'll have to sell everything off before you know it. Probably get that car back for pennies on the dollar."

"What do you mean?" I ask.

"His business is about to go under. Made some bad real-estate investments in Evanston. Bought a couple of old slummy houses near the college thinking to turn a quick buck, but the city just passed an ordinance banning rental dwellings with more than three separate living spaces in that zone. He's up to his eyeballs in debt now. Can't rent those places out since they've each got five or six little crappy apartments in them. And he doesn't have the cash to renovate them."

I guess that explains why he was down our throats looking for the rent money this month.

Wynona swings out of the kitchen with my basket of onion rings. "Here you go, sweets," she says to me. She eyes Flynn. "Why do you look so serious?" she asks.

"Garrett."

Wynona sighs. "I told you I'd call him again."

"Don't bother," Flynn says. "We'll just call his tab a loss. Lance Johnson was in last night saying Garrett's business is going under."

Wynona smiles. "Well, I won't cry about it. I know he's supposed to be descended from *the* Remingtons, but I still think he's a creep."

When I finish eating, I try to pay Flynn. "It's on the house," he says. "I'll let you know if I hear anything about an auction."

I wonder if that means our trailer will be gone soon, too.

When I get home, I feel sick to my stomach. I go to the bathroom, dropping my backpack with my phone and the car keys next to the tub and leaning over the toilet like maybe I'm going to puke. I retch twice, but nothing comes out. Maybe it was the greasy onion rings, or the worry that Garrett's about to lose everything. What will happen if he loses his rental business? How long until our trailer is auctioned off? Will we have a chance to buy it ourselves? Is there any bank in its right mind that would give Mom a loan?

Lux has left without telling me, just like she promised she wouldn't.

Mercy is pissed at me for keeping secrets from her.

I've nuked whatever it was that I had with Jett, a perfectly nice, funny, decent guy.

Fresh air, I tell myself, standing back up. I just need some fresh air. I leave the trailer and start walking. I don't know where I'm going, but some internal compass takes me back to the Truett farm, and I hike out to the pond where the three of us used to skinny-dip. I sit on the dock, staring out at the water.

I remember the three of us singing out here, our voices twining together into one beautiful melody.

Strange how everything can unravel so quickly.

Long past midnight, I leave the songs of the cicadas and the quiet lapping of the pond against the dock and walk back home. Steven is waiting for me just inside the front door, his whole body wriggling with excitement. I go into the kitchen. The hand-drawn map in its broken frame is on the table, all the glass cleared away like maybe Mom was trying to clean it up for me. There's a jar of smooth peanut butter and a spoon next to it, so Mom must have gotten her first paycheck. I unscrew the lid and dig out a mouthful. While I'm eating, I sit down and look at the map again. It's definitely different from the one in the book. The hills next to the ruins are here, and they were missing from the other copy.

But why?

I wonder if there's something on the back, like a date or maybe a name that's not Emmeline's. Maybe someone else drew this map. I pull apart the frame, wincing as a few remaining chunks of glass fall out.

Behind the map is yellowed paper. At first I think it's just the back of the map, blank, but when I tilt the frame, the paper falls to the table with the broken glass. The same spidery handwriting. Emmeline's.

> *May 2nd*
>
> *Maisie,*
>
> *I cannot begin to thank you for the care you've given me and my angel child in these last days. If I could not be with my true sister, it was at least a blessing to have something like one in my last hours. In return, I would like to repay you as best as I can. I've stipulated in my will that you are to live on the homestead as long as you wish. The taxes on the land will be paid through the trust fund set up for me by my family. Upon your passing, the town of Cottonwood Hollow has express permission to use the land as they will, so long as they pay the taxes. The deed to the land is in my dowry chest, should you ever need to find it. Look for the last hill to the south on the eastern border of our land. John had a dugout there before we were married, and it was easy enough to hide it. No one will find it there, and the place looks like it will tumble down on itself any day now. I suppose everything we once loved returns to the earth eventually.*
>
> *Sincerely,*
>
> *Emmeline*

It's like a punch of adrenaline in my gut. "Holy shit," I exclaim. Everything is right here, in my hands. Emmeline Remington gave all her secrets to a girl from Cottonwood Hollow. And Maisie had hung them there on the wall in the house, probably until some well-meaning member of the Cottonwood Hollow Historical Society packed it away.

I flip the map back over. There's a tiny cluster of flowers around the last hill to the south. This map was drawn at another time, just for Maisie, in case she needed it. My heart is beating about a million beats per minute as I wonder if the dowry chest is still buried there.

In another world, one where I hadn't let everything fall apart, I'd be sprinting across town right now to wake up Lux and Mercy. But Lux is gone and Mercy won't want to speak to me.

So I call Steven and we go to bed. I'm not sure I even deserve to find the chest anymore, and I don't think I could bear finding it without Lux and Mercy at my side, even if it might save me.

"Rome!" the voice booms, cracking through my skull.

Mom's face fills my vision. I pull back, trying to retreat into my pillow, but my body reacts slowly.

"What?" I manage to growl.

"Get up!" she says, "Rick is here! And the sheriff."

"What do you mean?" I ask. "Is this about Lux?"

There's a flicker of hope in my chest that maybe she came home. That maybe they want to talk to both of us together. Maybe she's out there waiting with them.

"No," Mom says, and as my vision sharpens, I realize that she's scared.

Mom is scared.

"What is it?" I ask, forcing myself up.

"They haven't told me," Mom says. "They said they need to talk to you."

I wince as I stand, and Mom pulls a pair of jeans and a T-shirt from a miraculously clean pile of laundry on top of my dresser and flings them at me.

"Hurry," Mom says. She leaves, and I can hear her out in the living room, trying to make small talk with Rick and the sheriff.

I change into the clothes, pausing at the bathroom to splash some water on my face and brush my teeth. I knot my hair on top of my head before hurrying into the living room.

Steven follows me, delighted to meet the guests. Rick is sitting on the couch, and the sheriff is standing awkwardly by the front door.

"Hi, Rick," I say, wincing a little at the light coming in the windows.

"Hi, Rome," Rick says. "Sorry to wake you so early." He motions to the other man in the room. "This is Sheriff Yost."

I glance at the clock and notice that it's barely seven in the morning on a Saturday.

"What's going on?" I ask. "Is this about Lux?"

Rick shakes his head. "We need to know if you've seen Mercy Montoya recently."

"Mercy?" I ask. "What do you mean? I saw her yesterday at school."

"But not after school?"

"No," I say. "I didn't see anyone after school." Fear sends goose bumps over my skin, even though it's warm in the trailer.

"Has she contacted you at all?" Rick asks.

"I . . . I don't think so," I stutter, realizing I haven't checked my phone since yesterday afternoon. "Let me get my phone and check." I stumble back down the hall to the bathroom, where I'd left my backpack when I thought I was going to throw up yesterday. My chest tightens, constricting in cold, metal bands that make it hard to breathe.

I find my phone. It's still set on silent from when I was at school yesterday. There are thirteen missed calls from Mrs. Montoya. I scroll through my text messages.

There's one from Mercy, sent at five thirty last night, when I was sitting out on the dock at Truett pond.

Do you want to come with me to drop off Lux's homework
after I pick up Neveah from church group?

My first thought is that Mercy really is the best of us. She's willing to forgive me at least enough for us to work together to help Lux. I hurry back out to the living room. "There was one," I tell Rick, handing him my phone.

"What time?" Sheriff Yost asks. He's pulled out a small notebook and a pencil.

"Five thirty p.m.," says Rick.

"And you didn't reply to this message?" Sheriff Yost asks me.

"No," I choke out. "I was at Truett pond. I think it was around two a.m. when I came home."

"Alone?" Sheriff Yost asks suspiciously. "There's no one who can confirm where you were?"

I look over at Rick. "What's going on? Where's Mercy? Has something happened?"

"Last night around six thirty, Neveah called home from a friend's phone. Mercy never came to pick her up."

"What do you mean?"

"Mercy is missing."

The words are like a fist to my gut. Mercy, sweet, gentle Mercy, is missing. Mercy, who wears floral nightgowns and reads romance novels in secret. Mercy, who charms feral cats and isn't afraid of heights.

Mercy, who was supposed to fly away someday.

NINETEEN

ONCE, A COUPLE OF YEARS ago, Steven ran away. Mercy, Lux, and I were having a sleepover and Steven had to go outside. Mom had picked up a waitressing shift at the bar, so it was only the three of us and Steven at home.

It was past midnight, and I didn't want to stand outside and watch him pee in the front yard like he'd done a million times before. So I let him out and went back to my bedroom.

We pulled the Ouija board from Lux's bag and placed it in the middle of my bed. I swear the temperature in the room dropped at least ten degrees, which completely freaked us out. But we wanted to see if Lux could communicate with the other side, so we all reached for the planchette. As soon I touched it, my fingers trembled with delicious fear.

The other side never answered.

Half an hour later, I remembered Steven and went back to the front door to let him in, figuring he would be waiting on the front stoop like always.

He wasn't there. I called for him, but there was no big, jowly dog loping over the wet grass to answer my call. Steven was gone.

I panicked, knowing Mom would absolutely flip if she found out that I'd let the baby of the family outside all alone in the dark and hadn't bothered to keep an eye on him. Other than not burning down the trailer, that was the one thing she asked me to do. *Keep an eye on Steven.* There were rumors of cougars near Cottonwood Hollow, because deer were plentiful out here. And of course there were coyotes, and they would attack a big dog if they were in a pack.

Mercy was the one to calm me down, to help me think logically about where Steven might be. She was the one who kept it together as we narrowed down Steven's probable location to the Ruizes' double-wide trailer, because it was closest and they kept Fluffernut's food outside on the back deck.

And thanks to Mercy, that was exactly where we found Steven, sleeping off a bowl of cat food that he would puke up an hour later.

"See?" Mercy whispered as Steven snored peacefully in the dark. "You just had to know where to look."

I have no idea where to look for Mercy now.

"Did Mercy happen to mention anything to you at school yesterday about plans to stay out last night?" Rick asks. "Did she say anything about meeting anyone?"

"No," I answer. "She just said she had to get Lux's homework."

"Do you know anything else about Mercy that might be helpful to us? Is she seeing anyone? Does she have a boyfriend? Maybe someone she didn't want her parents to know about?"

"No," I say, even though it feels like a betrayal. She would be mortified if she knew the police were asking me about boys. "She's not seeing anyone. She would have told me."

Mercy would never keep secrets from me.

Or would she? Didn't I keep secrets from her and Lux?

"You're not going to get into trouble," Rick assures me, as if he's reading my face. "If there's anything we should know, tell us now. You're sure you don't know where she could be?"

"There's no boyfriend, as far as I know. But could she be with Lux? I stopped by there yesterday, and it looked like Lux had left. Like she had packed a suitcase." I don't want to say *ran away* because the words scare me. Could Lux have really left town without saying good-bye? Could Mercy be with her? It's hard to imagine sweet, generous Mercy doing something as cruel as running away and not telling anyone. We swore a blood oath. Didn't she just show me her scar while we stood by the creek, reminding us that we kept our promises to each other? But maybe she only went to talk some sense into Lux. Maybe her phone died. Maybe she's at some bus stop right now, convincing Lux to come home and put this whole nonsense to rest.

"Lux and her mom went to stay with Lux's grandma since Aaron hasn't been apprehended," Rick answers. "We reached Lux this morning by phone and she said Mercy never arrived with the homework."

"You talked to Lux?" I ask. It's not possible. The only logical reason for Mercy to do something like this is if she's trying to drag either Lux or me back to sanity. No, no, no. Not Mercy. Mercy would never run away.

Suddenly Aaron's name registers in my brain. "They still haven't found Aaron?" I choke out.

Rick shakes his head. "We've checked with friends that Tina mentioned, and with his parents over in Evanston."

"You have to find Aaron," I tell Rick, grabbing his arm. "He was angry about his truck. Somebody put bleach in his gas tank. He thinks Lux and I might have had something to do with it."

Rick looks confused, and I don't blame him.

"It was *me*," I whisper, avoiding the looks I might be getting from Mom or the sheriff. "I saw Lux after Aaron hit her earlier this week, and I was angry. Rick, what if he thought Mercy was in on it, too? What if he did something to her?"

Rick opens his mouth to answer, but before he can, Sheriff Yost's phone rings. The sheriff stops jotting down notes and answers it, turning away from us as he speaks, as if there's any privacy in this tiny living room.

Sheriff Yost mutters, "Yeah, yeah. Fifth Street? Uh-huh. Yeah. Okay. We'll check it out." He ends the call and looks at Rick. "They found the Montoya minivan. Parked on Fifth in Evanston, just a few blocks from the church. No signs of a struggle, but the keys were still in it. Doors unlocked. Like someone wanted it to be stolen."

Rick's face hardens, and he's not my friendly neighbor anymore, or Letty's dad who checks out books on science and technology for her from the Evanston library every Wednesday after work. He's in full-on police mode.

"What do you mean, they *found* the minivan?" I ask.

"We know that Mercy drove the family minivan to Evanston to pick up her sister while Mrs. Montoya walked Malakai to T-ball practice at about five o'clock. But Mercy never showed up at the church to pick up her sister. We sent out a call to look for the van on the highway, but somebody already found it in town," Rick explains slowly.

"But what does that *mean*?" I ask him.

"Normally the police would never get involved this early. But it's a small town, and this is Mercy Montoya we're talking about. Nobody in Cottonwood Hollow is going to believe she disappeared without telling anyone where she was going. This is a missing person case."

It is as if everything in my body has seized up, like all my joints have rusted and locked. I look at my hands again. Strong, capable hands. Fixer hands. I don't know how I could have messed this up so badly. Our sisterhood is shattered. Lux is gone. Mercy is gone. I am alone.

There's nothing left for me to put back together.

"Oh my God," Mom whispers, and her voice loosens the working parts of my brain so that I can function again.

"We're going to need volunteers to help canvass the streets," Rick says. "Bring a recent picture of Mercy to share with the other volunteers. Several, if you can. Come over to the Montoyas' as soon as possible. We'll organize things from there."

"Mom?" I ask as Rick and Sheriff Yost shut the front door behind them. For once, I feel like a child. For once I want Mom to lie to me and tell me everything is going to be fine, like she used to even though I resented it. Like at the father-daughter dance in junior high when she promised me that any girl could bring a man, but it took a badass rebel to bring her mom. I need to know that there's a silver lining in all this that somehow I'm not seeing.

"Get your shit together and come on," Mom says, putting a leash on Steven and grabbing her purse. "Mercy needs you. Go get those pictures of you girls from your room. Hurry. We've got to get to the Montoyas'."

She might not be the perfect mom, but she's my mom, and she's exactly what I need.

I find Mrs. Montoya standing in her kitchen, red-eyed and unusually pale as she plucks dozens of muffins from cooling racks and arranges them on plates. She's feeding the volunteers, I realize, because the house is packed with Cottonwood Hollow folks milling around the living room, helping Mr. Montoya divide the town of Evanston into a grid for search parties. Rick's taken several of my photos to the police station in Evanston to get flyers made.

When Mrs. Montoya sees me, she drops the muffin she's holding onto her spotless counter, and it smears warm berry juice on the sparkly granite. "Rome," she cries, seizing me in a hug. "Thank God you're here."

"Of course, Mrs. Montoya," I tell her, holding her as tightly as I can. Holding her like Mercy would hold her. "Of course I'm here." She doesn't ask me why I wasn't with Mercy last night, and

I don't mention that this might all be my fault. I can't tell her that Aaron might have hurt Mercy because he thinks that she put bleach in his gas tank.

Mrs. Montoya pulls away and looks at my face. "I know we'll find her," she says. "We'll find her."

"Rome!" Mr. Montoya says from behind me. "Thank you so much for bringing pictures of Mercy. We didn't have any with her new haircut. Sheriff Yost told me he'd already spoken to you and that you'd had a text from Mercy?"

"Yes," I answer, pulling my phone from the pocket of my jeans.

"A text?" Mrs. Montoya gasps. "This morning? Oh my goodness, is she okay?"

"From last night," Mr. Montoya says gently, laying a hand on Mrs. Montoya's trembling arm.

Mrs. Montoya pinches her lips together in an effort not to cry.

"It's good," Mr. Montoya says, reading the text. "We know she was okay at five thirty. She hasn't been gone that long."

Nearly fifteen hours. I calculate the time in my head, and it doesn't sound good to me at all.

But it's enough to make Mrs. Montoya nod and blink back her tears. She takes the phone from Mr. Montoya with shaky hands. "That's my sweet girl," she says when she reads the text. "She was going to give Lux her homework so she doesn't get behind. Mercy's always thinking of others."

Numb, I just nod in agreement. I can't bring myself to tell her that Mercy had been angry with me earlier that day, and that her last text nearly kills me. Mercy wanted me to go with her to visit

Lux, even after everything, because she was kind and forgiving. Mercy was the one who was supposed to fly away. She was never supposed to be taken away.

Mom and Steven join us, and if it were any other day, Mrs. Montoya would be having a heart attack over the giant, drooly dog in the middle of her kitchen. "Thank you so much for coming to help," Mrs. Montoya says, hugging Mom and then patting Steven listlessly on his massive, wrinkly head. Steven's tail wags, because he doesn't know Mercy is missing. Steven is pretty damn lucky.

Mom turns to Mr. Montoya, "Have they tried pinging her phone? Isn't that something the police can do?"

"Rick's calling it in now from the station."

"Maybe that's how they'll find her," I say quickly, hoping it's true.

"We texted and called her all night," Mrs. Montoya explains. "We'd called the police at midnight, but they said until she'd been gone for twenty-four hours, it wasn't really a missing person case. So we waited, and even though it hadn't been long enough yet, Rick stopped by early this morning to see if we'd heard anything. If it weren't for him, we wouldn't have gotten the case upgraded to a missing person case as soon as we did."

"Maybe they'll be able to track her phone," Mom says, giving Mrs. Montoya an encouraging nod.

Neveah comes into the kitchen, and her resemblance to Mercy hits me in the gut. She's carrying an almost-empty pitcher that she must have been using to serve the volunteers. If Mercy was here, the pitcher would still be full because Mercy is an Enough.

I hope Mercy's talent gives her Enough time for us to find her. I don't say it, though, because even with my usual lack of filter, I'm scared to say it out loud.

Mrs. Montoya takes the pitcher from Neveah and goes into the pantry, Mom trailing behind her as if she might be able to help.

"Can you feel anything?" I ask Neveah.

Neveah shakes her head, and she looks so devastated that I feel like a jerk for asking. "I tried," she says, her voice close to tears. "Finding works on *things*, but not on people." I don't let myself think about how just a couple of days ago we thought Neveah would be helping us Find the chest this morning, and that all our problems would be solved.

Nearly an hour passes, and Rick comes back. I can tell from his face that his news isn't good.

The Montoyas, Mom, and I gather in the kitchen with Rick. "We pinged her phone," Rick tells us. Mr. and Mrs. Montoya draw a shaky breath of anticipation, and it feels like I might be sucked into a whirlwind.

"It was in a trash can near the van," Rick finishes. "So was her backpack. We identified it by her name sewn into the inside liner. It had papers for Lux Reed inside it."

Wherever Mercy is, she's completely alone, with no way to reach out to us. I feel like I might throw up. What happened to Mercy? Is she hurt? Is she dead? I want to sob, or scream, or run as fast as I can until my heart explodes and I can't feel this much terror.

"We need to start looking now," Mom says. "Enough snacks. Let's go."

Rick nods. "These first twenty-four hours are critical. I've got stacks of flyers for the volunteers to distribute. Everyone will be assigned to a grid section. Let's move out."

I refrain from pointing out that the first few hours were actually quite some time ago. Neveah's chin trembles and hot tears track down her small face. She flings herself at her mom and buries her face in Mrs. Montoya's chest. "The kids," Mrs. Montoya says. "Maybe one of the neighbors would stay with them?"

"I can stay with them," Mom offers, surprising me. Mrs. Montoya and her nice house have always made Mom a little nervous, like Mom felt like she might break something or say the wrong thing. But she's stepping up, volunteering to take the reins. "Neveah, Malakai, do you want to help me take care of Steven today?"

Malakai nods eagerly, taking Steven's leash from Mom.

"I want to help look for Mercy," Neveah says after she pulls her face out of Mrs. Montoya's now-wet blouse. "Maybe if I try hard enough, I can Find her."

"Oh, honey," Mrs. Montoya says. "That's not how your talent works. Nobody expects you to be able to find her. What we need you to do is stay here with Ms. Galveston in case Mercy comes home."

"Do you think she'll be home soon?" Malakai asks, tugging on Steven's leash. Steven is trying to steal a muffin that's perilously close to the edge of the counter.

Mrs. Montoya's face looks like it might crumple again.

"We hope so," Mom answers. "But if no one's here when she gets home, Mercy might leave again and go look for you. So it's important that someone mans the fort."

Neveah nods. "I don't want her to leave again."

"Thank you," Mrs. Montoya says to Mom, reaching out and squeezing Mom's shoulder. "I'm so grateful."

Mr. and Mrs. Montoya hurry away to speak with the rest of the volunteers, and Mom whispers to Neveah and Malakai, pointing at the cookie jar Mrs. Montoya keeps well-stocked on the counter, "We'll eat *all* the cookies while your mom's not here. And watch all the cartoons we want."

"We'll get to eat the cookies in the *TV room*?" Malakai asks eagerly. Even I know that's against the rules, and I cringe when Mom nods.

Malakai grabs the cookie jar and Neveah snatches some napkins to follow him to the TV room, but Mom stops and puts one soft hand on my cheek.

"Go find Mercy," she says. "She'll know you're coming. No matter what."

I try not to cry as I leave.

TWENTY

I PARK NEXT TO MR. Montoya's truck at the church Mercy's family attends, and I'm surprised to see how many Evanston families have shown up to help. Morgan is here, and Miss Strong, and the school librarian. It looks like the entire debate team is here and most of the baseball team, too. But Mercy has always been the kindest, friendliest one of us, so perhaps you really do reap what you sow. Cottonwood Hollow is no slouch, either, and most of the town has arrived to help look. I catch sight of Flynn and Wynona, all of Mercy's neighbors, Sam Buford and the boys from the gas station, Marisol and Letty, most of the Cottonwood Hollow Historical Society, and the entire troop of Cottonwood Hollow Girl Scouts.

I send out one lonely message to Lux, unsure if she'll answer.

Looking for Mercy. I need you.

I examine the bell tower of the massive brick church, wondering what Mercy found here that was so comforting. I find solace under the hood of a car or behind a freezer that's not making ice the way it ought to be. I am most comfortable where I can be useful.

My eyes trace the bell tower down to the front steps of the church, where I see a familiar face handing out water bottles. It's Jett, and he's standing next to a pretty blond woman. The shock of seeing him pulls me across the parking lot, and suddenly I'm standing before him. He wears jeans and a Royals T-shirt. The blond woman smiles. "So good of you to come help, sweetie. Do you know Mercy from school?" She hands me a water bottle and I take it even though what I really need right now is caffeine.

"Mercy is my best friend," I answer, squeezing the bottle harder than I should.

"Oh, you must be Rome," the woman says. She hazards a quick glance at Jett, who's staring at me like I've grown two heads. "Jett told me about you."

"Jett told you about me?" I ask.

The woman elbows Jett, hard. "Aren't you going to introduce us?"

"Oh, sorry," Jett says. "This is my mom, Aubrey. Mom, this is Rome."

"It's nice to meet you," Aubrey says, holding out a hand that's cold and wet from passing out water bottles. I shake it gently, aware that my Fixer hands are somewhat stronger than the average person's. There's a smudge of blue paint near her wrist, and I recall that Jett said she was into painting now.

"Why are you here?" I ask. I fumbled it, like so many other

things that come out of my mouth. "I mean, how do you know Mercy?"

"I know Mercy through church," Aubrey answers. "She's a sweet girl. And Jett said she's your best friend, so he wanted to come along, even though he's not much for attending church services."

"Thank you," I reply with a short nod.

"Come on," Aubrey says. "It looks like they're ready to send us out."

Mr. Montoya and Rick assign me to the four-block span of houses near where the minivan was found. And before they can give me a partner, Jett steps up from the crowd. "I'll go with her," he says.

Mr. Montoya nods, as if all is as it should be. "Thank you . . . um . . . ?" He waits for Jett to offer his name.

"Jett Rodriguez," he says, shoving his big hands in the pockets of his jeans. Being this close to him is like standing near a space heater, the kind Mom and I use to heat the trailer when we run out of propane before payday.

"Oh, that's right. Aubrey's son. Well, thank you for your help. With all these friends, we're sure to find Mercy soon." I can't decide if he's so optimistic because he truly believes what he's saying, or because he'll break down if he doesn't pretend. I suspect the latter. Mr. Montoya continues. "I would prefer that Rome not visit strange houses alone. But I won't worry if you're with her."

It's all I can do not to roll my eyes.

Mr. Montoya hands me a stack of flyers. One of my pictures of Mercy is on the front. It's from Lux's birthday, when we'd gone out for pizza. She'd had her hair cut just an hour before, and it had only taken six months of cajoling for her parents to allow her the sleek, shoulder-length bob instead of her long, girlish braids. We'd squished into one side of a booth, and Tina had taken the photo from the other. In the original photo, Mercy is in the middle of the picture, smiling primly. On her left, Lux is poking her in the ribs, and on her right, I'm doing an imitation of Steven when I bring home leftover pizza. But Lux and I are cropped out, and it's just Mercy on the flyer.

Underneath reads:

<u>MISSING MAY 7</u>

- Mercy Montoya, age 17
- 5 feet tall, 100 pounds, brown eyes, black hair
- Wearing blue plaid skirt, white blouse, navy knee socks, and a navy headband
- Last seen in Evanston area
- Please call Rawlings County Police Department with any information: 555-3483

Seeing Mercy laid out on paper in such bare, brittle strokes makes me ache. It doesn't mention that she's generous to a fault, that she rarely swears, or how she chews her pencil erasers while she's studying. It doesn't say that she brings over lasagna when my fridge is empty, or that she makes peace between Lux and me because we're both too stubborn for our own good.

"If you see anything suspicious, call the police," Mr. Montoya tells me pointedly.

Because he knows if I thought Mercy was locked up in someone's basement, I'd burn the house down to get to her. He's right, and I don't know whether to laugh or cry.

"We will," Jett promises. "Come on," he tells me. "Let's get to work."

We hit the first block of houses. They're mostly rentals, some divided into multiple apartments. The first two people we talk to are tired-looking moms who come to the door in sweat pants. Kids shout in the background of each apartment, asking for cereal or help flushing the toilet. Both women take the flyer but admit they haven't seen Mercy. The third door reveals a young guy in a ratty white T-shirt and boxers that leave his scrawny pale legs exposed. He takes the flyer and comments that Mercy is hot.

"Dude, she's *missing*," Jett replies, looking annoyed.

"Sorry, man, just saying."

"Well, keep an eye out, okay?" I plead, the words almost sticking in my throat. This all feels so unreal. I can't be here asking people if they've seen my friend.

"Definitely," he says with a series of emphatic nods.

"What a creep," I mutter as we climb down the front stoop.

Jett nods. "I don't think we'll get much out of him."

"So why are *you* here?" I ask, but I'm looking at the ground and not at him. The question's been eating at me since I saw him in the parking lot of the church.

"What do you mean?" he asks. "Why am I partnered with you, or why am I looking for Mercy?"

"Both," I reply.

"Well, I'm partnered with you because we're friends. And

I'm looking for Mercy because she's your friend."

"And because your mom and Mercy go to the same church."

"That's the only reason I even knew she was missing. It's not like you picked up the phone and called to tell me."

"You know, I don't think I actually have your number," I respond. It had never occurred to me to reach out to anyone other than Lux when Mercy went missing. For the first time in my life, I am without them, and I have no idea how to deal with it. It's like missing a limb. Two limbs.

"Well, I know I don't have your number," Jett replies. He accidentally bumps into me as we avoid a sticky spill on the sidewalk. "I was going to call you last night after my game to see if you were okay. You were obviously pissed about something, but I don't think it was about me."

The words are hard to get out, so I hurry. "I'm sorry about yesterday," I tell him. "I was upset. While I was out on our date, something happened to Lux. And I blamed myself for not being there for her. And you were right there, so I lashed out at you."

"And all the 'your town versus my town' stuff?" he asks. "What about that?"

I cross my arms, almost wishing that he would fight with me so I would feel something other than scared out of my mind for Mercy. "Some of that is true, you know."

"Look, Rome. Let's lay a few things out on the table here." He stops and stands in front of me. We're toe to toe, and when he looks down at me, he says, "I'm from Evanston, and you're from Cottonwood Hollow. We're not from two different planets. We live in the same county, go to the same school. I *do not* think you're a freak. I would gladly pummel the face of anyone who actually had the balls to say that you, no matter where they're from. But since I'm being really honest here, I want to tell you that if you let your guard down just a little bit and gave people a chance, you'd probably find that not everyone hates you just because you're from Cottonwood Hollow. Look at Mercy. Look at all the people searching for her today. More than half of them are from Evanston. And we're all here trying to help Mercy. Trying to help *you*."

I exhale a long breath, the fight gone out of me. Not because he's won, but because I want to let go of the anger if I can. It's not helping me survive in Evanston. It's certainly not helping me find Mercy. I nod and take a few breaths to steady my voice and keep the tiny pricks of heat in my eyes from turning into embarrassing tears. These people are here to help me. And to help Mercy. And I've spent most of my time building fences to keep them out.

"That's very flattering," I reply finally. "You would pummel someone's face for me. Gladly, even."

"I do what I can."

"I'm sure I could return the favor."

"See? That's what I'm talking about." He flashes his grin, and the dimple I'm fond of shows up, too. "I know I don't understand everything you go through, Rome, but I'm trying to. And I want to be with you. Whatever that means. Acquaintance. Friend. Boyfriend." He puts a hand on my arm, his palm hot against my skin.

"Bat lender?" I add. "Red's Auto customer?"

"Yeah, definitely that. My brakes are so much better now." He runs his other hand over his black hair. "But to be totally upfront and honest, I'd prefer boyfriend out of those choices."

"I do have that effect on men."

"Of course." He struggles to hold back another grin as his hand slides off my arm and we turn and go up the front steps of the next apartment building.

We get the same response, apartment after apartment: *Never seen her.* Eventually we reach a block that's mostly nice, single-family houses with carefully cropped yards. We walk up to a split-level that's tidy and freshly painted a mint green. It's strangely comforting to have Jett by my side as we climb the front steps. I'm glad I'm not doing this alone. I wish Lux were here with me, too, but since she never replied to my texts, I'm guessing that she's still so angry with me that she can't bring herself to read my messages.

Jett rings the doorbell, and when a woman in her mid-fifties answers in her yoga pants and T-shirt, I'm ready with my well-practiced speech.

"Good morning, ma'am. We're sorry to bother you, but we're looking for this girl." I hand her the flyer. "Her name is Mercy Montoya. She went missing late yesterday afternoon. Is there a chance you might have seen her recently?"

The woman bites her lower lip as she studies the picture of Mercy. The scent of apple cinnamon wafts out the door, and I wonder if she's baking a pie or if she has one of those magical scented candles that make your house smell like food.

Jett shifts restlessly next to me.

"Yeah," she says. "I've seen her."

"What?" I ask, my heart in my throat. I'm louder than I mean to be, and the woman winces at the volume. I turn it down a notch. "When? When did you see her?"

"Yesterday afternoon. Not far from that brick church on Monticello."

My pulse races. "What was she doing when you saw her?"

"Well, she was standing in the street talking to someone in a car. Not very sensible, standing in the street like that. But you know how teenage girls are."

"What kind of car?"

"Oh, honey, I don't know cars all that well."

I ignore her. "Was it big, small, old, new? What color was it?" Cars are something I can understand. Even finding out what kind it was might give us some insight on who took Mercy. On who might still have her.

She sighs, tossing a dismissive hand. "I don't know exactly. It was some kind of sports car. Maybe a Camaro? Red. I couldn't see who was driving it. Probably some high-school boy." She gestures at Jett as an example.

"Are you sure it was Mercy?" I ask. "She looked just like the girl in this picture?"

"I'm pretty sure it was. She was a real tiny little thing. Hard to forget those eyebrows of hers. I'd like to know who waxes them. They were *phenomenal*."

"Could you write down your name and phone number?" I ask her, turning over one of the flyers and holding it out to her. "The police may want to ask you some questions. No one else has seen anything so far."

She takes the paper and goes back into the kitchen to get a pen to write down the information.

My mind is reeling. Why would Mercy have been talking to

someone in a sports car? And who was driving it? Sure, Mercy has a thing for Sam Buford, and she might talk to him, but he doesn't have a sports car. Could it have been Aaron? Did he borrow a car from a friend? I can't control the fear that seizes my body, making it hard to breathe.

I thank the woman and snatch the flyer out of her hand. "Let's go!" I yell at Jett over my shoulder as I jump off the woman's porch and sprint toward the sidewalk.

"Hold up!" he calls after me. "Shouldn't we call it in?"

"I can run faster than you can dial," I reply. "Now let's *go*!" I finally feel like we have a solid lead on what might have happened to Mercy. But it's my imagination that tortures me, wondering if Mercy got in the car and was cut into tiny pieces hours later. Or if she's locked in a closet somewhere. Tied up in a basement. Dead in a ditch.

God, I hate my brain sometimes.

We hurry back to the church, Jett rambling on as we go, as if he's trying to keep me from imagining the worst. "This is good. This is a lead, Rome. The police will find her soon. It'll be okay. We'll find her soon." It's nearly the same thing over and over until we near the church.

"But what if we find her and she's not okay?" I finally ask, the words strangling me even as I speak them. I shouldn't speak them out loud. It's probably bad luck, or bad juju, or bad karma.

"She'll be okay," Jett says stoically, his dark eyes meeting my rusty ones. He reaches down and squeezes my hand in his big one. It's probably the only hand I know that's as strong or stronger than my Fixer hands, and its warmth is comforting.

I nod, and it's a struggle not to let the hot pricks behind my eyes turn into real tears.

Rick is at the church, speaking with other volunteers who have returned from their rounds. When he sees me, his face lights up. "Anything, Rome?" he asks. Because he knows I'm tenacious, and I won't quit until I've found Mercy.

"We've got a lead, I think," I tell him. I give him the flyer with the woman's contact information and repeat what she told us.

"This is good, Rome," he says. "The first good lead we've had all day."

"That's it?" I clarify, my insides turning to concrete. I'd hoped ours might be the clue that unlocked the case. Not that it might be the only clue we had so far. Finding a sports car is like finding the proverbial needle in a haystack. It's nothing. Nothing to go on other than that Mercy might have been forced into someone's car. And who knows where she went from there. She could be anywhere.

"It's a good start, Rome. Don't lose faith," Rick says.

Faith. Faith is something Mercy has. It's not something I ever had. I understand the functions of gears and pulleys and internal combustion engines. I don't understand the mechanics of faith.

I'm scared.

"Rome," says a familiar voice behind me.

I freeze. The voice is the last I expected to hear today, and at the sound of it, my heart leaps into my throat.

Slowly, I turn.

And come face-to-face with Lux.

TWENTY-ONE

STRANGELY, LUX HASN'T ASKED HER mom to Heal her face. Maybe Tina is too weak to do it, but I want to think that it's because Lux is finally done keeping secrets. Instead, she's covered the black eye with foundation. A purplish bruise hides beneath the blush on her cheekbones. Her busted lip is only slightly swollen under her lip gloss. She says my name again, this time a question. "Rome?"

I make my mouth function like it's supposed to. "Lux," is all I get out. I seize her in a hug. I squeeze tight, like I'm afraid she might disappear again if I let go. She tucks her face into my neck and holds on, too.

"What are you doing here?" I ask when we let go.

"You said you needed my help," Lux replies, holding up her phone to show she got my message. She glances at Jett as she begins to steer me away. "Your boyfriend will have to wait. We have things to do."

"I'll go see if I can do anything else for Officer Ruiz," Jett says with a small nod like he knows that Lux and I need each other most right now.

Leaning on Mom's car behind the church, away from the stares of the other volunteers, Lux spills her guts. "Mom wanted us to go stay with Grandma until they've arrested Aaron. But they haven't found him. And Mom's so freaked that she wouldn't let me leave the house. But I got your text, so I snuck out. Mom thinks I'm watching TV in the back bedroom. As if I could ever just sit around with Mercy missing."

"Do you think Aaron has something to do with Mercy disappearing?" I ask, guilt nearly ripping me to shreds.

"I don't know," Lux admits. "But he's sure it was us who messed with his truck, so maybe Mercy just happened to get in his way. No one's seen him anywhere around Evanston, though."

"I talked to a woman who saw Mercy talking to someone in a red sports car."

"Well, Aaron would have been in his truck. It was fixed that afternoon. Before he came home and . . ." She trails off.

I want to shout, to scream that I hate Aaron, and that I'll do everything I can to hurt him like he's hurt Lux, but I know that's not what she needs right now. She needs me to listen.

Lux swallows, takes a deep breath, her voice trembling a little. "We're building a case against him. After Mom realized he'd been touching me, that he almost raped me, she sort of snapped. The police are saying she's a victim . . . that she's not at fault. I was scared that maybe . . . maybe they'd think she was just as much at fault as him."

It's painful to hear, but it's also the first good news I've had all day. "So they'll prosecute him?" I ask.

"If we're willing to press charges," Lux says, her voice getting stronger. "Mom says she wants to. She's sorry she wasn't stronger before, that she ever let him stay after he hit me. She was scared about being alone, about not being able to make it without him."

"That's good," I tell her. "That's really good."

"You'll probably have to teach me how to live without cable, though."

"Yeah, probably. There are these things called books, you know. I can show you how to read them. You can kill hours that way. Or, hell, you could even get a job."

"Don't get crazy, Rome."

I hug Lux again, unable to express how relieved I am to have her by my side again.

"Mercy should be here for this," Lux says when we let go of each other.

"So let's find her, then," I reply. Lux opens the passenger door and I circle the car to the driver's side and get in. I wish I had the Mach so we could drive something faster than Mom's Focus. And then it all seems very clear. "A red sports car. Someone talking to Mercy. What if it was someone in *the Mach*?"

Lux agrees, buckling her seat belt. "Maybe Garrett sold it to someone, but she walked right up to it, automatically thinking it was you. Or maybe it *was* Garrett driving, and she thought she could negotiate getting the car back for you."

I hit the gas and we head for Cottonwood Hollow. The thought of Mercy alone with Garrett now scares me. I recall the last time I saw him at the gas station. *Where's your pretty girlfriends? The man-eater and the little Finder girl?*

I can feel all the little pieces clicking together, the tiny parts that make up the whole. "Lux, the diary."

"What?" Lux asks, rolling down the window so that the air rushes in, tangling our hair.

"The diary. It was in my room. We thought I brought it to school, but maybe it was taken even before I left the trailer. The morning after I showed it to you, Garrett came for the rent. And he looked through the house, saying he needed to see if anything should be repaired before he put it up for rent again. And he went through my room. It pissed him off that I'd painted it without asking."

"You think he took Emmeline Remington's diary? Why? How would he even know what it was, let alone that you *had* it?"

"He's a Remington, right? I mean, he's always bragged he was related to the *original* Remingtons—Emmeline and her loser husband. But if he was telling the truth, his great-great-great-grandwhatever might've told his kids that there was a hidden dowry chest somewhere on the land. The day of the tornado, when we found that box, what if he saw it and figured we'd found something of Emmeline's? Something that might lead him to the dowry chest?"

"If he read the diary," Lux says, "he knows it's all real, and not just some family legend. That chest has the deed to the eighty acres, not to mention all the other good stuff like the gold bar."

"Yeah, and he's in real estate. Yesterday, Flynn told me that Garrett's business is going belly-up. He's about to lose everything over some bad real-estate investments he made in Evanston."

"So you think he read the diary and thought the deed was in Emmeline's house somewhere? Like he could find it and claim it since he's a Remington? How much would that be worth?"

I shrug. "The Truett farm went for four grand an acre."

Lux's mouth falls open. "So that piece of paper is worth . . . what, something like three hundred and twenty thousand dollars? And that's not counting the gold and silver."

"Probably enough to save his business."

Lux shakes her head. "That's who went through the homestead before us. We were there looking for the dowry chest, or some kind of clue. And so was Garrett." Lux gestures with her hands like she's strangling him. "But why Mercy? Why would he take Mercy?"

"At the gas station the other night, he asked about my friends *the man-eater and the little Finder girl*. Everybody in Cottonwood Hollow knows the little Montoya girl is a Finder," I supply. "And Mercy *is* a little Montoya girl. She's tiny. What if he didn't know that it was Neveah he wanted instead of Mercy?"

I tell Lux about the letter hidden behind Emmeline's hand-drawn map, about the dugout that had been present on it but not on the other version of the map that was in the Cottonwood Hollow Historical Society's book, and her mouth falls open. "All this time, it was right there?" she squeaks out.

"Garrett's had the diary for days now. And that was probably him we saw poking around the Truett farm. It was too dark to tell what kind of truck it was, but I know the sound of a gas engine, and that's what's in his Ram. Where else did Emmeline go besides the homestead? What would have seemed like the perfect hiding place?"

"The dugout," Lux agrees.

"John took Emmeline there, and she said she was happy. It was in the very first entry. Garrett's got to be closing in on the dugout by now. The town's not that big."

"Call Rick. Tell him we think Mercy's out at those hills."

"Garrett's not out there digging in broad daylight. Even if Mercy pretends to have Found it, he'll wait until dark to dig. So he probably stashed Mercy inside somewhere. The only place nearby would be the ruins." It feels like there's something heavy on my chest. "Do you remember how Mrs. Montoya said they were going to burn them down?"

"Not until tomorrow," Lux says.

"That makes it the perfect place then, doesn't it? Whatever happens, all the evidence will be destroyed."

Lux grabs my arm. "Do you think he's that desperate?"

"Do you want to wait and find out?"

TWENTY-TWO

WE PARK MOM'S CAR BY the barbed-wire fence that separates the Remington land from the rest of Cottonwood Hollow. I dial Rick's number twice, but he doesn't pick up. He must be on the other line. The third time I just try 911, but it doesn't connect at all because the signal is getting worse the farther we get from town.

We follow the fence line quickly, tromping through the tall grass. Then I notice that the rusty barbed wire is sagging. I jog a little farther and see that it's been cut. One of the posts has been torn up from the ground and the tall grass has been mashed down by tire tracks.

No, I wasn't brave enough to drive out here. But someone was.

"Look," I whisper to Lux, as if someone might hear us in this vast, open field. "Somebody drove through here."

"Oh, shit," Lux hisses. "It's got to be him, right? Come on, we have to run."

Lux volunteering to run anywhere means she understands how likely it is that Mercy is in the ruins.

Waiting for us to find her.

When we get close enough to be seen by someone in the ruins, we crouch down, picking stealthily through the tall grass. We reach the outermost trailer, the one that was hit by the tornado Sunday night. The scattering of debris from the tipped trailer spills out onto the grass, still reminding me of the entrails of a wounded animal. We move carefully near it, trying to circle around to the other side of the ruins.

"Stay low," Lux whispers. "In case he looks out and sees us. It's hard to say where they are in there."

I'm crouched about as low as I can be, the tall grass scratching against my cheeks. It's nearly noon and the weather is already hot and sticky. All I can think is that if Mercy is out here, she's got to be exhausted and frightened. A whole night in the ruins would be terrifying, and that's without having some psycho demanding she Find a dowry chest.

When we finally circle around to the other side of the ruins, there's no car, and that means probably no Garrett, either. Deep ruts are carved in the ground, like maybe he's driven his big one-ton Ram out here. The Mach is nowhere to be seen. There are three red fuel caddies, the big ones that hold ten or fifteen gallons of gas. The smell of gas is strong, and I don't know if it's just the caddies, or if Garrett has already soaked the area. The mayor is about to burn the ruins, whether the town is ready for it or not.

There are seven trailers altogether, lined up next to each other on towers of crumbling cinder blocks, waiting to be burned.

The far west one has been ripped open by the tornado, but all the others are intact, so close together that you could pass through one with only a foot or less of open space to the next. They're rusted and rotting, and every step inside their dark interiors will mean a chance that we'll fall through the floor and break an ankle like the Pelter boy.

The hills just next to us are high and unyielding, the sun beating down on the tall grass on their crests. Somewhere among them is the dugout that John Remington first lived in, the dowry chest we've been hunting buried inside. Cottonwood Hollow is a mile behind us, and we don't know if Rick will even see that I tried to call him.

Lux and I creep close enough to the ruins that if anyone's inside, they won't be able to look out and see us pressed up against the cinder blocks.

Lux glances down at something by her shoe and gasps. She holds it up. It's Mercy's navy headband with its prim little bow.

"We have to call Rick again," I whisper to Lux. "Mercy's got to be here." I pull out my phone and dial Rick's number.

Thankfully, there's enough signal now for the call to go out. But the phone rings four times and goes to voice mail.

"Shit," I mutter. "He's not answering."

"Text him," Lux says.

My hands are shaking as I type out the message. Lux grabs the phone from me and finishes it with quick, nimble movements.

Come to the ruins. We think we found Mercy. Hurry.

"What if he doesn't know where the ruins are?" I ask Lux after I read the message.

"Jesus, Rome, he lives in Cottonwood Hollow. Everybody knows where the ruins are."

We sit a few moments, just the two of us, listening to each other breathe and to the sound of the wind pushing the tall grass.

"Do you think Garrett's out there, on the other side of those hills?" I ask Lux. "Maybe he's found John Remington's dugout and he's already got the dowry chest."

"I don't care where Garrett is," Lux answers. "All I care about is where Mercy is. And she's got to be inside the ruins."

"It looks like it," I agree. "And wherever she is, she needs us."

"Let's go. Rick will probably make it here before Garrett gets back anyway." She eyes the big gasoline caddies. "I don't think we should leave Mercy in there any longer than she has to be. What if all it takes is a spark to light the whole place up?"

We sneak up to the first trailer. "I'm sure she's not just in this one," I mutter. "That would be too easy."

Using the cinder blocks lying around beneath the trailer, we stack a pile to reach the doorknob, which is about six inches above our heads. The cinder blocks wobble under our feet, shifting slightly, but we manage to keep our balance. Lux turns the knob as quietly and slowly as she can, pushing the door open. It creaks, but only a little. The inside is completely dark except for the swath of light now cutting across the entryway from the open door.

We pull ourselves up and climb inside, getting to our feet slowly as we look around. The room is full of junk, but most of it's been pushed to the sides, leaving a little bit of a walkway.

An empty couch sits in the middle of what would have been

the kitchen. There are beer bottles piled in the sink, and what looks like part of an old stereo system sitting on the counter. My fingers twitch a little as I notice all the broken things scattered around.

Together we walk to each end of the trailer, peeking in the empty bedrooms. Like we expected, no one's here. If Mercy really is somewhere in the ruins, she's deeper inside. I can't hear anything, no rustling, no voices. Just the sound of Lux and me breathing in the stifling, damp heat, the gas fumes even stronger now that we're inside.

Lux moves back into the kitchen, where she gingerly pulls a beer bottle out of the sink.

It's the closest thing we have to a weapon so far.

I struggle with the back door, hoping that it lines up with the door on the next trailer. Miraculously, it does, with barely a foot of bright air and open space between them, but the door to the next trailer is locked, the brass knob in the cheap, bleached wood holding strong. Like someone doesn't want it to be opened.

I feel around on the floor of the trailer we're standing in, looking for something small and sharp that I can jam into the keyhole. Lux pulls her driver's license from her pocket and reaches out across the open space to the next trailer and wedges it next to the lock, sliding the license in and adjusting it slightly as she tugs on the handle. I move away from the door to give her space.

The knob turns, and Lux lets out a sigh of relief.

"Nice," I murmur, and Lux shrugs.

We step across the open space between the buildings, the ground nearly six feet below us, a tangle of dead grass and twisted metal and broken glass. The next trailer is even darker, and I realize this is because we're in a laundry or mudroom. There's another door just inside, and thankfully this one is unlocked. But it creaks when we open it, and Lux and I both freeze, holding our breath.

"How far back did he take her?" Lux mutters to me.

I step forward and the floor sags under my weight. I leap back, bumping into Lux.

"What?" she hisses, raising her beer bottle, ready to strike.

"The floor is rotten," I whisper. "Be careful where you step. You might fall through."

I light up the screen on my phone and shine it on the floor. Not five feet away, the dirty linoleum is bowed completely. "Go around that," I whisper to Lux.

There's black stuff everywhere on the floor, so much that my feet slide around in it. At first I think maybe it's rat shit, but when I see it's on the walls I realize it's mold.

We creep slowly around the sunken area, moving toward the front door. I don't know what the odds are that it will line up with the next trailer. We've been lucky so far.

When we reach the back door, Lux holds her beer bottle aloft as I slowly twist the knob. It turns, which I take as a bad sign, because if Garrett didn't bother to lock it before he left, Mercy's probably not in this trailer. I crack open the door, and we are met with a wall of rusty metal siding. We can't make it into the next trailer.

"There's got to be a way," Lux says. "If Garrett and Mercy made it through, we should able to, too."

"Unless they came in a different door," I say. "Or what about a bedroom window?" I think of our trailer at home. If the windows line up, we may able to sneak through that way.

"Good idea," Lux says, and together we inch down the hall-way through the trash and mold.

I try the first door, but it's a linen closet, and a bat whooshes out over our heads.

Lux stifles a scream and jumps about a foot in the air. The force of her movement makes the floor drop beneath our feet, and the subfloor crumbles. We leap away before the linoleum gives out, our shoes squeaking and skidding on mold.

Standing on what must be a joist, because it feels firmer here, we take a moment to catch our breath.

Lux gestures at a door farther down the hall.

This one opens with resistance, and I realize it's because there's a big, black bag of trash on the other side of the door. We push carefully, hoping that we're not about to knock over a pile of something that will make a lot of noise.

When the opening is just wide enough for us to squeeze through, I go first and Lux follows me. It's even darker back here, and it takes my eyes a minute to adjust. There's a low bed, and above it, a window hung with dusty, shredded curtains. The air is sour and sticky.

Lux uses her phone's light to see more clearly, tucking her makeshift beer-bottle weapon under one arm. The bed is covered by a blanket that no longer has any discernible color beneath the dirt and mold and mouse pellets. Lying on the bed is an old doll, its hair matted and dark. It's wearing a diaper and one shoe. One eye is closed and the other eye is open, like it's watching us or maybe winking, like it's saying, *Good luck, but you'll never make it.*

We climb up on the bed and Lux pulls the curtains back from

the window. "Look!" she whispers. "It lines up with a window on the other side!"

Opening our window is easy, but getting the other window open is a real feat. It takes us working together, leaning halfway out of the window of the trailer we're in, to jimmy it open, shifting it back and forth in the swollen frame until we push it up just enough for one of us to squeeze through. It's not very quiet, but the fact that Garrett doesn't appear confirms he's not here, and Mercy must be tied up or trapped somewhere alone. Lux pokes her head through. "It's a bathroom," she says. "And it smells fucking awful." She climbs all the way inside, stepping down onto the open toilet ring and then the floor.

"Do you see anybody?" I ask. "Any sign of Mercy?"

"No," Lux whispers back. I lean out farther to cross over and Lux helps me slide through the small window without falling headfirst into the toilet.

It's quiet, and dark, and unbelievably hot in this trailer. Sweat rolls off me in rivulets, dampening the shirt between my shoulder blades and under my arms. I wipe my brow with my forearm, wondering if we'll have to climb through all seven trailers before we find Mercy.

But then there's a shuffle, the sound of someone shifting in a chair, maybe farther down the hall. My heart jumps up into my throat. Tears prick at my eyes. Someone is alive in here. Mercy. Please let Mercy be alive.

Lux looks at me, grabbing my hand in hers. "We should call for her. Let her know we're coming. Maybe she can signal where she is. Rick has to be here soon, right? He'll get here before Garrett does."

I nod. If we're wrong, Garrett might light the ruins on fire with all of us inside. But Mercy is worth any risk. If there's a chance we can get her out safely, we have to go for it. Lux squeezes my hand again, as if she knows what I'm thinking. We've got to try.

"Start shouting for her," I say. "I'm going to try to call Rick again."

I pull my phone out of my pocket and start dialing as Lux yells, "Mercy? Can you hear us? We're coming!"

But instead of an answering call, there's an unmistakable rush of footsteps in the hall. Lux shoots me a look of terror, and before either of us can think to brace it, the bathroom door bursts open, knocking us backward into the bathtub. Lux's beer bottle goes flying and shatters against the wall above us. My phone lands on the floor with a clatter, sliding away. The tub is full of dead beetles and mouse shit, and we scramble to get up before the click of a safety being let off a gun stops us.

"And now there's more of you," Garrett says, and when I look up at him I see the gun is trained right at us. It's some kind of pistol, small enough to be hidden in a holster beneath his jacket, but big enough to kill either of us easily. "You probably won't be any more help than the one I've got, but why don't y'all come on up out of there real easy and join us?" His Oklahoma twang and blond Ken-doll hair seem out of place in this dirty hole. He lifts the heel of his boot and crushes my phone with one swift stomp. I don't know if it connected with Rick or not.

We climb up out of the tub, and I feel Lux shaking next to me. Her eyes meet mine in the dark, and they're wide and scared.

We are in deep shit now.

Garrett pauses to touch Lux's hair as she passes, and when she makes a small sound of revulsion, I crouch and grab my phone, stuffing it in my jeans pocket. The screen is shattered, our plan is broken, and I'm not sure I can Fix any of it.

TWENTY-THREE

THE LIVING ROOM IS LIT by three gas lanterns perched on piles of trash. The smell of gasoline is dizzying. Another gas caddy waits in the corner of the room. We were right about Garrett getting ready to burn down the ruins sooner rather than later. As my eyes adjust to the flickering light, I find Mercy sitting on a dilapidated couch. Her arms are behind her, presumably tied, and her dark hair is a tangle around her face. She squirms when she sees Lux and me, using a shoulder to try to tug down the red bandanna gag on her mouth.

"Oh my God," Lux croaks. She holds her hands up to show Garrett she's not trying anything as she carefully crosses the room to Mercy. As Lux pulls the gag down from Mercy's mouth, the strangled sound of relief Mercy makes nearly rips my chest open. There's a rotting wooden coffee table in front of the couch, and Emmeline Remington's diary sits on top of it, the cottonwood leaf etched into the leather making it easy to identify. I pull my broken phone partway out of my pocket. There's a faint light that suggests it might still have power. Garrett looks over at me, and I jam it farther into my jeans, pretending to be rubbing nervous, sweaty palms on my pants instead.

Garrett looks back at Lux and Mercy. "Sit the fuck down, girlie," Garrett says to Lux. "You don't do anything unless I tell you to, got it?"

He uses the gun to gesture at me to sit down on the couch, and then stands across the coffee table from us. "Well," he says, one hand on his hip, after I've sat down on the other side of Mercy. "Now I've got three of you. What the hell good does that do me?" He spits on the floor. "The Finder girl was supposed to have Found that stupid chest by now. She's not much of a Finder, is she?" he asks me. "We wandered all over those hills last night, and we didn't Find a damn thing. She said it was the roofie I gave her messing her up, but she wasn't much good this morning, either."

"So you really think that if you suddenly find the missing deed to the Remington land, the town won't question it?" I ask, hoping that if we stall for long enough, Rick and a SWAT team and some helicopters with machine guns will show up. Okay, probably the helicopters with machine guns are a little farfetched, but some backup would be good. Garrett has a gun, and we've got nothing. "You don't think they'll wonder when the three of us go missing?"

I reach forward and touch the diary, as if we're all sitting around at a party and not being held at gunpoint. I open it, laying it out flat on the table. Hoping the three of us together with it again will make something happen. The pages rustle a little, like a cool breeze is stirring the air.

Garrett's eyes dart around the room, as if he's searching for a cracked window. "My granddaddy told me when I was a boy that the deed to the Remington land is in that chest, and that it's rightfully mine. And that bitch's diary confirmed it. All eighty acres of prime fucking real estate. We'll clear all the crappy trailers out and build a real town here. Something the Remingtons can be proud of."

"Then let us help you Find it," Lux says, hazarding a glance at me that says, *Whatever I do, just play along.*

"How the hell are *you* going to find it if this little Finder girl couldn't?" Garrett asks.

"We're stronger when we're together," Mercy tells him. And it's true, but not like he thinks. "We'll look again. I'll Find it this time. And then you can let us go. We won't tell anyone where we were. I'll just say I ran away."

"You just *ran away*?" Garrett laughs, pointing the gun at her forehead. "Nobody's going to believe that."

Lux smiles slowly at him, like a predator looks at its prey before it launches a killing blow, and a shiver runs down my spine. "*Garrett*," she croons, her voice soft. Her Siren talent is stronger when she knows the name of the man she's trying to ensnare. "We can do it that way if you want. Or you and I can just get rid of these two after we Find the chest. Let's do it, Garrett. Let's all just go outside and Find it." She flicks a dismissive hand toward us, her eyes still locked on him.

Garrett's eyes briefly shift to her hand, then track back to Lux's face, his gun still pointed at Mercy's head.

The pages of the diary flutter, as a breeze moves through the cramped, dirty trailer.

Lux's full lips are in a playful smile, her green eyes even more catlike in the glow of the lanterns. "Come with me, Garrett," she whispers, her words like a caress. "Let's all go outside. I want to see you in the daylight. I bet you're even handsomer in the daylight, aren't you? Let me help you find the chest, Garrett. You're going to make this town something the Remingtons can be proud of."

The gun lowers slightly, his finger sliding infinitesimally on the trigger, as if he's ready to take it off.

"Come on girls," Lux trills, standing up. She will be the one to do it now, to protect us no matter the cost, as Emmeline wanted. Lux will use her curse to save us, even though she hates it and everything it's done to her. She gestures for us to get up, and we do, though Mercy stumbles a little with her hands behind her back. I glance down and notice that her hands are free now, but she's still pretending they're not, unwilling to spook Garrett. Lux purrs, "I want to go outside with you, Garrett. You'll take us outside, won't you?"

"There's a quicker route," Garrett replies, his words slurring together a little under her spell. "I can show you. You'll like it," he says, grinning at her.

My heart is thumping wildly in my chest as the gun lowers a little more.

"Can you show me, Garrett?" Lux croons again. "I'm a little scared of the dark. I know you'll protect us, but I'd be so much happier if you took us outside. Take us outside, Garrett. I want you to."

Lux steps forward, reaching out with a trembling hand, and I know she's going to touch his skin to strengthen the hold she has on him. Lux is going to save us. She will do whatever it takes to get us out of here.

But at the last second, Lux falters, her hand poised just above his bare forearm as it glistens with sweat in the heated room. For a few seconds she is gone, not here with us, but in some other moment that only she can see, and she recoils slightly with a sharp gasp. Her hesitation is all it takes for the hold she has over him to waver.

Garrett jerks his head as if trying to clear it of the fog Lux has created. "You little bitch!" he roars, and the hold snaps.

The spell is broken. Garrett swings the gun back at her, and I watch the tendons and muscles moving through his hand, pulling his trigger finger in slow motion.

And then I jump, shoving Lux out of the way as the gun goes off.

TWENTY-FOUR

THE FLESH JUST BELOW MY shoulder is ripped open by fiery claws, cleaving and shredding through muscle and bone. It's hot, so hot, and it's as if time has briefly stopped so that I can appreciate the full extent of the pain, the way it spreads through every fiber of my body like oil spilled on the floor of the shop. I'd been moving forward, pushing Lux out of the way, but the force of the bullet has me reeling, and I fall backward onto the coffee table. The rotten wood of the table splinters beneath me, and I slam against the dirty floor.

Suddenly my blood is everywhere. It's pooling beneath me, and just as fast as the fire burns within me, it's replaced with an icy, aching cold. So this is what it feels like to die.

Mercy is shrieking, and Lux is scrambling to get up from where I'd pushed her into a pile of trash. Lux throws herself at Garrett, ramming her shoulder into his gut and pushing him back into the wall. Mercy reaches me, her face splattered with my blood where it hovers over mine. She presses her small hands on my wound, tearing a scream from my chest. At least, I would be screaming if I could get any sound to come out of my mouth.

I never wanted to die in a trailer.

But here I am.

My vision is starting to blur, but Mercy shakes me to keep me awake. Lux is wrestling Garrett, trying to get the gun, and I bet wishing for those same helicopters and SWAT team I'd been hoping for earlier. Maybe even the beer bottle.

"Rome!" Mercy begs. "Stay with us, Rome!" She takes my hand and places it over my wound, and hot, sticky blood pulses out between my fingers. Then she jumps up and tries to help Lux tackle Garrett, because there's no way any of us will make it out alive if we don't get that gun. Garrett throws Mercy back on the couch, and she reaches between the cushions and pulls out a beer bottle. She flings it at his head, and it strikes his temple, sending him reeling back. As his arms pinwheel, the gun goes off again, this time into the floor a foot from my head. I would have flinched, but it seems like a lot of work right now.

Mercy reaches back into the couch as he raises the gun again, and she pulls out another bottle because she is an Enough. The bottle is broken, and this time she flings herself at him with it. She knocks the gun out of his hand with the broken bottle, and the pistol goes skidding across the floor, leaving a trail in the mold and dust. Lux jumps on his back, clawing at his face and screaming like a banshee, and Mercy is hitting him with the broken bottle and saying swear words I didn't even think she knew. They're trying to keep him from finding the gun, but neither one is strong enough to hold him while the other grabs it.

My hand slides away from the hole in my shoulder, and I think that the blood on my hand might be freezing into tiny crystals.

Why is it so fucking cold in here?

I find the phone in my pocket, and I rub the screen with my hands. If I can do one last thing before I die in a goddamned trailer, I'm going to try to get them help. I smooth the cracks with my fingers like I did with the car radio in Red's shop, but I'm just smearing blood on the screen. Maybe my talent's leaking out like all this blood on the floor around me.

The gaslights are flickering like strobes now, and the struggle is the only thing I can hear, Garrett grunting as he finally flings Lux off him. She flies back onto the couch, her head hitting the arm with a crack.

The phone falls from my blood-slicked fingers, but in all the noise I can't even hear it clatter against the floor.

It's getting harder to focus on what's happening around me. Why are the gaslights flickering? The wind, I realize, as it yanks Lux's hair back from her face. She looks like a wild thing, climbing into a crouch to launch herself at Garrett again. Her eyes squint against the force of the gale that's building in the room. Before Lux can leap, Garrett tosses Mercy on the couch next to her like a rag doll.

I manage to turn my head enough to see Garrett free of both of them, scrambling around on the floor in the moldy debris, his eyes wild as he searches for the gun. The wind rushes through the trailer, knocking over the gas lanterns, their flames extinguished by the roaring air before they can ignite the gasoline-soaked piles of trash. Mercy, realizing that the storm Emmeline's building around us is more powerful than Garrett now, has the sense to pull Lux down to the floor with me. Mercy puts her small hands back over the hole in my shoulder, pushing until it's even more painful, and I shout at her to stop, words finally making it out of my mouth.

The whirlwind circles around us. If it's a hurricane, we're in the eye. The couch is lifted off the floor, the piles of trash, a broken bicycle in the corner. Dusty, discarded bottles that Mercy pulled out of nowhere lift from the sink and the floor as the windows shatter, a cacophony of terror. The trailer's roof is ripped off, exposing a dark and brutal sky above us, and suddenly I think that this must not be Emmeline Remington at all. We're in a tornado. Damn, we're in a tornado and we didn't even hear the sirens.

Lux and Mercy huddle over me, Mercy pressing against the hole beneath my shoulder, Lux wrapping an arm around Mercy. Lux's other arm cradles my head, as if any of us were strong enough to protect the other, let alone survive this. My blood is smeared on both of their faces, and I wish it wouldn't be the last memory I'd ever have of them. Not even Emmeline could save us from this.

The walls rip away, a sound like the rending of metal and bone, and all I can think is that I hope Steven is okay. I hope Mom took him to the tornado shelter.

Mercy and Lux huddle over me in the icy wind. In the bare space behind them, I see a woman in a long dress that bells and collapses again and again in the force of the tornado's power. Emmeline, I think. She's coming to welcome us to death.

Everything goes black.

At least we're together in the end.

TWENTY-FIVE

"Rome? *Rome.*"

This time it's Mom's voice. The way it breaks takes me back to a night when I was six years old and I had the flu. The two of us were lying on the floor of the bathroom, our cheeks pressed against the cool linoleum while she rubbed my back. Her rusty eyes reflected my own when she told me that she was going to search the couch cushions again to look for money to buy some ginger ale. But I reached out to her because I didn't want to be alone.

Mom squeezed my damp hand, and she didn't leave.

I open my eyes and am greeted by a blindingly awful fluorescent light.

"Am I dead?" I feel pretty dead right now. Everything is numb, and my mouth moves slowly. My words are slurred. I am lying in a bed.

"No, you're not dead," Mom says. She's standing beside the bed, and I struggle to turn my head and look at her.

"That's good," I mumble. "Where's Steven?"

Mom laughs, her eyes wet. "He wanted to come, but the hospital has weird rules about dogs in the ICU."

"I'm in the ICU?" I ask, squinting as if that will make my situation clearer.

Mom nods. "Lux and Mercy are in hysterics in the waiting room. The doctor didn't think you should have a lot of visitors for a while."

"Dumb," is all I can manage to get out.

Mom nods again. "He said you lost a lot of blood. You're lucky to be alive."

"So lucky," I slur. "Lucky enough to get shot."

Mom laughs, and it ends on a near sob. "God, Rome, I was so scared. We followed the ambulance to where you were. When I saw you lying out there in the middle of that mess . . ." Her voice trails off and I know she's trying not to cry. "Can you tell me what happened out there? The ruins were just . . . destroyed."

"Knew I wouldn't die in a trailer."

Mom's hand finds mine beneath the white sheet, and she squeezes it.

I squeeze back, as hard as I can.

I don't know how long I slept, but when I wake up the next time, I'm less foggy and the walls have changed. I must be in a different room, but I don't know how I got here.

This time Lux and Mercy are here, so I know I'm no longer

in the ICU. They're sitting on a low bench beside the bed, talking in hushed voices. Their faces are clean, no traces of my blood remaining. On the windowsill, there are several bouquets of flowers in vases. Bright, gaudy balloons are tied to the foot of the bed. I'd be embarrassed if I wasn't so damn sore. My shoulder aches fiercely, and the pain radiates down my arm and across my chest and into my gut. With my eyes, I trace the drip lines of IV fluid and something else from my arm to the stand, watch the blip of the monitor as it records each beat of my heart with a sterile *beep*.

"Rome!" Mercy exclaims, noticing me. "You're awake!"

"Wish I wasn't," I mutter, my mouth dry and stiff, but at least not slurring my words.

"Let me get you a drink," Mercy says, hurrying to what must be the bathroom behind a small door in the corner. I hear water running.

"Let me get you something for that awful face," Lux says, and at first I think she means makeup and I open my mouth to protest that this is not the time or place for eyeliner, but she lifts her hand to a small button on one of my drip tubes and clicks it twice.

A blissful coolness settles over me, and the pain in my shoulder ebbs. "What is that?" I ask, my voice decidedly less sharp.

"That's your morphine drip. The nurse said you might need an extra shot now and then."

"Sweet Jesus, tell her thank you," I sigh.

"You should be thanking me. I'm the one who clicked the button," Lux sniffs, tossing her hair over her shoulder.

Mercy returns with water and helps me drink it. I try to hold the cup myself, but my hand isn't quite steady enough.

"Thanks," I tell her after I've had a few gulps to moisten the cracked cave of my mouth.

Mercy sets the cup down on the table by my bed.

"So what happened today?" I ask. "Everything is sort of foggy. I was kind of in and out there for a while."

Lux laughs. "It's Tuesday."

"What? Then I missed *two* shifts at the shop."

"Yeah, Red'll probably fire you," Lux agrees. "Getting shot is no excuse."

"Saturday was kind of a blur for all of us," Mercy says. "It was like what happened in Emmeline's bedroom with the wind and the shaking. Only a hundred times stronger."

Mercy gets her purse from the bench and holds out Emmeline's diary. The cover is dark with dried blood. My blood.

"It would have been nice if she would've shown up *before* I got shot," I mutter.

"Thanks for that, by the way," Lux says, clicking the morphine drip one more time. She grins and I would roll my eyes but I'm too damn relaxed now.

"Anytime," I tell her. "What happened to Garrett? Did they catch him?"

"He died in the storm. Rick says the police report is citing that part as 'a random, strong microburst' because there's no way to report that the ghost of Cottonwood Hollow came and blew apart seven trailers to kill someone."

Mercy makes a face. "It was pretty awful," she whispers, holding the cup out to me to see if I want another drink.

"Did anyone see her?" I ask after taking another sip. "Did either of you?"

Mercy and Lux shake their heads. I know that I saw her. Even if it's all kind of hazy when I look back now.

Lux shrugs. "I think she was there, too. She came back to protect us against Garrett. She came back to take care of the daughters of Cottonwood Hollow."

"That's why she wanted us to read the diary. It wasn't just about the talents. It was wanting us to be strong enough to take care of each other. No matter what," I tell them.

Mercy interjects, "Well, things will be a hell of a lot better if you two would stop keeping things from me. I mean it. This ends now."

Lux looks away. "I couldn't tell you," she says in a low voice. "I was so ashamed."

"There isn't anything you can't tell us," Mercy says, hugging Lux. When she lets go, she points her small finger at me. "And *you*, keeping all that from me. You pull that crap again and *I'll* be the one putting you in the hospital. Same goes with the rent money and the bleach."

I make a face.

"But you did the right thing calling Rick," Mercy tells me before looking back at Lux. "So don't be pissed at her. If I can forgive you two, you've got to do the same."

Lux twists a lock of her long hair around her finger, looking away again. "I haven't told you yet," she says, her voice barely a whisper. "I wanted to wait until Rome was awake."

We wait for her, the steady beep of my heart monitor echoing in the room.

"They picked up Aaron yesterday."

"Oh, I am *so* relieved," Mercy says, putting her hand over her heart.

Lux shakes her head. "No. He's already out on bail thanks to his brother."

"He's not!" Mercy hisses, her dark eyebrows sharply arched.

"The police said we can file a restraining order against him while we wait to take him to court. That's it. A piece of paper is supposed to protect us," Lux says, and by the way she holds her mouth I know that she's struggling not to cry.

"You can do this," I tell her. "File the restraining order. Press charges. We'll help you. Whatever you need."

Lux's face does crumple this time, and tears run softly down her cheeks. "I don't know if I can even face him again," she says. "Out there in the ruins, when I thought I could control Garrett with my curse, all I could see was Aaron. And what Aaron said I did . . . how I *made* him do those things to me. I couldn't do it. I couldn't touch Garrett. And it almost *killed* you, Rome."

"Come here," I say, scooting over as much as I can in the bed. Thankfully the last shot of morphine makes it bearable. Lux crawls in, sniffling. Mercy follows, climbing up next to Lux and squeezing her.

I reach out to Lux, palm to palm.

Scar to scar.

"I'm still here for you. Mercy's still here. We're not going anywhere."

Mercy takes Lux's other hand. "We'll be with you every step of the way. Because nobody messes with the girls from Cottonwood Hollow," Mercy says, tucking her head under Lux's chin.

And we stay that way, the three of us tangled together in my hospital bed, letting the steady beeping of my heart be the only song we need.

TWENTY-SIX

I'M IN THE BATHROOM OF my hospital room, struggling to get the thin button-down flannel shirt on over my bandages. It hurts to use my right arm; all movement is painful, and I wonder if I'll ever be able to shift gears in the Mach again without feeling the ache of what happened in the ruins. The ache is in other places, too. Sometimes I wake up in a cold sweat, chest heaving, reliving Garrett and the gun and the storm at the ruins, sure that he's going to be standing at the end of my hospital bed, drawling in that Oklahoma twang, "What are you doing, pretty puss? Looking for trouble?"

I push the image of Garrett out of my head and finally get my arm in the shirt with the assistance of a few creative curse words. I fumble with the buttons until the shirt is sort of closed. Mom is supposed to pick me up today. I am thankful to be leaving. The hospital, while accommodating and regular with their meals, makes me feel boxed in and restless.

More than that, every passing hour, doctor visit, and bandage change makes me worry about the bill. Mom and I were just about to get back on our feet with both of us having jobs again. This hospital stay is going to knock us flat on our asses. I tried to broach the subject with Mom several times, but she always waved me off, saying we would figure it out later. "Just get better," she said. "Let me worry about the rest."

Avoiding a problem until the last possible moment is typical Mom behavior, so I let the worry settle in my stomach, agonizing over every meal and every tiny paper cup full of pills.

When I exit the bathroom, I'm surprised to see not Mom, but Jett sitting beside the bed. He stands, giving me a bright smile.

"You are not my mom," I say, double-checking that I've closed a sufficient number of buttons.

"So you didn't hit your head, then," Jett teases.

"Nope, the head is still pretty good," I answer, waiting for him to explain his presence.

"I met your mom in the lobby. She said she was coming to take you home on her lunch break, so I offered to take you home so she wouldn't have to skip it."

"Oh," I falter. "That was nice of you. Thanks."

"I like to eat lunch every day, so I figured she does, too. But really it's just a good excuse to see you again." He gives me a roguish smile. "Your mom said to help you with your sling, and that I'm not supposed to let you carry anything or open doors."

"Did she also say to lock me in a closet when we get home?" I ask.

"Yeah, but to flip the light on so you don't get scared. And to leave you with some peanut butter and a spoon. Oh, and to make sure you can get the lid off okay with just the one working arm."

"That's thoughtful."

Jett moves toward me, and I shift a little self-consciously, worried about the buttons I didn't close.

"Can I help you with those?" he asks.

"That would be nice, thanks." Asking for help has never been one of my strengths, but it's something I'm slowly learning.

He starts at the bottom of the shirt, his big fingers surprisingly deft with the small buttons. When we're this close, I realize I've forgotten how big he is, and how he radiates heat like a furnace. And I'm thankful Mercy and Lux helped me shower last night. I've only seen Jett a few times since I've been in the hospital, and Lux and Mercy were here each time to tease him with leading questions during most of the visit. He's careful not to touch my skin where the shirt still isn't closed and manages to make it all the way up to my chest before he blushes, fighting a dimple-producing grin that's either embarrassment or pleasure.

"I, um, think that's probably good." He pulls away, his fingertips grazing my collarbone.

"Thank you," I whisper, my voice tighter than it should be.

He grabs the sling off the bed, helping me get my arm in it and then adjusting it over my neck. "All right," he says when we've finished. "You have any bags?"

"Mom and Red came and took it all last night."

"That's your boss from the auto shop, right? The one with the tire iron?"

"The very one."

The nurses want me to ride in a wheelchair down to Jett's car, but I refuse with my entire being, and eventually they agree to escort Jett and me out while I walk on my own two feet. Jett brings the Challenger around to the front of the building, and a bevy of nurses checks to make sure I have all my prescriptions and a schedule of all my follow-up appointments. It's not a huge surprise that they like me. Mrs. Montoya made sure Mercy delivered a basket of homemade baked goods every day.

One of the nurses leans into Jett's car and helps me with the seat belt, adjusting it so it doesn't irritate my shoulder. "Be good, sweetie," she says before she closes the door. "Do me a favor and don't take any more bullets, okay?"

"Got it," I reply before the door shuts.

Jett starts driving toward Cottonwood Hollow.

"Are you pumped about going home?" Jett asks.

"Beyond pumped. I am completely inflated. Or whatever's better than pumped."

Jett laughs. "I'm glad. That was a scary couple of weeks, I bet."

"I've had better weeks, that's for sure. But look at me now. I'm better than new. I asked the surgeons to do some special shit to my shoulder to make me like Iron Man."

"Iron Man actually wore a suit—" Jett begins.

"Shhhh. Don't ruin it for me."

"So you'll make it back to school in time for finals?"

"Yeah. I'm thrilled. Mercy brought me all the homework I missed, so at least I'm not behind or anything."

"If you need a study partner for history, let me know."

"I don't know how good you are at taking notes, though. Seems to me like you spent that class trying to pick up girls."

"Just one girl. But she blew me off most of the time, so my notes are still pretty good."

"Well, her loss is my gain."

Jett laughs again.

"What are your summer plans?" I ask him. "Besides dating me, obviously."

He reaches over to hold my hand, and something flips in my stomach. "Painting houses again. And baseball. And *definitely* seeing you more than I've been able to lately. Those visiting hours are killer. But now that you're out, I heard you're going to come help me with the baseball team's big car-wash fund raiser next weekend," he teases.

"Let me know when the team has a big oil-change fund raiser. I'd be better at that," I reply. We drive past the last gas station, and I remember him taking me there the night I ran out of fuel.

"What about you?" he asks. "Any big summer plans?"

"Working, I hope. My left arm is fine. The doctors say I'll need weeks of physical therapy before I can use the right one all the way. But I'm hoping Red will let me do some things around the shop in the meantime."

"You're really lucky, you know," Jett says.

"Everybody says that," I reply, because it's all I've heard for the last two weeks. Apparently the whole town was out at the ruins after I'd been shot to see them load me into the ambulance, thanks to Rick and Sheriff Yost blaring their sirens all the way out there. The only good thing that came of it was when the Mach was found farther down the road from where Lux and I had parked Mom's car, the entire town was present to identify it. They swore the abandoned Mach 1 near the scene of the mysterious microburst was absolutely, 100 percent the property of Rome Galveston. And Mercy pinching the keys and title out of the glove box didn't hurt, either.

"I know. But I was there, out at the ruins right after the ambulance left. The blood . . ." His voice trails off.

"There was a lot of blood," I agree.

"Hard to imagine that could all come from one person and she could still be alive."

"Well, I assure you, it was more painful to experience first-hand than it was to see the aftermath."

Jett shoots me a glance. "I'm sure it was. I just want to say, in whatever weird, awkward way I'm managing right now, that I'm glad you're okay. And I'm glad you found Mercy. You're kind of a badass, Rome."

I laugh this time. "I am, definitely," I agree.

Jett's phone beeps, and he casts a glance down to see who's texting.

"Is that Mercy's number?" I ask, unable to keep myself from looking.

"I, um, sent her a text earlier," he says awkwardly. "I'm helping her out with a special project." Jett pulls his phone out from the cup holder and hands it to me so I can text a reply. "Can you text her back that I'm taking you home? And while you're at it, why don't you finally add your number?" He smiles at me, his eyes crinkling.

I notice that the screen is cracked from a chip on the corner. "What happened to your phone?" I ask.

"I dropped it. Not long after you left the church to go look for Mercy with Lux."

Mercy's text to Jett only reads, *ETA on the delivery?* A crack runs right through the middle of the message.

I text Mercy, *On my way home—Rome.* Then I slip into his contacts and add my name and number. The crack in the screen taunts me, and I lick my lips. Jett's watching the road, and my Fixer hands are twitching to Fix something after two weeks of lying in bed. I rub the shattered screen with my thumb, tracking the broken glass carefully. The cracks lighten and thin until they're nearly smudges, and then they disappear completely.

Without saying a word, I put the phone back in the cup holder.

When we turn onto the dirt road that leads to the trailer, I feel that same twinge of embarrassment as I did the last time he dropped me off, but I push it away, because there's nothing wrong with where I come from. I am Rome Galveston, badass. Fearless enough to protect my friends. Strong enough to ask for help with my buttons.

When we round the bend, I am momentarily confused by the crowd of people and cars. Lawn chairs dot the front yard, which needs to be mowed, and what looks like hot dogs sizzle on a grill. A banner hangs over the front door of our trailer. It says *Welcome Home, Rome!*

I see Mom near the banner now, standing next to Red, who's frowning at Jett's Challenger.

"So my mom was going to miss eating lunch, huh?" I ask Jett. Mercy's cryptic text now makes sense.

Jett laughs. "She asked me to help with your surprise party. Everyone wanted to welcome you home."

"I think I might've preferred the closet and the peanut butter thing you mentioned earlier."

"Yeah, I kind of thought you might. But your friends are very persistent. Lux told me the only way I was invited was if I agreed to bring you so that she and Mercy and your mom could all help get ready."

"That sounds like Lux," I agree.

But it's not just Mom and Red. Lux and Mercy come to help me get out of the car, both of them hugging me as gently as possible so they don't mess up my sling or hurt me. Mr. and Mrs. Montoya are there, all of the Ruizes, Sheriff Yost, several of the volunteers from Mercy's church, and most of the residents of Cottonwood Hollow. Tim and Eddie, from Red's Auto, are there, failing miserably at running the grill, even with Flynn and Wynona offering advice. Neveah and Malakai are playing ball with Steven, and I catch sight of Sam Buford, who had better step up and finally ask Mercy out or I'm going to smack him with my only functioning arm. Tina, Morgan, and a woman I presume is Lux's grandma are there, and I think that Tina looks more relaxed than I have ever seen her, despite the pink cast on her arm.

I have never been an expert at making small talk, but for the next forty-five minutes, I'm passed from person to person, asked to give a one-minute summary of what happened two weeks ago, and then told again how lucky I am. It would be awkward and annoying if I didn't suddenly have a deep appreciation for a community that had rallied around me and been a family, even before I'd been shot in the ruins. Sure, Mom and I were two women living in a trailer on the edge of town, but everyone here had been a part of our lives, a piece of a family much larger than just the two of us.

Red tells me that the Mach is in his shop, and that when I'm getting around a little bit better, I can start Fixing the damage Garrett did during his brief ownership. It's probably the best news I've had since Mercy handed me the keys and the title. Or maybe since the doctors told me I was going to live.

Just when I think all the attention is going to cause my head to explode, Mom announces that it's time to eat. The residents of Cottonwood Hollow have put together a long table of food, and I am thankful that everyone turns their attention to the various bowls and trays.

Jett appears at my side and helps me make a plate of food with my one good arm, which thrills Mom to no end. When his back is turned, she gives me a thumbs-up and an exaggerated wink. Red scowls a tad less when Jett offers me his lawn chair and sits in the grass.

Later, I sneak into the trailer to use the bathroom, and the first thing I notice are the boxes. Mom's packed almost everything; our few dishes are in dusty cardboard boxes that she's taken from Red's Auto, and the nice plastic totes are filled with her beloved, tattered paperbacks, organized by genre and author. It's really happening. We're really leaving. There's a small pang of sorrow when I realize that we'll be saying good-bye to the only home I've ever known, even if I wasn't always proud of it. The trailer will go up for auction next week, and tomorrow afternoon Mom, Steven, and I will be moving into the small rental apartment above Red's Auto.

Soon I won't be one of the girls of Cottonwood Hollow. Someday I'll look back, and this will just be somewhere I used to live, a fading memory of a run-down trailer with a leaning front stoop and a massive cottonwood tree out front.

Mrs. Montoya is waiting in the living room when I come out of the bathroom.

"I'm sorry!" she says when I jump about a foot in the air and jerk my shoulder painfully. "I wasn't trying to scare you. I just wanted to speak with you without a big audience."

"Oh?" I prompt, uncomfortable already. I wonder how Mrs. Montoya sees the trailer, the mismatched furniture and the faded wallpaper. The precariously stacked boxes of paperback novels and plastic bowls. There's no smell of freshly baked cookies coming from the avocado-colored stove in the kitchen. I'm sure she visited before she let Mercy come over to play when we were kids, but I don't remember her ever being inside the trailer before.

"I wanted to give you this," Mrs. Montoya says, holding out a plain white envelope.

"What is it?" I ask. "Do you want me to . . . open it . . . or . . . ?" I'm never sure if I'm supposed to open gifts in front of people, and even though I don't know, I know that Mrs. Montoya does know, and I don't want her to think I'm rude. Or something.

She smiles. "Yes, please open it."

Inside is a check with more zeroes than I've ever seen.

"Holy shit," I mumble. My eyes flash back up to Mrs. Montoya, "I'm sorry—" I begin.

Mrs. Montoya manages a little laugh. "It's a pretty big surprise, Rome. I understand."

"But I don't understand. I can't take this. I don't deserve it."

"What do you mean?" Mrs. Montoya asks, frowning. "That money is all donations. Some from our church, and the rest from Cottonwood Hollow. Some of your teachers and classmates' families from Evanston donated, too. It's to help cover your hospital bills."

"I can't just take money from people. I *don't* just take money from people."

"You're going to take this, if not for me, then for Mercy. And for your mom."

I think of Mom, of her quiet persistence that I didn't need to worry about the hospital bills. "Does Mom know about this?" I ask.

"No," Mrs. Montoya answers. "We didn't want to say anything until we were finished collecting. But Rome, she's trying so hard. And so are you. Don't let Garrett Remington derail you. Let us help you. Just this one time." She purses her lips and for a second I think she might cry. I'm struck again that this woman is family, that the people who've rallied around me are family. And that part of being in a family is letting them into your tiny, narrow trailer that doesn't smell like cookies. It's showing them your deepest, darkest fears and letting them shine a little light on them.

"Don't be an ass, Rome," Lux commands, coming in the front door. Mercy follows her.

"You were right," Mercy says, crossing her arms and giving Lux a look that speaks volumes.

"I always am," Lux replies. She tells me, "We all helped raise that money for you. Now don't be a jerk and screw it up for us."

I nod. "Thank you," I tell Mrs. Montoya. "I can't tell you how much I . . ." My voice cracks a little, but Mrs. Montoya knows what I can't say, and she folds me gently in her arms.

When we go back outside, everyone is starting to pack up and leave, and Jett stops to say good-bye. He pulls his phone out of his pocket. "I'll text you later," he says, gesturing to me with his phone. "Maybe we can set up another date that doesn't involve peanut butter."

"I don't know what you've got against peanut butter," I reply. "It's protein. I thought athletes were all about that."

Mom and Red come over to tell Jett good-bye. When I show Mom the check, she looks like she's going to bawl. She buries her face in The Collared Shirt, and Red blushes profusely.

"You deserve it, kid," Red says. "Don't blow it on car parts, though."

Jett moves to put his phone back in his pocket, but frowns suddenly and holds it up for closer inspection. "The screen was cracked," he says. He touches it hesitantly. "That's crazy. The cracks are totally gone."

"Somebody must've Fixed it," I say.

Jett nods, looking at me again. "Pretty good for only one hand." We leave Mom and Red and I walk Jett back to his Challenger so that he can leave.

"Technically both hands work. It's this shoulder that's a real bitch. But since your car is an automatic, I could probably still drive it on our next date," I tell Jett.

He gets in the Challenger, leaving the door open as he agrees. "All right. I'll let you drive it home from my next game. After you're off the painkillers."

I lean down and kiss him, hoping that Red can't see us. "Deal."

TWENTY-SEVEN

It's sunset, and Mercy and Lux are pulling Emmeline's dowry chest out of a hole not far from what's left of the ruins. It was right where Emmeline's map showed us it would be, the last small hill to the south, in what was once the dugout where Emmeline and John Remington spent a lovely afternoon before everything that happened between them. A little help from Neveah was all we needed to make the search a success.

I sit on the grass, my shoulder aching a little, watching them finish the job. Neveah is pleased that she was able to Find the chest so quickly, pinpointing it to an exact location and depth. She dances around us all, spinning and twirling and letting the sun cast a halo around her small form.

"You know," Lux says with a grunt when they get the large wooden chest out of the ground, "I think you could help a *little*. I mean, your left arm is fine." The shovels she and Mercy used to dig up the chest lay in a pile in the grass.

Mercy chastises Lux with a look. "She's not supposed to do anything strenuous," she reprimands. "You'll survive a few blisters. I bet your mom can even Heal them for you."

Lux makes a face.

"Is it locked?" Neveah asks, darting forward to examine the chest. She finds a twig on the ground and scrapes dirt from the lock. "Can we open it?"

Mercy hands me the bobby pin from her bra, and I go to work on the lock with my good hand. The tug is familiar, the ache a pleasant one that doesn't tire me too much.

When the lock tumbles, Lux makes a sound of relief deep in her throat.

Neveah cheers, dancing around us again. I'd like to think that if Emmeline's daughter had lived, she would have danced around her mother that way in the prairie sunset.

"Okay," Mercy says. "This is it."

Together, we open the chest.

The contents are shrouded in the same fabric that the diary was wrapped in. Mercy carefully lifts and unfolds the fabric, every layer bringing us closer to the contents. When she pulls away the last of the cloth, she reveals only yellowed letters, wrapped in ribbon. Three silver spoons. The deed to the Remington land.

"Where is everything?" Lux asks. "The gold bar? The two sets of silver?"

"Gone," I whisper. With my good hand, I pull out one of the letters and fumble to open the envelope. A note written in a scrawling, shaky hand and a black-and-white photo fall into my lap. I read the note first.

May 4th

Dear Emmeline,

*I don't know what brought you to us after all these years,
but I thank you. The gold bar saved the farm, and now my
daughters will have a place to grow up. Two years in a row it's
been so dry that we barely harvested anything, and what with the
Depression there's no place to find work. I'd taken out so many
notes against the land that I thought we'd have to sell for sure. I
promise we'll stay and take care of Cottonwood Hollow like you
would have wanted. My two girls and I will make you proud.*

Yours truly,

Patsy Truett

I pick up the photo. It's of two little girls standing in front of
a stone barn. I've seen a photo like this before, and I recognize the
pond and windmill in the distant background.

"It's the Truett farm," I tell Mercy and Lux, my voice shaking. "Those are the Truett sisters when they were little. Abigail
and Bernadette."

The other letters are similar. All from daughters of Cottonwood Hollow, all explaining what was taken from the dowry chest
and why. All are stories of struggle, accompanied by photos and
trinkets and dried flowers from Readers, Fixers, Strong Backs,
Wits, and every other talent we know.

The most recent letter is a surprise to us all. Nearly eighteen
years old, it's from Tina, who took some of the silver to help with a
down payment on the small bungalow she bought after Lux's father
died, before she married Aaron. She promised she was doing it to

make the best life for her daughter. She enclosed a photo of herself holding an infant Lux outside the bungalow, Lux's hand stretched toward the camera as if inviting Emmeline into the frame.

Lux's chin trembles. "I never thought to ask her if she knew anything about the dowry chest."

Mercy wraps an arm around Lux's shoulder. "Look at all those stories," she says. "All those girls that Emmeline helped. Doesn't that make you happy?"

I nod. Knowing that every one of these women had survived what seemed like it would break them makes me feel stronger. And it reminds me of Emmeline's wish for us to take care of each other. Mom told me that she and Mrs. Montoya took Tina to the courthouse to file the restraining order against Aaron the day he got out on bail, the three of them climbing the steps to the courthouse together, only one of them born in Cottonwood Hollow, and yet as tied to each other as Lux and Mercy and me. We are bound to each other, perhaps not by our brightest moments, but by our darkest.

"I don't need it anyway," Lux says softly. "Aaron's out of the house. We did it without the money."

Mercy squeezes her.

"Let's put it back," I say. "The important thing is that the deed stays safe. And the land and Emmeline's home are still a part of Cottonwood Hollow and all the daughters born here, like she wanted."

It doesn't take much to put the chest back in the hole that we and so many other girls have dug it up from. I even help shovel the dirt back in by pushing it with the instep of my worn-out sneakers, as if this tiny gesture will ever show Emmeline how grateful I am.

I lie back against the hill where John Remington's dugout once was and rest for a while when Lux and Mercy leave to walk Neveah home. It feels good to sit outside in the golden sunset and let the steady, gentle wind tug at my curls after so many days of being cooped up in the hospital. The trailer, with its empty bookshelves and stacks of boxes, doesn't feel much like home anymore, and I'm not in any rush to get back and say good-bye.

When Lux and Mercy return, they settle on either side of me, and together we lie back and watch the sunset fade into a purple twilight.

Quietly, Mercy begins to hum our favorite song. Lux gives a low laugh and looks at me before she starts singing the words aloud in her beautiful, silvery voice. I join in, and when all our voices twine together on the last night of all three of us living here in Cottonwood Hollow, I know that everything is changing.

But we'll always be connected, the three of us.

Palm to palm.

Scar to scar.

ACKNOWLEDGMENTS

Once while I lived in a mobile home, a bad storm rolled in quickly. Golf ball–size hail and strong winds made it too dangerous to go outside to find a shelter, so I had to stay put and hope that everything would be okay while the tornado sirens wailed outside. Recalling the experience with my husband in the summer of 2016, I had an idea for a story about a teenage girl riding out a wicked storm in an old trailer, afraid of how things might end for her. Wondering how a storm could change her life.

Three weeks later, I had the first draft of *The Deepest Roots*.

First of all, I have to thank my amazing, super-talented agent, Kristin Nelson, and everyone at Nelson Literary Agency, who make things run so smoothly and take such excellent care of authors. Kristin, thank you for taking a chance on me and my girls from Cottonwood Hollow. You took my manuscript and your excellent vision for what it could be and turned my story into a dream come true. Another huge thank-you goes to the very insightful and witty Angie Hodapp in literary development at

NLA, whose maps helped me discover all the secrets of Cotton-wood Hollow.

Emilia Rhodes, my perceptive and entirely awesome editor at HarperTeen, I thank my stars that my story found a home with you. Your editorial guidance and enthusiasm helped me shape this book into more than I'd imagined. Thank you for finding the beauty that I see in rural America. More gratitude goes to the rest of the HarperTeen family, including most especially Alice Jerman, who fearlessly took the reins, Alexandra Rakaczki, Megan Gendell, Jenna Stempel-Lobell, artist La Scarlatte, and everyone else who helped make my dream a reality. You people rock.

My husband, Antonio, thank you for finding that Mach 1 in an alley seventeen years ago and teaching Rome and me everything we know about cars. Thank you for encouraging me to follow my dreams, even when they seemed farfetched. Thank you for herding our small humans and ordering Chen's takeout while I wrote this book. Thank you for the long drives so I could plot. Sorry about that time I accidentally threw your new Bluetooth headphones into the washing machine with the laundry. I was thinking about edits.

My daughters, Amira and Rosalie, sharing stories with you made me remember how much I love them, and you were the inspiration for me to begin weaving words again after years away from writing. Thank you both for cheering me on. And for bringing me leftover Halloween candy when I looked tired. None of this would have happened without you.

To my family, I am so grateful to you for putting up with my weird stories since I was a kid. Mom and Dad, thank you for the notebooks, the pencils, and the encouragement. You read everything I wrote, even the bad stuff. Sorry about that, especially for my period of apocalypse literature. Dad, thank you for driving hours on your one weekend off a month to collect the certificate every time I won an award from a kids' short-story contest. Mom, thank you for keeping us all alive when I'm "in the zone."

More gratitude goes to my kind and generous critique partner, Katie, who patiently gave feedback on all my manuscripts, even the ones that got trunked. I salute you with Twizzlers, my friend, and count myself lucky that we ended up officemates in grad school. My beta readers, Alexis and Rhonda, you read everything (multiple times) and always gave me honest feedback, especially about the parts that made you cry. (Cue the evil laughter.)

Many thanks to my friends, colleagues, teachers, professors, and mentors near and far, past and present, who have supported me, including, but not limited to, late-night texts and chocolate delivery. More gushing and love to the wonderful crew of writers I met via the magic of social media, especially the Electrics, the Skulls, my IG pals, and fellow mom-writers. Thank you for commiserating with me, cheering me on, and celebrating with me. Your caring messages, hilarious GIFs, playlists, and witty banter make writing not such a lonely profession.

And finally, thank you to the girls like Rome, Lux, and Mercy, who fight for each other and for a better place in this world. Thank you for being unbelievably courageous, resilient, and compassionate. I can't wait to read your stories, too.